What Reviewers Are Saying About Larranaga's
***In The Company of Wolves* series**

"Larranaga's intricate development of characters and the way he compares them to wolves and pack hierarchy is captivating." - GoodbooksToday Reviews

"Another little twist and you're once again reading late into the night to see what is coming next." - LibraryThing

"Full of lies, deception and drug induced hallucinations, you are kept on your toes till the end with the outcome never certain. The analogy with wolves which runs through the story is clever." - Basingstone Book Reviews

IN THE COMPANY OF WOLVES

FOLLOW THE RAVEN

JAMES MICHAEL
LARRANAGA

20 19 18 17 16   10 9 8 7 6 5 4 3 2 1

ISBN: 978-0-9913256-5-8

CHAPTER 1

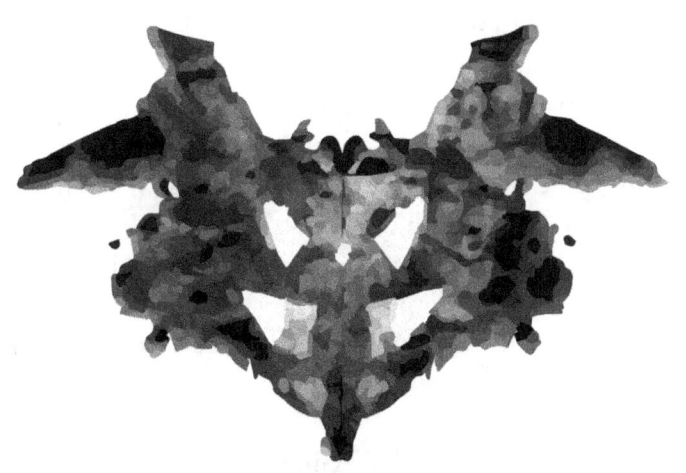

People are creatures of habit, and Gino wasn't breaking any molds as he shuffled across the parking lot of a Moose Lake convenience store. Quin watched him through a pair of Steiner Predator Binoculars—perfect for hunters sighting big game or bounty hunters following men on the run. Gino grabbed a newspaper and made a beeline to the men's room, where he'd sit in a stall and catch up on yesterday's news. After ten minutes he'd flush, wash and dry his hands with paper towels—not the hand dryer—and buy a large coffee and a lottery ticket. For three days Quin had observed Gino's predictable routine from the comfort of his truck, and today that routine was about to change.

Gino was a short, pudgy drug dealer who had missed his court date. And with bail piece in his back pocket, Quin was itching to escort the forgetful delinquent back to Minneapolis. He opened the glove box, sifting through heavy-duty cable zip ties, debating if he should use them or the Smith & Wesson handcuffs. If he forced Gino to his stomach, zip ties would be ideal for securing both his wrists, but if he needed to apprehend him in the restroom stall, then handcuffs would be a better option for securing one wrist before locking the other to the stall door or handrail.

This guy was definitely Gino, but Quin grabbed the fingerprint scanner connected to the Minnesota criminal history database and the FBI's list of wanted persons. Skips—people who skip out on bail—usually give up once they know a bounty hunter has tapped into the database; there's no bullshitting a fingerprint.

His phone vibrated on the dashboard. Agent Kruse again.

He raised the phone to his ear, still watching the convenience store. "Yeah," Quin answered.

"Where are you?" Kruse asked.

"None of your business."

"You're late for training."

"I took the day off, remember?"

"You didn't mention any day off."

"I have a funeral today."

"If you want bereavement time off, you need to fill out Form 105b," Kruse reminded him.

Quin had learned months ago that the FBI had a form for everything. "I e-mailed it to you. Gotta go," he said, hanging up on Kruse. He grabbed the cuffs and stepped out of the truck, jogging to the convenience store, his cowboy boots pounding hard against the pavement. He'd considered contacting the sheriff prior to making this arrest, but other bounty hunters listened to police radios and he didn't need any competition stealing his show. He'd call the sheriff soon enough.

The store was quiet and smelled of hazelnut coffee and doughnuts. No sign of Gino. He walked back to the restroom and stepped inside. He had studied this room the day before and it had a deadbolt lock on the inside so the staff could clean it, which apparently they never did. There were two urinals and two stalls. Beneath the door of the larger, handicap stall at the far end next to the wall was a pair of white Sketchers and blue jeans around the ankles.

Quin stood in front of the door. Drug smugglers always carried guns, so he'd have to secure both of Gino's wrists in one swift motion and then frisk him. Quietly, he removed the cuffs from his back pocket and with a silent count to three, kicked the stall door open with the heel of his boot, then lunged at the man inside.

Gino raised his hands as the door blasted inward. Quin cuffed one of his wrists before Gino shouted, "What the hell?!"

Gino sprang upward like a rabid dog with his uncuffed right arm swinging, his fist connecting with Quin's jaw. The punch stung, dropping Quin to his knees onto the cold tile floor. Gino kicked wildly, his pants at his ankles, high-tops bashing Quin's chest, when Gino's silver Beretta 9000S dropped onto the floor.

Quin reached for it and staggered back out of the stall, slipping on the wet floor before he was able to stand. "Pull up your pants," he said, gasping for breath.

"Who are you?" Gino said, standing with one wrist cuffed to the stall, his pants still around his ankles. "You want meth, is that it?"

"I'm not a customer. I'm here to re-arrest you," Quin said. "Notice the free bracelet around your wrist?"

"Re-arrest me? You got the wrong man. I wanna lawyer!" Gino shouted, his youthful face and acne red with anger.

"You already have a court-appointed attorney and judge waiting for you," Quin reminded him. "Your biggest problem isn't legal representation, it's punctuality."

Gino fumed, "C'mon, man..."

"Pull up your pants." Quin waved the gun. "I don't need to see your junk."

Gino stretched his underwear and jeans over his fat ass, but with one arm he couldn't tighten the belt around his belly. "What are you, a cop?"

"Bounty hunter."

Quin knew this wasn't over yet. Gino only had one wrist cuffed and he was desperate enough to lunge at a man with a gun.

"Cuff yourself to the handrail," he said to Gino.

"Why? Or you'll kill me?"

Lowering the gun, aiming right at Gino's crotch, Quin said, "I could injure you so you piss sitting down the rest of your life."

Gino flinched at the thought of life without his dick and snapped the dangling cuff around the handrail on the stall. "You got the wrong guy!"

This was as good a place as any for the fingerprint scanner to make its grand entrance. Quin slid it out of his blue jeans pocket and scanned Gino's thumb. The name on the display was Ambrogino Baxter.

"That's you, right?" Quin flashed the scanner at Gino.

"Shit, c'mon," he moaned. "I paid a bounty hunter yesterday to let me off. I doubled it."

Doubling it meant he'd already bribed another bounty hunter to look the other way. Plenty of bounty hunters made a better living taking bribes and setting skips free than turning them in for money. Catch and release was very profitable and a lot less hassle than transporting skips back to jail. For Quin, it really wasn't about the money anymore. This was fun. The mental and physical challenge was therapy for him. While most twenty-five-year-old guys were fishing on weekends, Quin was bounty hunting.

"Who set you free?" Quin asked.

"Hell if I know," Gino said.

"What did the bounty look like?"

"I dunno, he cuffed me, put a bag over my head. It was a real shake-down."

"You bought yourself a few extra days of freedom, but it's over," Quin said, easing the gun behind his back and into his belt.

"I'll pay you, too. Let me go. I gotta family, you know?" Gino said.

"Really? You're a hardworking family man? That's not what your mother says." Quin pulled out his phone and swiped through his photos to a picture of an old curly-haired woman with bags under her eyes. "Recognize her?"

The man squinted in disbelief. "What the...? That's my ma!"

He reveled in Gino's confusion. The first place to start a search for a skip was their family; parents, siblings, or cousins often had reasons to turn in their own kin. In this case, Gino's mom had footed the collateral for her son's bail, and now she was more than happy to have somebody searching for her black sheep.

"You should talk to her," he said, dialing her number.

"No!" Gino shouted.

"Hello, Mrs. Baxter? Quin here...yes, it's a pleasure hearing your voice, too. I found him. May I put you on speakerphone?" He held the phone up to her sweet boy's face.

"Gino! You no-good hoodlum!" Mrs. Baxter screamed, her voice filling the restroom. "I put a lien on the house and you run from the law?"

"Ma! Cool it!" he shouted back. "Listen to me, Ma!!"

"No, *I'm* talking now," she said. "This home is all I got. Don't you put me out on the street. Why can't you do the right thing? Take your punishment like a man!"

Quin was enjoying the sight of Gino, chained to the stall, braced for more verbal ass-whipping from his mother. She screamed expletives while he shook his head, and then she started up again.

"Turn her off," Gino begged Quin. "Hang up!"

"He's in good hands now, Mrs. Baxter," Quin said. "You'll keep your home."

He hung up, laughing at Gino. Justice had been served.

"Who are you?" he asked again.

"Quin Lighthorn."

He studied Quin's earrings and long hair. "You're the Indian I've seen sleeping in the truck."

"You got a problem with that?"

"No, no, my great-grandmother had Indian blood in her," Gino said, as if they were somehow distant blood brothers.

"Everyone's great-grandmother had Indian blood," Quin replied. "Welcome to the tribe."

Gino huffed, spitting out every skip's desperate cliché plea: "You didn't read me my rights, you know."

"I'm a bounty hunter, I don't have to read you your rights." Quin dialed 9-1-1. "Can you send a squad car to the Holiday Station at Moose Lake? Some poor guy locked himself in the men's room."

Within a half-hour Gino was slouched in the back of a Carlton County Sheriff's squad car. Quin slid the cuffs into his back pocket and motioned to Gino's Porsche. He told the sheriff, "That's his car over there. Sal Foster of Freedom Bail Bonds will contact you Monday about transporting Gino back to the city."

The sheriff nodded and looked into the window at Gino. "What's he dealing?"

"He's a mule, transporting meth to dealers between here and Canada," Quin explained. "Doesn't know when to quit, a real workaholic."

"Good job," the sheriff replied, seemingly envious of this catch; but Quin had an advantage. He knew all the habits of drug mules from where he had grown up in Arizona. Gas stations were the oasis for people carting drugs across the border.

His phone flashed with a message from Agent Kruse: *"I'll see you at work first thing in the morning."*

He climbed into his truck as the squad car pulled away. Rather than respond to Kruse, he sent a text to Sal Foster at Freedom Bail Bonds: *Gino Baxter is back in captivity.*

Standing in Oak Ridge Cemetery, a lonely five acres of land surrounded by birch and oak trees, Quin watched a raven perch on a branch, wiping its beak as it built its nest of twigs and grass. The bird was a welcome distraction from the funeral and all the loneliness he felt here. Some of the headstones were so old and weathered he couldn't read the names of those who had passed before his friend Rebecca Baron.

In front of him her relatives and friends watched as her mahogany casket was lowered into the ground; it made a clanking sound that spooked the raven in the tree. The bird hopped further out on the branch and made an angry croaking sound, but Quin was the only one who seemed to notice the wildlife. Everyone else stared at the casket.

Rebecca, a woman Quin had once rescued, was finally reunited with her deceased daughter and was being lowered next to her, in a separate box, below the frost line. This cemetery was once a wide expanse of prairie land, roamed by the Sioux tribes and later divided into farms by Europeans who carved the earth into cemeteries sub-divided into small plots like Rebecca's. Quin knew of old burial rituals where Indians wrapped their deceased loved ones in cloth and laid them to rest up in trees. This was to prevent animals like wolves from digging their dead. Nobody did that anymore. White people preserved their dead underground in expensive boxes.

There was a sniffle from a woman standing in front of him. He looked to his right and noticed Christopher Gartner loosening his tie. Quin hadn't seen or spoken to him in six months and the man looked ten pounds heavier; he wasn't a skinny stray dog anymore. He wore a black Armani suit and a red tie, and Quin felt under-dressed in his cowboy boots, jeans, and navy jacket.

"Quin!" Christopher whispered. "How are you?"

"I'm all right. You put on weight." He meant it as a compliment because Christopher had looked too skinny before. "You look good, though."

"Unemployment does that to you," he replied, unbuttoning his suit coat and wiping sweat off his pale brow. "I was a nervous wreck working at Safe Haven. The place gave me ulcers. Where've you been?"

"Training with the FBI," Quin said, watching the mourners talking and hugging.

"I'm on the witness list to testify against Ben Moretti," Christopher said. "How about you?"

"I'll testify, too, if they need me."

"Ben posted $5 million bail and he's free," Christopher said, snapping his fingers. "Just like that."

"With certain court-ordered restrictions," Quin said. "That's how the system works."

"Well, you're the expert. I don't like the idea of Ben Moretti walking around free. Gives me anxiety."

"You got nothing to worry about," Quin said.

"What makes you so sure? I'm the whistle-blower. I helped bring Ben to his knees."

"He's too busy working with his attorneys before the trial to even think about you."

Christopher reached out and grabbed Quin by the elbow. "Can I have a word with you, away from Rebecca's family?"

They walked across the cemetery lawn, acorns crunching under their feet. Christopher walked fast, his black leather shoes slipping on the wet grass.

"God! Three hundred sixty bucks for these Salvatore Ferragamos," he complained, "and I step in goose shit."

Quin glanced at the ground. "That's deer. Scat."

"Of course it is," he replied, embarrassed, wiping his shoe in the grass.

"What do you want, Christopher?"

"I'm low on dough," he said, looking over Quin's shoulder back at the funeral in the distance. "And I submitted Rebecca's death certificate to the insurance company. They'll send you a claim form and because of the amount of the death benefit, the insurance company will want to do a wire transfer—"

"I haven't forgotten."

"Of course you haven't forgotten the *payout*," he said. "I want to make sure you don't forget about *me*. We agreed to partner on that deal. I was the death broker who filed the paperwork. That was a perfectly legitimate business transaction that you couldn't have pulled off without me."

"My friend Hawk funded the insurance policy. You couldn't have done it without us, either," Quin said.

"I know, we're partners." Christopher backed down. "Whatever you think is fair. Ten percent would be cool, but whatever…"

There was desperation in his voice. Quin had heard this tone when they'd worked on the Safe Haven case. "You were a successful death broker before all of this. Why do you need money now?"

"Everyone's broke at different levels," Christopher said. "I need to find another line of work."

"When the insurance money comes in, I'll pay you ten percent," Quin said. "You can use the money to make a fresh start."

"You're working for the bureau full-time now?" he asked.

"I'm in training, sort of."

"What kind of bureau training?"

"Bounty work," Quin said, considering whether he should tell Christopher how the past six months had been a psychedelic mind warp. He wanted his friend to know how challenging life had been for him while Christopher assisted in the investigation, but he wasn't allowed to talk about any of his recent paranormal training with the FBI.

"What could the bureau teach *you* about bounty hunting?"

That was a good question, and one Quin had contemplated many times since partnering with the FBI. He was already damn good at catching skips, and his experience in tracking wolves had taught him a thing or two about predator behavior that he'd never have learned working in the city. So what *could* the FBI teach him about bounty hunting?

"I'd tell you about the training but it's confidential," he replied.

"Have you spoken to Candace Johnson?" Christopher asked.

Quin shrugged. "Don't know anybody by that name."

"Sure you do. Candy? A blonde?"

"One of Ben's girlfriends? The woman who kept calling me?"

"Yeah, but she's not Ben's girlfriend, far from it," Christopher said. "I assumed you knew that."

"No, I'm not involved in this case anymore."

"She's a writer doing a story about Ben and she wants to interview you too, Quin. When are you available?"

He remembered her brief visit to his hospital bedside. Candace was nothing if not persistent. He opened the calendar on his phone. "I'm usually free for dinner after seven."

"I'll check her schedule and get back to you. I'd better say my good-byes to Rebecca's family."

A task reminder popped up on Quin's phone: *Take medication.*

Christopher walked off, slipping again on the wet grass, dodging deer scat as Quin reached into his jacket pocket and found his antipsychotic Prolixin pills, folded into a napkin. He set one on the tip of his tongue before swallowing it. He *lived with* a mild form of schizophrenia but didn't *suffer from it*, as many people assumed. He endured the acute phases when he felt paranoid and saw things others couldn't see, or heard voices others couldn't possibly hear, but he lived comfortably in the quieter periods, or what was known as the 'maintenance phase,' when he felt almost no symptoms at all. He took a deep, calming breath, looked up at the trees, and noted that his raven friend was gone.

Agent Sean Kruse was an elder statesman by FBI standards, at least that's how Quin viewed the man. He was pushing sixty, with gray hair combed straight back, and he was wearing a crisp white shirt with the sleeves rolled to his elbows and a loosely knotted paisley tie. His deep, comforting voice could talk anybody off a ledge or coax a nervous patient out of a hospital room, and Kruse used his calm demeanor to teach his FBI recruits.

Quin loathed the debriefing sessions followed by group practice in paranormal training. Kruse taught them Coordinate Remote Viewing (CRV), a paranormal form of spying and data recovery. The team trained at the Minnesota State Security Hospital, built in 1911 as an asylum for the "dangerous and insane" that now housed the state's most violent criminals. None of the recruits had shown extreme violence toward others, but Kruse preferred to work with them here, away from the scrutiny of FBI headquarters.

Quin had joined an existing team in January: five women and three men. Kruse had pruned the team down to four agents in training and never said what happened to the other paranormals. They were "released" was all he would say when Quin asked. Were they fired or had they quit? Nobody talked about it. The team that remained was made up of:

Dillan Mercer, age nineteen, who lived with Asperger syndrome and was strong in pattern recognition, whether it was numbers or abstract objects. Dillan was a skater-boy hacker who got busted scaling PayPal's firewalls and had agreed to help the bureau in exchange for his freedom, which meant he could still live at home with his mom and their elderly cat, Tesla. Quin had eaten dinner at Dillan's house a couple of times and been served a macaroni and cheese doused with A-1 sauce by Dillan's mom. It was pretty good.

Rachel Crump, age twenty-one, who also had Asperger syndrome and the ability to recognize patterns, but her social skills were minimal. She'd been busted for card counting at Mystic Lake Casino and then again at Treasure Island until she checked herself into the psych ward and cut a deal with Kruse. She had bleached-blond hair with streaks of blue highlights. While Dillan liked her, Quin thought she was odd.

Susan Johnson, age twenty-seven, with autism and the ability to draw and sketch objects. She was chronically depressed, and Quin had no idea how she had made Kruse's dream team.

And there was Quin, age twenty-five, a bounty hunter living with schizophrenia, who had cut his own deal with Kruse after nearly killing Ben Moretti in the fight to apprehend him.

Kruse himself had no ability for remote viewing, or RV. He had admitted this to Quin, but after devoting five years of training to the CIA, he could teach it to people who possessed the raw talent. He embodied the dictum "Those who can't do, teach."

Quin took a seat with the other recruits at a table with notepads and pens while Kruse stood at the front of the dark conference room, holding a wireless remote for a ceiling-mounted projector. He flipped to the next identifier projected on the wall: 9467K. The number was randomly assigned to a specific object or location downtown, and none of the recruits knew what the object was or its location. Kruse would have to cross-reference the number to the file on his laptop to confirm after the trainee finished his or her viewing.

The game was to guess or "see" the object without knowing in advance what it was or where it could be found. "Just see with your mind's eye," Kruse had taught them.

Rachel Crump was the first to give it a go. She stared at the symbols projected on the wall, her eyes fixed as if she were looking right through it. Quin watched closely as Kruse guided her through a series of questions to help her focus on the target.

"Give me a stage-one description," Kruse said, "such as color or shape."

"Rose or red, yes red, red, definitely red," Rachel said.

"What else?" Kruse asked.

Rachel turned her eyes from the wall to her notepad and sketched a sweeping arc with her pencil. "Round or oblong."

The other trainees sketched too, following along, but Quin knew Kruse didn't want them to. They were breaking his rules. "Only Rachel is in the hot seat. You're influencing her. Pencils down, please."

Dillan and Susan set their hands on the table. Quin's arms were already folded and he leaned back, watching Rachel.

"Draw the object," Kruse said to her.

She continued sketching a sweeping arc into a circle as she looked up at the wall and back down to her pad before sketching again. "I see trees and buildings," she said, shading the drawing.

Kruse gave her another five minutes of quiet as she drew the images her mind could see. The other trainees remained quiet and Quin yawned.

"Now go to stage three," Kruse said as if he were asking her to increase the magnification of a microscope. "What smells or tastes come to mind?"

"Water...like pond water," Rachel said.

"How does she know what pond water tastes like?" Dillan whispered to Quin.

"I can *smell* it," Rachel said, turning to him. "Screw you, Dillan!"

"Dillan, you're not to interrupt or break a viewer's concentration," Kruse said.

Quin sensed the irritation in his voice. How many times did he have to remind Dillan of that?

"I'm in a park," Rachel said.

"Draw what you see," Kruse encouraged her. "Draw quickly before it fades. Write keywords."

The room was silent but for the vibrating fan inside the projector above. Rachel turned her attention away from the wall as if she had already captured the image in her mind and she continued drawing. Kruse walked to the table, standing over her. She wrote and said the keywords: "red, white, water." He had to cross-reference her hand-drawn sketch with the image 9467K.jpg on his laptop. Then he held up her drawing for the others to see.

"Recognize this?" Kruse asked the group.

"Spoonbridge and Cherry," Dillan said. "I had it before she did. I wrote 'cherry and spoon' before you told us pencils down." He pointed at his notepad.

"Anybody else come up with an image?" Kruse looked at Susan and Quin.

"I wrote 'truck'," Susan said.

"How about you, Quin?"

"I got nothing. My mind was totally blank." Which was the truth. He really wasn't seeing what the others could see.

Kruse walked back to his laptop, clicked onto file 9467k.jpg, and the image projected onto the wall: Spoonbridge and Cherry.

"There is no spoon, nothing is real," Dillan joked.

"Shut up," Rachel said.

"Haven't you seen the movie *The Matrix*?" Dillan asked. "When Neo realizes nothing is real?"

"*You're* right, Dillan," Kruse said. "Even though the spoon sculpture is 5,800 pounds and the cherry 1,200 pounds, they're made up of nothing more than atoms. They exist in our 3-D world as flashes of light that our eyes see. What we're doing here is finding these objects but also seeing *through* them, because on a quantum level, they don't really exist."

It was obvious, even to Quin, the newest member of the group, that Dillan was the fastest viewer of the four and Rachel was right behind him. Susan was slow and rarely confident in what she was viewing. Quin, while not successful in a controlled environment like the dark conference room, had proven successful when remote viewing in the real world, on location while undercover at Safe Haven LLC. Quin was able to track the men over great distances, in the dark on a frozen lake. That was why Kruse had so much hope for his remote ability.

"Let's take a fifteen-minute break," Kruse said, allowing the trainees to stand and walk to the door. "Quin, can I see you?"

"Sure, what's up?"

"Were you distracted by something?"

"You know how I feel about all this," Quin said, pointing at the projected image on the wall. "Still seems like bullshit to me."

"But you watched Rachel and Dillan identify the location. Are you still saying they're liars?"

"Maybe they cheated."

"How could they cheat, Quin?"

"What if Dillan hacked his way into your laptop and shared the file names with Rachel?"

Kruse considered the idea for a fleeting moment. "Not possible."

"Okay, let's assume she really could remote view. Then why would she use her mind to see a sculpture thirty miles away? Why not use her psychic powers to look into your computer hard drive?"

"Again, not likely, but it would still be impressive. We're always looking for ways to gain access to computer data."

"If this is real, and that's a big *if*," Quin said, "then I don't see how identifying landmarks is all that helpful. You need feet on the street and agents who can apprehend criminals. When I'm bounty hunting, I'm not just spying on people, I'm *catching* them."

"You're not still doing bounty work, are you?" Kruse asked, folding his arms.

Quin shrugged. "Here and there."

"The bureau pays you a good salary to be in this elite pilot program," he reminded him.

"Elite program tucked away in a hospital? Besides, I can do what I want on weekends."

"We need you to focus your efforts here. Dillan and Rachel are good at sighting locations and stationary objects, but as you're suggesting, crooks and terrorists are mobile. Remote viewers sense the world as a grid, like a chessboard with all its pieces, but they cannot predict how those pieces will move or change course. But you can, Quin. You could be on location and anticipate and react to the infinitesimal moves that our human targets might make."

"You'd make me an agent in the field?"

"Well, officially, all the paranormal investigators are informants, not agents."

"And all the other agents think this department is a joke. That's why you train us here at the hospital," Quin said. "The bureau agents won't work with your psychics."

"Once we prove to the bureau how effective this is, you'll all get the respect you deserve."

"*We'll* get the respect or *you'll* get it?"

Kruse ignored the question and gave him a pat on the back. "Hang in there."

"Why?" Quin sighed. "The salary is good but I can make money bounty hunting. And I can choose my own hours."

"You're different from them." Kruse motioned to the other paranormals down the hallway.

"I haven't felt *it* lately."

"Be more specific, Quin."

"My mind is…numb."

"When you're bounty hunting on the weekends, do you see or feel anything?"

"I saw a raven yesterday," he said, remembering the funeral. "And then she was gone."

"The numbness might be a temporary side effect of the medication—cognitive dulling. Hang in there, Quin. It'll come back to you."

"God, I hate Mondays," Sal Foster groaned, staring into an old computer monitor plastered with sticky notes and cigarette ash. "Arnie at A-Plus Bail Bonds is kicking my ass."

Quin listened to this rant from him every Monday. Sal would sit in his downtown office encased in bulletproof glass, whining about how slow business was and how the bail game had too much competition. Arnie Cook, a former business partner of Sal's, had started his own bail business and ran Internet ads all weekend long. That was today's topic, how the Internet and Arnie Cook were kicking Sal's skinny ass.

Quin glanced around the shabby reception area at the wood paneling and framed pictures of all the accused Sal had set free. The photos were faded yellow newspaper clippings and mug shots. A real Wall of Shame. But it was the FBI Most Wanted posters the bulletins from the State Department's Rewards for Justice program that always held his attention. Payouts for international terrorists ranged from $5 million to $25 million. That kind of work would be far more lucrative than chasing Sal's bail jumpers.

Quin thumbed through the calendar on his phone:

Take medication—done.

Meet Sal for payment—doing.

"How can Arnie fund so many bonds and also run online ads?" Sal mumbled to himself.

"I dunno, maybe he has a deep line of credit." Quin knew most bail companies had credit lines with banks. Sal did it his own way, using his own cash, which always left him angry and nervous. It was also why he relied so heavily on bounty hunters like Quin.

"You're back already?" Sal said, lighting a cigarette and squinting at him.

"You can't smoke indoors," Quin reminded him. "Against the law."

"Fuck the law," he said with a rattling laugh. "People smoke in your casinos."

"We're a separate nation with different laws," he said, standing and walking to Sal's window.

"I've been to your paradise. People smoke when they play cards. You know I've lost a shitload of money playing blackjack?"

"The Wakan Nation thanks you."

Sal drew on his cigarette, his cheeks collapsing, and blew smoke through his nostrils toward the glass. Maybe all he needed was a vacation from this firetrap he called an office. For all Quin knew, he lived in the back, eating, sleeping, and smoking bail bonds. All work and no play made Sal a grumpy boy.

"I found Baxter up in Moose Lake over the weekend."

"And?"

"You didn't get my text? I tagged him and bagged him," he said. "He's in the county jail up there. You need to arrange transportation down to the cities."

"Me?" Sal said. "Why didn't *you* bring him in?"

"Had a funeral to attend. Some of us have lives outside of work."

"It costs me *money* to transport skips. It's coming out of your bounty."

"The hell it is." Quin knew Sal could afford to pay for the transport. "I tracked him and caught him faster than any of the other Fugitive Recovery Agents running around this city. I don't have to work exclusively for you. I could work for your old buddy, Arnie Cook."

"Traitor! You wouldn't dare cross me like that after I gave you a shot when you were as green as that fucking tea you drink. I only hired you because Hawk begged me to. You aren't half the tracker that old coot was."

This was true. Hawk had taught Quin how to track and set him up with Sal on his first few assignments, but that was five years ago. Quin had more than proven his worth since then. Shifting his weight, he leaned on Sal's glass. He didn't give a shit about the money, just liked seeing the old smoking frog squirm.

"We'll split the cost," Sal said. "You want another assignment? I got a heroin dealer, a pimp, and a sex offender."

"I already have a full-time job Monday through Friday."

"Oh, helping the feds—I forgot. How's that workin' out? Can't be too good if you're doing this on weekends."

Sal's confrontational tone hung in the stale air. It was none of Sal's business why Quin did this. "Once Baxter arrives, process my payment and make sure you lift the lien off his mother's house."

"Of course."

"No, I mean it. Don't let that poor woman worry any longer than she needs to."

"Okay, cool it," Sal said. "What's eating you?"

Seeing Rebecca's family mourning at the funeral Saturday. All this chasing skips and training with the FBI was beginning to seem meaningless. You catch a criminal, bring him in, and he eventually reoffends. And the victims in the machine called "criminal justice" were the family members like Mrs. Baxter, who were naïve enough to mortgage their homes for relatives in jail.

"You suddenly grow a soft spot in your heart?" Sal asked.

"Not in my heart," Quin said, "but maybe my conscience."

"Ha! That's a good one. But I'm not the goddamned Wizard of Oz passing out hearts or a conscience. I got people who owe me money running around out there. If you can't chase skips or bring me the witch's broom, you're dead to me, at least until Friday. Good day!" Sal shut the window hard.

Nice touch, thought Quin. He turned around and the office was still empty except for the two of them and a haze of smoke in the air. "You realize it's only you and me here, right?"

"What? I can't hear you through the glass."

"It's bulletproof, not soundproof," Quin said, walking to the door as he mumbled, "F-you," under his breath.

"Fuck you too, Quin!" Sal shouted. "See you Friday?"

"Yep, see you Friday."

CHAPTER 2

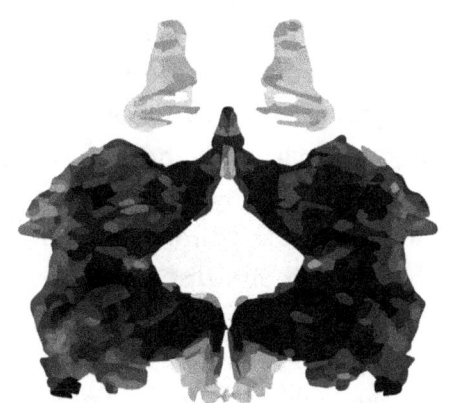

Maybe it was the smile on Christopher Gartner's face that put Candace Johnson at ease when she entered Spyhouse Coffee for their private meeting. Usually when she met and interviewed people they were nervous, but he seemed more than eager to help.

"Candy?" Christopher said, shaking her hand. "What can I get you?"

She was about to correct him because she preferred the name Candace instead of Candy, but she let it slide. "How about I buy this one?"

"Great, I'll have another latte." She ordered the same and followed Christopher back to his table where they sat with their drinks. Months ago, on snowy days in January, she had watched Quin frequenting this coffee shop, and she'd returned here many times since, hoping to run into him. That had never happened, so she invited Christopher here on the off chance he might bring Quin. Her goal was to write a story about Ben Moretti's crimes, and also learn more about the man who brought him down. Her job as a freelance journalist focused on true crime stories for magazines and websites. The edgier the better; and if she could get an editor an exclusive interview with photos, they paid double. In a world of online page views and trending keywords, websites needed original content to rank higher on the search engines. Candace always delivered what she promised.

"Thank you again for meeting with me. Interviews are so much easier in person than by phone," she said. "Mind if I record this?"

"Hmmm, not sure about that." Christopher loosened his tie, his pleasant demeanor fading.

"By recording, I capture all the details, for accuracy. I won't broadcast the interview."

"Who do you write for?"

"I'm a freelance reporter. I've published stories in the *Wall Street Journal*, the *New York Times*, and *Vanity Fair*."

"You're a media pimp," he said with a smile.

"Excuse me?"

"You pimp your work to the highest bidder," he said. "I would too. It's gotta be hard making money in journalism these days."

"Tell me about the case you and Quin worked on."

"I'm not supposed to talk about the case," Christopher said. "I'm on the witness list. They've granted me immunity."

She left her phone on the table without recording the conversation. "Were you charged with any crime?"

"No, but the feds said they could find something, some way to link me to it if I don't testify against Ben."

"Then why did you agree to meet with me here?"

"How do you know Ben?" he asked her.

"I've been following his story for a while. I met him a couple of times before he was finally arrested. But he would never sit down for an interview."

"I bet you found Ben charming, though."

She remembered her first meeting with Moretti, their late-night drinks at the bar and the trip to the casino with Quin. "Yes, he has a certain magic, but the best con men usually do."

"The next time you talk to Ben, would you relay a message for me?"

"Sure."

"Tell that son of a bitch good-bye for me," he said with a huff.

"Good-bye?"

"He's going to prison for sure."

"They have a good case against him?" she asked.

"His days of stealing and killing are over," Christopher said. "In the company of wolves, Ben was the alpha. But now that he's gone, another wolf will take his place."

This much she knew from her background research on Ben and viatical settlement products, or what's also known as structured settlements. Sometimes death brokers cheat the insurance companies, and other times they cheat their clients. "You mean there are others?"

"Ben won't reveal his investors."

"You and Quin know who they are?"

"Some of them, mostly the Washington elite."

"How big is this crime?"

Christopher sighed and shook his head. "It's *all* a Ponzi scheme, like everything else, Candy. The stock market goes up, and then it comes down, and if it comes down too far, people panic and pull their money out. And then congressional leaders start looking to blame corporate America for all the job losses. Hell, everybody knew Bernie Madoff was a thief for years before he was arrested. They finally made him one of the 'whipping boys of Wall Street,' forcing banking reform down everyone's throats. Then gradually the market gained confidence and the money came flooding back in. Looks like it's Ben's turn at the whipping post. I'm sure his investors are praying he won't shout any names while he takes his beating."

He seemed so cavalier about what amounted to serious accusations against Ben and his investors, Candace thought. It was as if Christopher lived in a different kind of reality from the rest of the world. "Let's say Ben goes to prison, then what?"

"Life goes on and another greedy death broker will take his place," he said. "It's the circle of life. What you've got to focus on, Candy, is Quin."

"Believe me, I've tried, and he doesn't return my calls."

"He's not well. Whatever they're doing to him at the bureau, it's taking its toll. I saw him recently at a funeral and he looked and acted different. They got him on something."

"Like what?"

"Prescription medications. He's kind of crazy, and they got him all juiced up on something to control it. Makes him all glassy eyed and distant."

"The FBI prescribes medications?" she asked, doubting it.

"If the CIA can bring crack cocaine into this country and torpedo the banking industry, then the FBI can prescribe whatever it wants, but don't quote me on that," he said.

She knew the CIA had been linked to a number of conspiracy theories. Some were proven true, like its LSD mind-control experiments in the 1950s. Other claims that the CIA had planted crack on the streets or that it had instigated the savings and loan crisis in the 1980s were never proven.

"Why would the bureau do this?" she asked.

"That's what I want to know, and that's what you have to find out."

"How can I get ahold of Quin?"

Christopher slid back in his chair and reached under the table where he kept a briefcase on his lap. He opened it, removing a large hunting knife with a pearl handle.

She reached for it, feeling the heavy weight in her hand. "What is this?"

"A knife."

"Of course, but why—"

"It's Quin's. He'll want it back."

"But why do you have it?"

"When he caught Ben, Quin dropped it," he explained. "So now you can use it as a peace offering, a reason to meet and talk. The knife is very important to him."

"What's its significance?" she asked, still holding it in her hand.

"You didn't hear this from me," he said, looking around the coffee shop, "but one night when Quin was young, his parents were murdered and his sister was kidnapped. He's been kind of a mess ever since. But the bureau likes working with him. Anyway, this knife was left at the scene."

"God," she said, setting it on the table quickly. "I don't want it."

"You want to meet the Zen Master of Tracking? You gotta bait him," he said. "Take a picture of it and text him. I'll give you his new number."

She did as Christopher suggested before setting her phone back in her purse. As strange as this was, she kept peppering him with questions. "How does the bureau work with him?"

"Tracking, hunting humans," he said, as if she were missing the obvious. "It's his thing. He's very good at it."

"And this FBI work Quin is involved in has to do with that?"

He shrugged. "I suppose. Like I said, Quin wouldn't talk about it with me. And I won't do anything to jeopardize my immunity by poking around and asking too many questions. You can do that part."

Christopher had rekindled and fanned her curiosity. She'd been unsuccessfully tracking this bounty hunter for six months, trying to meet up with him to learn more about the events that led to Ben's arrest. Who was this bounty hunter now working with the FBI?

"I suppose meeting with Quin might be worth something," he said.

"I don't pay for stories," she said out of principle.

"But you're not paying for the story," he said. "You're buying the knife, the peace offering that secures a meeting that could lead to a story *quid pro quo.*"

"You're selling Quin's property?"

"C'mon, don't look at me as if I'm Judas."

"But you're selling him out and profiting from it."

"Helloooo? You're the media pimp selling Quin's story," he said, leaning back on his chair.

Her opinion of Christopher had suddenly dropped a couple of notches. He was sleazy, and obviously worked in sales because he knew how to insert himself as a middleman. She swallowed hard and he certainly noticed it; she could see a glint of pleasure in his eyes. The smile he had when they'd first met had faded to a darker stare.

As much as she kept trying to cover this story objectively, she knew she was also slowly becoming part of it. She could've easily walked away at that point, out of the coffee shop and back to her normal life but she didn't.

She was interested in Quin, and the knife could give her a reason to finally meet with him. She pulled out her checkbook and said, "I'll pay you for the knife but from now on, my name isn't Candy, it's Candace. Got it?"

Dr. Kristen Hayden looked up from her notebook at Agent Kruse sitting with her at a pinewood conference table. He was reviewing her notes on Quin in comparison to the other paranormals in the program. As part of the research study, all paranormal trainees had signed authorization forms allowing Dr. Hayden to share medical information with the research team. She watched how Kruse's silver eyebrows would rise and fall as he read her notes. Occasionally he smiled, and then his demeanor would become serious again as he scanned further down the page.

"O-D-D?" Kruse asked, pointing.

"He shows signs of Oppositional Defiant Disorder," she explained. "He's become more confident lately and defiant towards authority."

Kruse grimaced. "Well, the training program is stressful. Is he clean?"

"He failed the drug test twice in January," she said, "but he's passed all random tests since then. I doubt his behavior change has anything to do with recreational drug use."

"Maybe it's the *lack* of recreational drugs that's making him so angry," Kruse said.

"He shouldn't use while on a prescription medication or his hallucinations will return."

She waited for him to finish reading. He must be searching for better news on Quin, something positive to hold onto, but in her opinion, Quin wasn't an ideal candidate for the Paranormal Investigators Division. She had already expressed her concern in several e-mails to Kruse.

"Talk with him for a few minutes, then administer the Rorschach," Kruse said, paging through the file.

"What good will a Rorschach do?"

"Every RV trainee must take it."

"It's an outdated test."

"I need him added to the database."

"Forgive me if I'm stepping out of line here," she said, "but I don't care what you do with the paranormals in the field. What I care about is what all this RV training is doing to them emotionally."

"And you're putting your foot down when it comes to Quin?"

"I'm concerned about *all* of them."

"We have records of you e-mailing Quin after hours," Kruse said, "and divulging to the thieves at Safe Haven that he is your patient."

"I e-mailed him because *you* demanded that I maintain contact," she said, trying to hold back her rage. "I *told you* those actions violate HIPPA and I could lose my license!"

"We're on the same team, Dr. Hay—"

"Don't you dare blackmail me," she said in an angry whisper so her voice wouldn't carry beyond the door into her reception area.

"Quin's in the program and we want to keep him here," Kruse said. "You have nothing to worry about."

There was a knock at the door and Agent Kruse stood, adjusting his tie. "We'll talk later about his medications, adjusting his dosage. You'll be around?"

She looked up at him towering over her. "Yes, I'll be here all day."

He walked to the door and opened it, greeting Quin with a friendly handshake. She watched as they made small talk, Kruse offering him encouragement and Quin nodding before turning to her. "Should I wait outside?"

"No, I'm off to another meeting," Kruse said. "You're right on time."

Quin closed the door. "What's with Kruse? He seems so upbeat."

"Oh, he's just checking in," Dr. Hayden said. "Have a seat."

He sat in a brown leather couch and Dr. Hayden stood up from the conference table, pulling up a chair and her notepad.

"How are you today?" she asked, studying Quin's clothing: boots, blue jeans, and a black t-shirt.

"Good. What's wrong?"

"Nothing, it's busy, that's all." She regained her composure. "How was your week? How's Quin doing?"

"Feeling great."

"What's with the bandage on your wrist?"

"Got in a fight with a skip over the weekend."

"Would you remove the bandage for me?"

"I didn't cut myself, if that's what you're thinking," he said, removing it. "And you know I'm not a junkie."

He let her inspect the wound until she was satisfied that it was only an abrasion.

"How come you're working bounty?"

"That's what Kruse wants to know. I like the challenge."

"Weren't you instructed to stop bounty hunting while you work for Agent Kruse?"

"Yeah, well, you can take a kid out of the woods but you can't take the woods out of the kid."

"It makes you feel empowered?"

"I suppose so…"

"Looking back on the past week, did you ever feel panicked or fearful?"

"When I saw Gino's gun, I panicked."

"I imagine so!" she replied. "Any hallucinations or voices?"

"No."

"Any symptoms?"

"Symptoms of schizophrenia? No panic attacks, no voices, but I did see a raven when I was at Rebecca's funeral. It was right before I took my pill. Then it was gone."

"Great! You were able to manage the hallucination." She wrote in her notepad. "Any low points you want to discuss?"

"At Rebecca's burial I saw Christopher Stray Dog, the guy I worked with on the Safe Haven assignment."

"You mean Christopher Gartner?" she corrected him. "We're working on seeing people as *people*…"

"…and not as prey," he said, finishing a mantra she had asked him to memorize. "Anyway, I met with Christopher *Gartner* and he seemed happy to see me."

"Did the funeral bring closure for you?"

"Sort of, but it set in motion a promise I had made to her."

"Really?"

"She wanted me to return to Arizona," he said, rubbing his palms on his jeans.

"You told Rebecca about your past?"

"Most of it. She encouraged me to go back and find out what happened to my sister."

"How do you feel about that?"

"A promise is a promise."

"But how does it feel to have made such a promise?"

"Gino's mom, the skip I caught this weekend, she was shouting into the phone, '*Why can't you do the right thing, Gino?*' It made me think, I should do the right thing, too. And Hawk agreed I should look for my sister."

"You're ready to go back there, to return to your childhood home?"

"Agent Kruse gave me the files on the case months ago. I've reviewed the notes and photos hundreds of times," he said. "I might as well go there."

"When?"

"Soon. This remote viewing isn't exactly working out for me," he said. "I can't give Kruse what he wants."

Dr. Hayden turned a page in her notebook. She knew Kruse would want details. "By that you mean…"

"How much of what I say here do you share with Kruse?"

"You're part of his research study. He has access to your medical records, how you perform on tests, and I'm required to give him my professional opinion of your state of mind."

"So pretty much everything."

"If it pertains to the research and training, yes," she said. "But your thoughts and feelings about your family aren't necessarily related."

"Agent Kruse chose me because he thought I could see future events, but ever since I enrolled in the training, I've felt dead inside."

"Depressed?" She wrote the word in her notebook.

"Whatever psychic powers Kruse thought I had, they're gone," Quin said. "Poof! Vanished. Or maybe I..."

"Maybe what, Quin?"

"What if I wasn't psychic in the first place?"

"Most recruits have self-doubt."

"You've never believed in my psychic ability. You had some psychobabble theory about why I see the ravens."

"It's not my theory but psychiatrist Carl Jung's. He said that we all have a shadow self, a dark side, and I'm suggesting that's what the ravens are, a manifestation of your own fears."

"Not a form of RV."

"Agent Kruse has worked in this field for more than twenty years. He's more of an expert in RV than I am."

"What if the ravens are spirits?" he asked. "Guiding and protecting me?"

She was careful not to insult him. "I respect your beliefs but as a scientist, I can't document or prove spirits."

"Well, what if I don't believe in RV and all this therapy? Then it all seems like a waste of time," Quin said.

"Would you rather exit the program?" she asked, careful not to sway his decision. Even though she didn't think he was right for the program, the decision was his alone.

"I can walk away?"

"You sign forms, of course."

"Just like that, I'm done?"

"Yes. You'd be resigning from the study and your paid position with the bureau." She stood and stepped to the credenza behind her desk where she kept her files. "You can sign it right now if you want. But there's also a chance you'll be reassigned to a new doctor. I'm not sure how important that is to you." She handed him a form before she sat back down in her chair.

Quin held the paper as if he were weighing his options. She knew that sometimes he was angry at her for making him relive his past, and for prescribing drugs that he had to take on a strict schedule. But she knew that sometimes the devil you know is better than the one you don't, and that's why most patients are reluctant to switch doctors.

"Thanks, I'll hold onto it for now," he said, folding the paper and sliding it into his back pocket.

"Well then, for the rest of today's session I'm going to administer the Rorschach."

"The inkblot test?"

"Yes. The Rorschach is one of several tests we give to paranormal trainees along with the Minnesota Multiphasic Personality Inventory, which you've already taken."

"You want me to stare at inkblots and tell you what I see?" Quin said, amused.

"It's that simple."

"That test is bullshit. It doesn't prove anything. Why should I take it?"

He was smarter and more inquisitive than the others who'd come in for training over the years. Most of the recruits were happy to have a purpose or a job, and their families were relieved that they had something constructive to do. The majority of the recruits worked tirelessly in the hopes that they would be mainstreamed into society, but she knew Quin didn't care about fitting in. He wasn't motivated by peer approval. But she knew he still had some respect for authority.

Dr. Hayden sighed and closed her notebook. "Why should you take the Rorschach test? Because Agent Kruse wants you to."

Jogging down a stairwell, Quin listened to Sal's croaking frog of a voice on speakerphone. Text messages were routine for the guy, but when he left an angry voice mail, it was urgent. Today, Sal had a theory: the reason so many of his clients were skipping town was that his competitor, Arnie Cook of A+ Bail Bonds, was bribing them to run off.

"Can you believe it?!" His voice echoed in the stairwell. "Arnie is bleeding me dry. I can bankroll a handful of perps skippin' town but damn it if I'm gonna let him set all of 'em free! Where the hell are you? Call me!"

Quin exited the stairwell into the lobby of the hospital, dodging patients and medical staff in scrubs. The doors opened and a warm late-afternoon breeze enveloped him as he walked across the hot pavement to his truck. It was one thing for a skip to bribe a bounty hunter—that happened all the time. But since when had the bail bond industry turned on itself like a snake eating its own tail? He climbed into his truck, started it up, and got the AC blowing before he dialed.

"It's a beautiful day of freedom, this is Sal, how can I help you?"

"It's me," Quin replied.

"Finally! Where you been?"

"I'm at work on my lunch hour. I only have a few minutes."

"What you do with them feds ain't work," he said. "You get my messages? We got problems."

"*You* do, not me."

"He said, she said, whatever. That fact is, Arnie Cook is screwing me."

"How do you know that?"

"One of the other bounty hunters told me as much."

It was no surprise that Sal had other bounties working for him. Most bounties were free agents anyway, picking up the best-paying assignments or the lowest-hanging fruit. "Which bounty told you that?"

"Finn."

There were two Finn brothers who worked together in the business. Quin remembered seeing them at Moose Lake while searching for Gino Baxter. The Finns were a good team, they had each other's backs. "Which Finn?"

"Beats me, they're carbon copies of each other," Sal said. "Nordic gods, those two with their blond hair and ice-blue eyes…"

Silence.

"Hello. You still fantasizing, Sal?"

"Huh? No, it was the taller one with the muscles."

"Muscles is Mike and the skinny one is Steven," Quin said. "That's how I tell them apart."

"Mike told me that there are rumors about what Arnie over at A-Plus Bonds is doing to me."

"Could be bullshit talk. Why would Arnie do something like that?"

"To drive me out of business!" Sal said. "Do you not understand capitalism?"

Of course he understood the laws of supply and demand, but he also knew time was a precious commodity. "I got other plans tonight."

"What could be more important than helping your old friend Sal?"

"Having dinner with Hawk."

"Oh, come on, Hawk has all kinds of widows out there bringing him meals."

The old man certainly was popular with the ladies, even with some of the younger ones in their fifties who gambled at the casino and invited him off the reservation for drinks. Still, he wanted to check on him rather than drive downtown to hear Sal bitch and moan.

"I got to see Hawk and make sure he's all right before I leave town."

"You leaving? When…where?"

"Maybe as early as next week, back to Arizona," Quin said. "Heading south on the freeway to the Wakan Indian Reservation outside of Shakopee."

"No, no, no, you're staying here to help me patch the holes in this boat!" Sal's gravelly voice filled the truck with demands and expectations. He told Quin how important he was, how he trusted him like his own prodigal son, even though he never had any sons (*that he knew of anyway*). Quin doubted he even knew what the word *prodigal* meant.

"If the Finns are telling the truth, ask them for help. They can round up those skips as fast as I can," he said.

"They're not as fast as you, Quin. And they always want more than I'm willing to pay."

"I'll be back in a few weeks."

"Weeks?"

Dr. Hayden had waited patiently for Agent Kruse to return to his office, checking e-mails from her phone as he entered. She was already seated in a chair in front of his desk, and now handed him a file as he sat down. "Quin's test results."

Kruse opened the file and read through her summary. She knew from his expression that words were leaping off the page: *hesitation, second-guessing, overanalyzing.* That was how Dr. Hayden had described Quin's answers on the Rorschach test. Quin's Rorschach Interpretations were as follows:

1. Moth
2. Two humans
3. Women dancing
4. Man standing
5. Butterfly
6. Animal hide
7. Kissing faces
8. Two dogs
9. Human face
10. Lobster

"These are all common answers," Kruse said to her. "I would've expected he'd see ravens and wolves."

"He was very spontaneous; he hardly gave them any thought at all. You know, we never administer the Rorschach test anymore."

Kruse looked up from the file. "Why, because the test is outdated junk science, just like remote viewing? Is that what you mean?"

This was a sore spot for Kruse and she knew it. Only 20 percent of correctional psychologists like Dr. Hayden administered the Rorschach test, while 80 percent of clinical psychologists relied on it routinely. This was a hospital but also a correctional facility, and she wasn't always comfortable with Kruse's test methods.

"I'm not criticizing your program. But some of the validation methods are outdated, yes," she said.

"Actually, I shouldn't be surprised at these results," he said, shuffling through the file. "He's been under our close supervision for almost six months. No wonder he's acting so *normal.*"

"In that regard, he's made progress."

"Really? We've got him on such a short leash, he's starting to lose his natural instincts. He's lost his sixth sense. What if we stopped his medication?"

She leaned closer to his desk. "I wouldn't recommend it."

"Step him down slowly?"

"He could become violent again."

She knew Kruse was aware of Quin's previous outbursts, and while those incidents were problems for the FBI's director of public affairs, Kruse never seemed bothered by them at all.

"Soon he'll be on the streets tracking terrorists. Violence is a necessary part of the job."

"You want me to reduce Quin's medication?" she asked. "I'd need to document that in his medical file."

"To the same dosage he was at before joining our team. He won't be a danger to himself or anyone else," Kruse said.

"But on that low dosage, he had hallucinations and nearly killed Ben Moretti."

"Nearly killing somebody in the line of duty isn't a crime," Kruse said. "Go back to his previous dosage. And there's no more need for random drug testing for Quin."

She looked at Kruse as if *he* were crazy. "You know he was high on ayahuasca tea when they dragged him into the hospital back in January."

"I remember."

"Without the threat of a drug test, Quin is likely to return to his old habits."

"That's what I'm hoping for, a return to Quin's old ways, no matter how fringe those ways might've been. I'm realizing now that we accidentally blocked his psychic abilities with medication. I need to see what he's like in his more natural state. If Quin needs to self-medicate, then so be it," Kruse said, handing Dr. Hayden her file back. "No more drug tests for this one."

"You're sure about this?"

"One hundred percent."

"But what if he's burned out? What if he wants to quit?"

"Why? What have you heard?"

"Seems like he could use a break from all of this," she said, shuffling papers into the file.

"We're very close to a field trial. It's too soon for a vacation."

"He wants to go back to Arizona, to search for his sister. You encouraged him to do it by giving him the file months ago."

"I said he could do it on *his* free time, not on *my* time."

"How much investigating can he possibly do from Minnesota? Why not give him a vacation back to Arizona where he can get some closure?" she asked. "He'll come back refreshed."

"But if we cut his meds, how can we monitor the effects?" he retorted, though considering her idea.

"I'll adjust his meds immediately so we can observe him before he leaves. Have him check in regularly on the bureau's secure videoconferencing line," she said. "I can even do his weekly therapy sessions by video."

Kruse nodded, his face lighting up. "We can make Quin's trip back home the field trial. We'll test the paranormal team by having them all focus on the search for his sister from Minnesota, while Quin is on the ground in Arizona. It's a brilliant idea, Dr. Hayden."

She blinked at him in surprise. "I'm not recommending a field trial while he's taking personal time off."

"Of course you are," Kruse said. "On some subliminal level, you want to know as much as Quin whether RV even works. I'll show you both."

In a hospital break room reserved for paranormals in training, Quin listened to Dillan fretting about how Kruse constantly expected more from them, demanding more accurate viewings. He nodded along as he read his e-mails and annoying texts from Sal Foster.

"You wanna get dinner tonight?" Dillan asked, rubbing the red eczema between his knuckles.

"Why, what's your mom making?"

"Hold on," he said, texting the Mother Ship. "She'll make whatever we want."

Quin read another text from Sal. The guy was still anxious about his growing list of skips and wanted a commitment from Quin to work the weekend. He'd wait before replying.

"I got plans."

"Ah, come on. What if she makes rib eye?"

"I might stop by the rez tonight to see a friend."

"I'll go with you," Dillan said.

He thought about this socially awkward kid with the baggy pants and a mop of hair riding along with him. "Probably not a good idea."

"Why? How come?"

How could he explain this to Dillan without hurting his feelings? The kid was so fragile and innocent, but also blind to social cues. The last thing Quin needed was him gawking at tribal members from his truck.

"Is it because I'm too white?"

Quin held back his laughter by biting his lip. "Yeah, something like that."

"Damn it!" Dillan scratched his knuckles.

Quin watched as Agent Kruse approached the break room with his hands in his pockets. He stood there for a moment before interrupting. "What's wrong, Dillan?"

The kid remained slumped in his chair. "My knuckles itch, that's all," he replied without turning to look at him. He knew to turn on the crazy when it suited his own selfish needs.

"Check in with the nurse before you leave. Get some ointment for your hands," Kruse said. "Do you mind if I speak with Quin?"

"Go right ahead," Dillan said.

"Alone, please?"

Dillan winked at Quin. "Alone right now?"

"Yes." Kruse jingled coins in his pockets.

"Fine, why didn't you say so in the first place?" Dillan stood and tugged his shirt down over his belt. "See ya tomorrow."

Dillan walked down the hall, counting the tiles on the floor, and Quin waited for him to round a corner before he said, "Have a seat."

Kruse sat across from him at the small table, pushing aside candy wrappers Dillan had left behind. "Was he bitching about work again?"

"Dillan? You know how he is sometimes."

"He might be right. I've been working the team pretty hard lately. You even mentioned being burned out."

"I'm not used to working indoors as much as the others," Quin admitted.

"And you're interested in possibly working on your sister's case full-time?"

Kruse had obviously spoken to Dr. Hayden. He knew they'd talk, but hadn't expected his boss to circle back so quickly. "It's time for me to go back there. I'm about due for some vacation time anyway."

Kruse nodded, hands folded in front of him on the table. "Good idea. But who knows how long you'll be down there? Your sister has been missing for a long time. Won't you need more than a couple of weeks?"

"I suppose." Quin shrugged to keep him at bay.

"What if we help from here? What if you go into the field and the paranormal team gives you support?"

"No thanks, I prefer to work solo," he said, knowing that Kruse wanted to keep him in close contact.

"Quin, this isn't like looking for some skip who busted bail two days ago. This is a cold case, extremely cold. You're about to go looking for a family member who hasn't been seen in twelve years. How will you even know where to start?"

"Same place the feds should've started, with my tribe," he said, remembering the sloppy investigation that lasted no more than two weeks. The bureau had partnered with the tribal police, as if this was a mere formality, but they didn't care what happened to his family. To them it was just another drug deal gone bad on the border between the Land of the Free and No Man's Land. There was a reason the FBI file Kruse had given him was so thin; nobody cared about the Lighthorns because they were dirt-poor and the poor...well, they didn't count. "I know what I have to do," he said, staring Kruse directly in the eyes.

"You interview a few tribal members, then what? They either know nothing or they'll send you off to dead ends."

That was a possibility for sure. Quin's family was a loose band of cousins, aunts, and uncles on his mother's side. He didn't even know specifically where his father's white family lived; he thought it was somewhere in Florida. Neither family had wanted Quin after the murders of his parents because some feared he was the murderer, and others thought the real killers would come back for him. He had been a boy stuck in the middle of nothing and eventually shoved into the foster system. Agent Kruse was the closest Quin had come to a father figure in a long time, but he was strict, and sometimes overbearing. Maybe that was how fathers were.

"What would the paranormal team do?" he asked.

"They'd stay here and view targets for you to investigate," Kruse said. "You can travel alone and report back what you're finding."

"Doesn't sound like much of a vacation."

"C'mon, you work every weekend bounty hunting anyway, right?"

He wouldn't answer that question. He didn't want to get cornered in one of Kruse's logical arguments where "this therefore that" always fit like some kind of 10,000-piece puzzle.

"I can make it a working vacation. How about no more drug testing?" Kruse said. "No Big Brother looking over your shoulder expecting you to pee in a cup. What do you think?"

There was no smile on the man's face and no hint of sarcasm in his voice. He said it so casually, as if he were offering him a cigarette. Now *that* would feel like a vacation.

"You want me to go back to using?"

"No, not at all. Your training is over, Quin. I'm setting you free. Fly like an eagle."

"But you want me to keep in touch, so…more like a homing pigeon."

"Well, before you start trashing my idea, let me show you what I mean. Tomorrow in training I'll show you how it would work. Agreed?"

Quin's phone chirped with another text message from Sal Foster. It was only mid-week and the guy was hounding him. It felt pretty good, though, to have all these people begging for his assistance. And Kruse was willing to bend the rules, or at least look the other way, while Quin was on the road.

"Okay, tomorrow show me what you mean, and then I have to start making plans to head south."

CHAPTER 3

Quin maneuvered his truck through traffic as a dream catcher that Hawk had once given him swung back and forth from the rearview mirror. It was his reminder to Quin to focus on good thoughts that came his way. And he was starting to feel good, tying up loose ends and looking forward to a road trip. Over dinner he'd tell Hawk that it was official, he would soon be leaving for Arizona.

When he drove up Hawk's street, the sun was still high on the horizon and all he could see were two silhouettes in the driveway. He pulled to the curb and realized that Hawk's grandson, Slim Jim, was barely helping his elder carry groceries out of his shiny black Bronco. Hawk held a twelve-pack of Coke under one arm and a paper grocery bag in the other. Slim Jim was wearing a hockey jersey to cover his belly and he texted and carried a fountain drink.

Why can't that fat kid focus on his grandfather once in a while?

Quin stepped out of his truck and jogged up the driveway, the heels of his boots knocking on the pavement. "Let me help you with that," he said, easing the twelve-pack from beneath Hawk's arm.

"Oh, I coulda got that. He insisted on carrying it," Slim Jim protested.

"I only wanted to carry one can," Hawk muttered to Quin. "I'm thirsty and he's sucking on that Mega Gulp."

"I'll take it from here, Hawk," Quin said, grabbing the twelve-pack and the grocery bag. He heard Slim Jim sigh and slurp his soda.

When Quin opened the door, the first thing he noticed was the mess in Hawk's living room: bags of chips and popcorn on the couch and beer cans stacked on the wood mantel of the fireplace. He'd seen frat houses on campus cleaner than this. The dead giveaway was the Xbox on the floor in front of Hawk's flat-screen TV.

"You entertaining guests, Slim Jim?" Quin asked, setting the twelve-pack and bag on the kitchen table. Hawk opened the carton and popped open a Coke.

"I had some bros over last night. Hawk's cool with it, right?" he said to his grandfather as if this were some kind of alibi they had agreed to. Hawk guzzled his Coke without responding.

"How late were they here?" Quin asked.

"All night. You can't serve beers and then send them out onto the roads," Slim Jim said, as if he and his buddies were suddenly sober drivers.

Quin pointed at Slim Jim. "Don't take advantage of Hawk. Clean up your mess and stop making this your crash pad."

"What the...? Why you sticking your finger in my face, bro? You got nothin' to say about it," he said, rocking back on his heels.

"Your aunt, the one in prison, is concerned about Hawk," Quin reminded him. "She asked me to check in on him and this is my house call."

"God knows why she brought you here," Slim Jim muttered under his breath.

"Because she doesn't trust you to watch after him." Quin hated to dig up this family's dirty laundry. Hawk had two daughters, one in prison and the other, Slim Jim's mother, lived in an art commune in the hills of northern California. It was obvious, though, that the old man couldn't rein in his grandson, just like he couldn't his own daughters.

"You're not family. Go back to your own rez," Slim Jim said.

"I will."

Nobody said a word; Slim Jim squinted as if he'd misunderstood what Quin had just said. They'd had arguments like this many times but Quin had never agreed to leave before.

"When are you going?" Hawk said.

"In a few days."

Hawk's brown eyes met his and Quin knew his elder was proud and sad at the same time. He had once told him that in life's journey, paths cross, sometimes over and over like twine and sometimes rarely, like the switchback trails on a mountain pass. For the past five years, they were as tight as twine, but Quin felt they were about to unravel. He looked around the house, at the dishes in the sink, a stack of newspapers and pizza boxes near the back door by the garage. Hawk was looking at the mess too.

"You going alone?" he asked, the Coke can shaking a bit in his hand.

"Unless you want to come with me."

The old man's expression lifted, his tan forehead wrinkling high in surprise, as if he couldn't believe Quin had read his mind.

"You're goofin', right?" Slim Jim said.

"No. If Hawk wants to tag along, he's more than welcome. How about it?"

"No way," Slim Jim said.

"I'm not asking you, I'm asking him." Quin turned to Hawk. "How about a vacation, old man?"

Hawk raised his can like a ceremonial cup. "I would be honored to see your homeland."

"You can't haul him halfway across the country down to the desert," Slim Jim protested. "That heat could kill him."

"Neglect could kill him, too. Shit, it's only for a few weeks. Think of it as a vacation for him *and* you," Quin said. "You can party here all you want while Hawk is away, but once he returns, you'd better have this place cleaned up. And start thinking about moving out."

Slim Jim glanced around the house, probably imagining all the wild times he and his homeboys could have if Hawk weren't there. He seemed to warm up to the idea. "A vacation sounds good, I suppose."

Hawk and his grandson shook hands and hugged. Quin knew this trip could ease a growing tension between the two, but he also knew he had spoken too soon. He should not have offered to take Hawk along without planning and thinking through what this really meant.

"Before you pack your bag, Hawk, I have to visit Helene Woman of the Storm and explain it to her."

"Good. I'll go with you and make sure she gives this her blessing," Hawk said. "Who wants tea?"

The next training session with Agent Kruse and the others from the Paranormal Team had been rescheduled twice, and this time Kruse had moved the location. Instead of a conference room, he'd upgraded them to a lecture hall on the first floor of the security hospital. Quin had walked by this room many times as physicians gave lectures or pharmaceutical reps demonstrated new technology. There were ten rows of leather seats with drink holders and pullout desktops. Rachel was already seated in the middle of a row with her sketch pad while Kruse stood at the front of the room talking to Dr. Hayden and two men in suits.

Dillan wandered in and stood silently before saying, "What's up?"

"A big room with a small audience," Quin replied. "Where's Susan?"

"*Dismissed*!" Dillan said, mocking Agent Kruse's tone. "We've been practicing our asses off for two days without you and she cracked. She had a nervous breakdown in here yesterday, shouting obscenities and throwing pens and crumpled sheets of paper at Kruse."

"Wait a minute. When he rescheduled this session, it was because he only wanted to work with the three of you?" he asked Dillan.

"So we could zero in on the target, your sister," he clarified. "He didn't want to waste your time, I guess. We're the support team, you're the star, and Susan was just sent back to the minor league, the psych ward."

"Why not treat her on an outpatient basis?" Quin said, looking at Dillan, who was fidgety, scratching his knuckles, ignoring the obvious. Quin knew the answer. Other recruits in the early weeks of boot camp were sent directly home, but Susan was too fragile for that; she'd need time to recover from the emotional side effects of remote viewing training. As the training progressed and became more intense, those who were dismissed were sent to the psych ward for what Kruse called "evaluation," or what the recruits knew was really a suicide watch.

"Despite her meltdown, we had a good session yesterday. We found your home in the desert," Dillan said. "What were your parents doing living way out in the middle of nowhere?"

He ignored the question and watched Dr. Hayden excusing herself from Kruse and the two FBI agents before walking to the back of the room.

"I'd better get seated. It's almost showtime," Dillan said as he joined Rachel in their front row.

"How are you today, Dillan?" Dr. Hayden asked.

"Peachy," he said, without looking at her.

Dr. Hayden was nervous as well, dressed to impress in a gray suit with a silver necklace and more red lipstick than usual. What was going on here? Why was everybody on pins and needles?

"Good morning, Quin. You ready?" she asked.

"Who are they?" he responded, nodding to the two men talking to Kruse.

"They're from bureau headquarters in DC."

"I thought this was our field test. Why is he inviting others to watch?"

"Agent Kruse has been very impressed with what Rachel and Dillan have found so far. And he only invited two people from headquarters for this session."

Quin still wasn't satisfied with her answer. Two was two too many. "What happened to Susan yesterday?"

"It was time for her to go."

"Dillan said she snapped."

"I can't speak about her situation."

"Then I'll visit with Susan myself," he said.

"Not yet," Dr. Hayden replied.

"What's going on? Dillan's a mess, scratching like he's got fleas. Look at Rachel sitting there like a robot."

"Remote viewing is hard, exhausting work, and I do my best to treat each of you based on your individual needs," she said, as if she were apologizing.

"When can I visit with her to find out why she crashed?"

"Agent Kruse will explain everything. I want you to know that I'm reducing your dosage, which you will take with you when you leave today."

Kruse had promised Quin there would be no more drug tests, but the news that Dr. Hayden was reducing his medication after increasing it in January was an even bigger surprise. "Why do that?"

"You said you're numb and we want you to feel normal again; we're listening to you."

"It's about time."

"When you're out in the field, you'll be in touch with your team. You and I will do our sessions by phone."

Dr. Hayden reached out and shook his hand. "Remember in January when you told me how young wolves eventually need to leave their pack to find a new one?"

How could he forget those long conversations where she had asked him about his childhood? At first he'd hated those talks; he didn't like somebody rummaging around in the dusty corridors of his mind. But over time, he liked retelling her his stories. And when she took notes, he knew she was really listening.

"I want you to know how much I've enjoyed working with you," she said, lowering her voice.

Enjoyed…as if it were over? Did she think he'd run off into the desert to hide, or was this assignment turning out to be more dangerous than they had expected? The video screen lit up, casting Dillan and Rachel as silhouettes against a wall of white. Kruse and his colleagues from the bureau began walking from the front of the room toward him, suit jackets swaying.

"Good luck," Dr. Hayden said.

Still distracted by the bright light, silhouettes, and the men walking up the aisle, he said, "Huh?"

"I'm wishing you good luck, Quin."

Blinking, he saw squiggles of light as she walked past him to the back of the room. Then Agent Kruse stood in front of him. "Good morning. Quin, I want to introduce you to Agent Clark and Agent Backstrom from FBI Headquarters in Washington."

Both men were built like linebackers, with wide shoulders, and hands in their pockets. Clark had a thinning crew cut and Backstrom had a wavy comb-over and a thick mustache. Quin noticed Kruse hadn't told him their first names…that must be how it was the higher you climbed the bureaucratic ladder.

"Congratulations on apprehending Ben Moretti," Agent Backstrom said, as if Quin already had a reputation in Washington.

"You're either really talented or incredibly lucky," Agent Clark said with a touch of jealousy.

"Maybe I'm both," Quin said.

The bureau men exchanged a glance, as if maybe they'd made a bet about him before he arrived.

"We're looking forward to this field assignment," Backstrom said to Kruse.

"Aren't we all?" Quin added.

Kruse loosened his tie, ready to get to work. "Today, Rachel and Dillan will zero in on potential locations for the ground search. As you collect evidence in the field, Quin, I'll share that with Agents Clark and Backstrom."

"And what will they do with it?" he asked Kruse.

"This is a pilot program. They'll share our data with bureau headquarters."

"So you can get more funding or so we can find my sister?" Quin's attitude apparently offended Kruse and surprised Clark and Backstrom.

"It isn't an either/or situation. This could be a win for you *and* the bureau," Kruse said.

Quin nodded. "Let's get started then."

The approach Kruse used in this lecture hall was similar to what he'd used in the small conference room for the past six months. He had Quin sit in the same row as Dillan and Rachel, while two chairs to Dillan's right, Agents Clark and Backstrom were seated, and Dr. Hayden sat three rows behind the remote viewers.

Kruse walked back and forth in front of the large screen above him, holding a remote to control access to the Internet. Quin felt nervous tension from him; Kruse's voice was dry and sometimes cracking. He sounded nothing like the calm mentor who trained with these paranormals every week. There must be a lot of pressure for him to deliver something credible to headquarters.

"Remote viewing is not a new science. In 1995, Congress asked two independent scientists and statisticians to assess whether $20 million spent on RV research had produced any quantifiable results. Unfortunately, politics plays an important role in funding projects, and after the terror attacks on 9/11, RV science was brushed aside. But

I'm here to show you that it works. Let me explain what RV is: similar to how our computers are connected to the global Internet, our subconscious minds are connected through global consciousness. And just like how a hacker can access your wireless router to access the Internet and burrow into almost any computer for information, a trained remote viewer can tap into a signal line to retrieve information. Does that make sense?" Kruse said, looking over Rachel, Dillan, and Quin to his colleagues from the bureau. "Yes, Agent Clark?"

"Can anyone be taught this technique?" Clark asked.

"Good question. Anyone can learn the basics of remote viewing, but a very small percentage of the population is accurate on a consistent basis. The people I train, such as Rachel, Dillan, and Quin, are not old-school psychics who self-proclaim their powers. They must be selected and tested to make it this far. In my experience, the most reliable viewers are right-brain dominant, more creative than they are analytical. They already see and feel the physical world differently than you and I do. Many of them live with bipolar disorder, schizophrenia, or somewhere on the autism spectrum. It's interesting to note that our viewers today, Rachel, Dillan, and Quin, are left-handed and excellent artists."

"Susan was left-handed, too. What happened to her?" Quin asked.

"She suffered from over-training, where the viewer becomes burned out and can no longer tap into the signal," Kruse answered abruptly.

"When will she be back?"

"It's unlikely she'll return to the program, Quin," Dr. Hayden replied.

He craned his neck and saw her standing at the back of the room with her arms crossed. It was obvious she wasn't pleased with Agent Kruse.

"Has she lost her ability entirely?" Backstrom asked.

"No, what I mean is that if a viewer reaches burnout, they can no longer tap into the matrix. We had many former viewers in our earlier research suffer from exhaustion before they were released from the program."

Quin looked over at Dillan and Rachel, who were whispering. Dillan turned to him, mouthing the words, *What the fuck?* Agent Kruse didn't just recruit and train talent at mental institutions, he left his wreckage there, too.

"I assure all of you, Susan is fine and we have no reason to believe our team here is in any danger," he said. "Continuing on…this matrix can be envisioned as a vast, three-dimensional geometric arrangement of dots, each dot representing a discrete information bit. Each geographic location on the earth has a segment of the matrix corresponding exactly to the nature of the physical location. Over the past two days, I've worked with Rachel and Dillan, who had no idea what targets I wanted them to search for. To them it was just another training session. But this time I assigned random code numbers to Quin's childhood home, his yard, and photos from the crime scene where his parents were murdered and his sister was abducted. Basically, we were doing a Stage I and Stage II viewing to see if Rachel and Dillan could tap into the matrix and see the desired location. And I think you'll find the results impressive. First, I will show you on the screen behind me what each of them sketched, and then actual photos."

Quin swallowed and his stomach churned as he sank into his seat, laying his head on the back of the chair. This was like preparing to watch a horror movie where you don't know how you'll react and you don't want anybody observing your reactions, either.

Kruse pressed the remote and the room went dark except for the glow of the white screen. He clicked to bring up the first sketch. "Stage I is where we're looking for a broad geographic location, such as an island, a mountain range, or a desert."

Two sketches appeared on the screen and Quin recognized the drawing styles. Rachel used sweeping lines and Dillan's sketches were always heavily shaded with jagged strokes of his pen. The images were similar: a square, and nothing much else. Rachel's looked like a large box with a smaller one to the left.

Kruse pressed the remote again. "And here's the target. I wanted them to see Santa Cruz County, Arizona. And notice how similar their drawings are compared to the map."

"My sketch is more accurate," Rachel observed. "The county isn't square. It juts out to the west."

"It took you like ten minutes longer to come up with that," Dillan replied.

Here we go again, Rachel and Dillan arguing like an old married couple. Why can't they admit they make a good team? Quin thought.

"Let me understand this," Agent Clark said. "In a missing persons case, tracking dogs might be used to follow a scent, but you gave Rachel and Dillan no scent to follow, and they zeroed in on the exact county where the crime happened a dozen years ago? They had no prior evidence to review?"

"Correct, but there *was* a scent. I have knowledge in my mind and I had assigned that knowledge to random numbers that essentially act as an address for a remote viewer," Kruse said. "Let me show you the next images from when we moved to Stage II and gathered more details of the location."

On the screen appeared the small, two-bedroom, ranch-style home that Quin remembered so well. Rachel's sketch was the house from the front with the stone path and small cacti in his mother's rock garden under the kitchen window. She had even written the word *purple* with an arrow to the front door. How could she know that? Dillan's sketch was from further back, a lonely house in the desert with a swing set in the front yard. *Amazing!*

"Quin, do these images look accurate?" Kruse asked.

"Yes," he said, looking over at Dillan and Rachel, who already knew how accurate they were.

"And for our guests, I'll show you the actual home as photographed after the crime in which Quin's parents were murdered and Autumn was abducted. Please notice how Rachel wrote the sensory detail of a purple door, which is shown in this photo."

The sketches were one thing but when Quin saw the old photo of his home, he felt heaviness in his chest and limbs. He wasn't sure he wanted to see the inside or even to know that Rachel and Dillan had been there in their minds.

"And now we'll move on to Stage III. Here you'll see the sketches showing the layout of the home with the family room and kitchen in the front," Kruse said, using his remote as a laser pointer, "and the bedrooms and bathroom in the back. Here are the crime scene photos of those same rooms."

With deep breaths, Quin watched as Kruse brought up photos of the broken front door, red sand on the family room carpet, blood in the bedrooms, and the open window through which his sister had fled that night. He looked away, down at his boots, mortified by what had happened to his family.

"Where do we go from here? How can Quin assist in this search?" Dr. Hayden asked.

"Thank you, Dr. Hayden," Kruse said. "To be most effective, RV needs people on the ground. While viewers like Rachel and Dillan can find physical locations, they cannot as easily find moving targets, like humans. Quin will be our man in the field tracking leads."

"That's all great, but this is a very cold case," Agent Clark said. "I've reviewed the file and there were no suspects other than…well, him."

Quin felt the heat of their stares and the assumed guilt he'd carried on his shoulders for most of his life. Yes, a twelve-year-old could murder his parents, even his sister, if he was crazy enough. Many children are capable of such atrocities, but he wasn't. He knew it was time to put all those rumors to rest. He stood up and turned to face his new accusers, Agents Clark and Backstrom.

"I think about my parents and my sister constantly, but this is the first time I've ever felt that somebody could put me on the right trail. I need a place to start, something to follow, and if she's still out there, I'll find her. I'm a bounty hunter, gentlemen. I hunt people for a living."

"I couldn't have said it better myself," Kruse said, folding his arms.

"How much contact will I have with the paranormal team?" Quin asked, feeling his working vacation already dissolving into a full-time assignment.

"You'll be in touch daily. We'll equip you with Bluetooth and these military-grade sunglasses," Kruse said, flipping to a new slide showing an earpiece that hides inside an ear canal. While the sunglasses looked ordinary, there was a tiny camera lens discretely embedded in the center of the frames, above the nose. "The consumer-grade version of these glasses records video at 1,080 pixels and 30 frames per second continuously for only one hour. These glasses record four times longer, capturing video wirelessly and backing it up in the cloud. The glasses will monitor your vitals, Quin; your heart rate, sweat rate, even your body fat. It shows us a color-coded composite score. Blue means you're relaxed, totally cool. Yellow means you're under mild stress. And if you enter the red zone, we know you're in a fight or flight situation."

"Is this really necessary?" he asked Kruse and Dr. Hayden. "Why record my vitals?"

"Your health is important to us," Dr. Hayden said.

"There might be times when we cannot speak to you," Kruse said, "but we want to know how you're doing."

"What you really want to know is if your guinea pig dies in the desert, where to go pick it up," Quin said.

"No, of course not," Dr. Hayden said.

"Use the gear as much as possible, but rely on your natural instincts, too," Kruse said.

That's what Quin intended to do, live by his wits, his own natural senses. He knew gadgets often failed in the real world of bounty hunting and all of this technology meant Kruse could track Quin's every move. They were sending him on a long journey with a very short leash.

The Minnesota Correctional Facility in Shakopee is the only women's facility in the nation to house maximum-custody-level offenders without a perimeter fence. Among its 568 beds, child molesters live among first-degree murderers, as well as arsonists. To an uninformed visitor to this small town, the one-story brick buildings might look like the east campus of the Sweeney Elementary School across the street. Security is maintained with tightly controlled supervision during times in which inmates move from one building to another, or what is announced as "movement." Guards are always nearby, observing inmates and visitors.

Quin picked up his ID, along with Hawk's and Slim Jim's, and handed them back so they could put them in lockers. He set his keys, dream catcher earring, and belt inside and watched Slim Jim tugging off his tight hoodie, stuffing it into another locker along with all his other cheap bling. Hawk carefully removed his bracelet and silver necklaces, kissing each item as he placed them into his temporary locker.

"I hate this place," Slim Jim said, combing his hair with his fingers.

"A good reminder of how you don't want to live your life," Hawk replied.

Slim Jim smirked. "How many of these chicks you think you've put in here, Quin?"

"None. I never bounty hunt women."

"How come? I'd do it."

Of course you would. Most skips are men, and the few women brazen enough to bust bail usually run into the arms of a protective boyfriend. Cops know how dangerous domestic disputes are, and most bounties know how futile it is to chase a female skip. But of course Slim Jim didn't know anything about the trade.

Quin led them to the security scanner, where Hawk went through first, then Slim Jim, and finally Quin, who set off the alarm. A male guard with thick lips and a bulbous nose sighed and told him to stand. He waved a wand up and down Quin's legs.

It beeped.

"Empty your pockets," the guard said, challenging him.

Stuffing his hands into his pockets, Quin assumed he'd find nothing but lint or possibly a gum wrapper. Instead, he felt metal: his earring. How did that happen? Embarrassed, he showed it to the guard. "Sorry." He heard Slim Jim laughing inside the waiting room.

"Pick it up on your way out," the guard said, taking it from his hand.

He joined Hawk and Slim Jim in the lounge with the other visitors. Movement would happen on the hour in five minutes when inmates like Helene were allowed to go from one building to the other.

"Did you plant that earring in my pocket?" Quin asked Slim Jim. "I could've been banned for that."

"No, I swear," he said, but the kid was already laughing again, proud of his stunt.

"Jimmy!" Hawk said, snapping his fingers. "Stop it."

"It's not like I *want* to be here," Slim Jim said.

It was Quin's idea to bring him along as a reminder to Helene what Hawk had to put up with every day living with his rebellious grandson. They waited to enter the visitors' room because inmates entered first, sitting in rows that faced the guard. When they got approval, they walked into a room that was already abuzz with loud conversations.

Helene Woman of the Storm was seated in the middle of a row between two other inmates, eyeing Quin and Slim Jim before she stood in front of her father and embraced him. Her black hair was parted down the middle and tied into two braids, one of them resting next to Hawk's cheek as he hugged her. That's all the physical contact inmates could have with the outside world: one hug and kiss at the start and end of each visit.

"You look good, Papa," she said, sitting, tugging at her sweatpants.

"You too," he replied.

Quin knew that was a polite lie because she was heavy; she'd probably gained fifteen pounds since he'd seen her in January. How could she gain weight in this place when meal times, she'd complained, were only thirty minutes long, with long lines? Maybe she was spending too much time in Segregation with no exercise.

She squinted at her nephew. "Hey, Jimmy."

"Hey…peace," he said, deadpan.

Quin watched as Helene, Hawk, and Slim Jim talked for ten minutes about family on the outside and her tedious life in here. Sometimes they'd drift into their Lakota language as if they didn't want Quin, the Navajo outsider, to understand what they were saying, but he knew some of their words, which said that Hawk was approaching the subject of a journey.

"Quin," she said, "this is a surprise. Thought you left the rez for good."

"That's why I returned today, to let you know I'm leaving Minnesota."

"Where to?"

"Arizona."

"Back to the Navajo Nation where you belong. No more Sioux life for Quin?" she said. He remembered how she'd convinced him to pretend he was her son, to live on the Wakan rez and keep a watchful eye on Hawk while she served her prison sentence. She trusted him better than any of her money-grubbing cousins and far more than her nephew, Jimmy. That was the pact Helene and Quin had made with each other, and it was only recently that Hawk admitted he'd known the truth all along.

"Not sure I belong with the Navajo either, but I'm heading back," Quin replied. "Hawk received the full death benefits from Rebecca's life insurance. I wanted you to know that."

"Is that true?" she asked Hawk.

"Yes, the money is in the bank."

"Good. But if Quin is leaving, who will check in on you, Papa?" She ignored Jimmy seated across from her.

"That was the other thing I wanted to talk to you about," Quin said. "Hawk was thinking of taking a vacation from the rez."

She folded her arms. "Vacation...with who? Him?" She pointed at her nephew, laughing at the idea.

"No," Hawk answered, resting his hand on his grandson's knee. "Sorry, Jimmy."

"Why is it so hard to believe that you and I would vacation together?" Slim Jim asked.

"You barely get your ass out of bed by three in the afternoon," Helene said. "That's why."

"He's better about that, but he still stays up pretty late," Hawk admitted.

It was awkward listening to Helene list the reasons why Slim Jim would never make a road-worthy travel companion. She told her nephew he was lazy, a reckless driver, money slipped through his fingers like sand, and he was bad at cards, too. How ironic it was to watch a prison inmate describe all of somebody else's faults. Quin's plan to use Slim Jim to bait Helene into letting her father go was working all too well.

The kid finally blurted it out, "Hawk wants to go with Quin to Arizona!"

Helene gasped loudly enough for the inmates and visitors on either side of her to pause their conversations, turning to see what the drama was about. "With you?" she said to Quin.

"How about it?"

"Why would I let him go with *you?*"

"Because Slim Jim is lazy and reckless," he said, using her own words.

"Hey, *she* can call me those things, but not you, bro," Slim Jim said, leaning forward, pointing at Quin.

"The point is, Hawk would like to go on a road trip, and your nephew here has agreed to work on his own self-improvement program while Hawk's away," Quin said.

"No, uh-uh," she said.

"It will only be a couple of weeks," Hawk said.

"You two gonna golf or gamble? Do that here. The summer is so damn short, why waste it in Arizona?"

"We have a bounty assignment," Hawk said.

She pinched the bridge of her nose up between her eyes, as if she had a headache. "What? You two are teaming up?"

"Told you she wouldn't like this," Slim Jim said, folding his arms.

"What kind of bounty assignment takes the two of you to Arizona?"

"We're searching for Quin's sister," Hawk said.

"Ah, Jesus," Helene said, looking up at the ceiling. "A goose chase."

"What's wrong with looking for a sister?" Hawk said, his voice cracking.

Helene lowered her head and looked her father in the eyes. "Oh, c'mon, don't start with that."

"You ever tried to go out west and talk to your sister?"

"Well obviously I can't leave here. I tried that once and it didn't go so well," she said. "She knows where to find me, where to find her son," she said, nodding to Slim Jim.

All of this was family history that Quin had only heard fragments of in conversations with Helene: two sisters who floated away like balloons and a widowed father grasping at their strings.

"Family is important," Hawk said. "Quin is searching for family and I want to help him."

"You said you wouldn't hunt anymore," she said.

Quin remembered this agreement, too. He and Hawk would bow hunt for whitetail deer along the muddy banks of the Minnesota River Valley. When the tension on the bow proved to be too hard on Hawk's shoulder, he agreed to be a spotter for Quin. On more than one occasion, Quin had found Hawk asleep in his tree stand twenty feet off the ground. Hearing that, Helene had put an end to her father's hunting days. Hawk and Quin's excursions became long walks through the forest, tracking, Hawk showing Quin how to find smaller, secondary deer trails or woodland streams where they could find deer at midday. He was his field guide, teaching him about predators and prey and how the wolf once lived there but had been pressed north by *Europeans*, he'd say, not *white people*; French fur traders who navigated the lakes and rivers in canoes.

"I'm going with Quin," Hawk said.

She folded her hands, pleading, "Papa, you're too—"

"Old? We don't stop hunting because we get old, we get old because we stop hunting."

Quin watched a tear slide down Helene's cheek, dripping onto her prison pants.

"I'm not asking for your permission," Hawk said. "I'm asking for your blessing."

"Oyawaste ota," Helen said in Lakota, meaning *many blessings.*

"You'll watch over him, yeah?"

"Like my own father," Quin assured her as he stood up. Once a visitor or inmate stands, it signals the guard that the visit is over.

Two more tears raced down her puffy cheeks before she wiped them away with her palm. This must be why they named her Helene Woman of the Storm, her emotions always shifted like thunder clouds before bursting into rain. He knew the Lakota could have several names in their lifetime, but this one seemed to fit. And through those tears she smiled at her father and her face became a radiant sun shower, the best blessing Hawk and Quin could have asked for.

"I'll order the plane tickets and we'll leave in a couple of days," Quin said.

"Oh, no, I can't do that," Hawk said, shaking his head.

"Why not?" Quin asked.

"Fear of flying," Helene answered.

"I'm not afraid," Hawk argued. "It's the pressure in my ears."

"If you're taking him," Helene said, "you gotta drive him to Arizona."

"That'll take too long," he said, looking at Hawk. "You sure you won't fly?"

"No, go without me, Quin."

Quin did not want to leave Hawk behind, not after getting his hopes up. "Jimmy, you do it," Quin said. "Drive your grandfather down to Arizona."

"No way," Helene said.

Slim Jim chuckled, scratching his belly. "Looks like my value here is starting to rise. How much you gonna pay me, Quin?"

Leave it to Slim Jim to take advantage of the situation, but Quin didn't have much choice. "I'll cover your expenses plus a hundred dollars a day," he said. "And if we get shot at, I'll double your pay on those days."

"You never mentioned getting shot," Helene said.

"Every bounty assignment has the potential for violence."

Slim Jim belly-laughed louder. "Say no more, I'm all in!"

Without the threat of a random drug test hanging over Quin's head, he started drinking Hawk's tea again. He had small bags of it stuffed into a coffee canister in his kitchenette cupboard. He was on a lighter dose of medications, thanks to Dr. Hayden, and officially "off the chain," free to imbibe, thanks to Agent Kruse. Tonight would be a quiet celebration with a cup of ayahuasca on the deck where he could watch the moon rise with the steam of his tea.

The microwave beeped and he set the mug on the counter where he steeped the bag in the water and breathed in the tart aromas. Just a whiff of it made him feel at ease, gave him a natural sense of calm he hadn't felt in how long—weeks or months? He sipped and walked barefoot with mug in hand across the apartment, past his overstuffed duffle bag that he'd load into the truck tomorrow to start his trip. There was a dry evening air on the deck and he set the mug on a small table, then sat in a teakwood chair, his bare feet cooling in the breeze.

The night was clear, the moon shining down like a searchlight focused only on him, a man on the deck drinking tea. He sipped and thought about his upcoming travels to Navajo land where he'd face his past, the family that had disowned him. The way to find out what might've become of Autumn was to start with his relatives, the very people who didn't care about Quin, back then or now. The same family members who'd turned him away and left him to foster care and a life of shuffling from one home to another. From there, he and Hawk would drive south to his childhood home to see what they could find, to at least bring closure to the event, as Dr. Hayden had suggested. And on some remote chance, maybe Dillan and Rachel could zero in on where to look for his sister.

Sipping, he thought about Minnesota, the Land of 10,000 Lakes, and how the summer sun could burn a person's skin and the winter winds could freezer-burn it as well. The North Country was a land of four seasons, where a wolf's summer coat thickened as the autumn's daylight hours thinned. And a north woods pine felt more like home to him than a desert cactus.

Out of the corner of his eye, Quin caught a movement below his deck. Something in the ash tree had hopped from one branch to another. It was too late in the evening for a squirrel to be out of its nest and there were no owls in this part of the city. He watched the tree through the bars in the deck railing and noticed a raven stretching its wings in the breeze. He sipped again, watching it preen itself, picking at its oily feathers in the moonlight. Another raven leapt from a building across the street and soared overhead. Quin tracked it with his eyes, admiring its ability to rise into the night sky on gusts of warm air.

Dr. Hayden would label this a hallucination; the product of schizophrenia brought on by a change in his medication and intensified by his tea. Quin called it something very different: a good omen. His raven spirit guides had returned from their travels to protect him from danger. He watched them as they called to each other and to him. They were agitated, warning of danger below.

He stood up and looked over the railing as the raven in flight landed on a street lamp above a row of cars parked along the curb. Somebody was down there in one of them, waiting, watching Quin's building. His calm evaporated and he felt a heightened awareness, all of his senses firing at once. He saw movement in the car, heard the ravens calling, smelled cigarette smoke, and swallowed the sweet aftertaste of tea, his palms sweaty. Time to see what all the fuss was about.

He left the deck and walked through his apartment out into the hallway, entered the stairwell, and ran down three flights, his bare feet padding with barely an echo. At the exit he looked out the window but didn't have a clear view of the car in question, so he stepped out and jogged completely around the building. He waited for a truck to pass before he crossed the street, keeping his eye on the suspicious vehicle. It was always safer to approach prey from behind. He crouched low, three cars back, and studied the vehicle in question: two people in the front seat of a BMW, nobody visible in the back. They were talking or debating, and occasionally looking back at Quin's apartment building. They must've seen him on the deck, watched him step inside the apartment, but they hadn't realized he was now only thirty feet behind them.

The ravens flew to a small tree branch above an old Schwinn bike chained to it and they perched there, watching the BMW, their heads cocked with a mellow curiosity. Quin knew he wasn't in any serious danger but he wanted to know if the people in the car were predators or prey. He picked up and tossed a pebble, listening to it bounce off the hood with a *click! click!*

Inside the BMW, Candace Johnson stared out the passenger window as Christopher Gartner drummed the steering wheel with his thumbs. "You hear that, Candace?"

"Something hit the car."

"Just an acorn," he said.

"That's not an oak tree," she said, pointing to the branch above the car. "I don't like spying on Quin."

She looked up through the sunroof of Christopher's car and saw that Quin hadn't returned to the deck. She knew he was home, she'd just watched him; but now she was nervous about approaching him. "I should've e-mailed him a photo of the knife. What if he doesn't want to talk?"

"He'll answer the door when he hears my voice," Christopher said. "And we'll go in together."

"What if he has a peephole and sees me standing next to you? Call him first. Tell him you're in the neighborhood and we want to stop by."

"You realize how you're overthinking this?" Christopher said.

"Let's not spook him."

"Believe me, you can't spook this guy," Christopher said. "We'll go to his apartment and I'll reintroduce you two. We'll give him the knife and you'll probably get a chance to interview him."

This should be easy. Quin was one of the good guys, but she felt uneasy about what they were doing. "Somebody's watching."

"I don't see anybody," he said.

"Can't you feel it?"

"No, I don't. It's probably a Peeping Tom staring down on you from one of the buildings. Button up your shirt."

She buttoned it, even though she knew Christopher was wrong. There wasn't a Peeping Tom looking down on her; she felt a powerful force stalking them from street level.

"I'll go up there first," Christopher repeated, stepping out of the vehicle.

"Christopher, wait. Call him again."

"I'll be right back," he said, shaking his head.

He locked the door and ran across the street to the apartment building. She sat listening, looking out the rearview mirror at the dim streetlights and the sporadic passing traffic. Whatever was out there, it didn't follow Christopher, but kept its eyes on her. The presence felt closer. Her heart pulsated faster as she reached into her handbag at her feet and lifted Quin's knife up into her lap for protection.

And then the presence stepped closer. Was the knife drawing a spirit toward her? The spirit wanted the knife. Was it Quin himself? She moved up in her seat, reached for the open sunroof with the knife, and stood on the console, her upper body positioned now through the roof. She stood facing the back of the car, toward the street, and stared at a low hedge along a parking lot.

"Quin?" she said, holding the knife flat in her palms, like a gift.

"Where did you get that?" a voice called out.

She spun around and he was standing directly in front of the car.

"Jesus, where did you come from?" she exclaimed, embarrassed.

He was a tall silhouette backlit by the streetlight. She couldn't see the expression on his face, only his wide shoulders and muscular arms at his side.

"It's, um, it's yours," she said, extending the knife.

"How did you get it?"

"From Christopher Gartner. Here, take it."

He didn't move. "Is that why you've been calling me?"

"Yes and no," she admitted. "I wanted to talk with you."

"About what?"

"Ben Moretti, among other things," she said. "I feel kind of awkward standing through the roof of this car, holding your knife."

In one fluid motion, Quin leaped onto the hood of Christopher's BMW, his bare feet landing softly. He towered over her and his eyes scanned her face. She felt both awe and fear in his presence, and he portrayed an animalistic beauty and grace. She handed his knife up to him and he lowered it to just below her jaw, the tip of the blade cool against her skin. If he harbored any grudges against Christopher or her, she would be dead in an instant.

"You have a scar on your chin," Quin said.

"Huh?"

He lowered his blade and touched her chin. "How did you get your scar?"

"When I was a young girl learning to ride a bike, I wiped out once and had to get stitches."

"I have scars, too." He showed his bare forearms, with large crisscross marks in the skin.

"How did you get those?"

"From this knife."

She wondered if he had been in a fight or if those wounds had been self-inflicted?

"C'mon, let's see what Christopher is up to," he said, slipping the knife behind his back into his belt. He jumped down to the street as she climbed back into the car and unlocked it. He opened the passenger door like a gentleman and she walked with him to his apartment building, up flights of stairs, neither of them saying a word to each other.

When they reached his door it was ajar, and Quin motioned to her to wait in the hallway. He pushed it open wider and stood watching and listening. Candace wondered why he was so cautious about Christopher; *or was he like this with everyone?* He slipped inside to the kitchenette, observing Christopher reading his mail, only a few feet away, yet oblivious to Quin's presence. He looked up, as if he had felt the same spirit she had felt out on the street.

He dropped Quin's mail on the table and his voice cracked. "Hey, buddy, how's it going?"

"What are you doing?" Quin motioned to the envelopes and bills on the table.

"Oh, I was just wondering if you got that insurance check yet," he said. "We agreed on my portion."

"I'll see to it that you get the money," Quin said.

"Great, wire it to this account," Christopher replied, handing him a piece of paper from his pocket.

Candace wasn't privy to their business, but she knew they'd made a deal with each other months ago. She realized now why Christopher insisted they go to Quin's apartment together; he was as uneasy around him as she was.

She stepped inside the apartment. "Everything all right?"

"Oh yeah, we're cool," Christopher said. "Did you give him the knife?"

"She did," Quin said. "Where did you find it?"

"I picked it up after you caught Ben," Christopher said. "Candace is here because she wanted to ask you some questions."

Quin glanced back at her and then walked into the apartment, past Christopher, and she followed him into the living room. There was a futon couch, a laptop on a coffee table, and stacks of books on the floor. And there was an overstuffed duffel bag along the wall. He was either returning from somewhere or he was just about to leave.

"Have a seat," he said, tossing pillows to one end of the couch. "Want something to drink?"

"Water for me," Christopher said.

"I'll have whatever you're having, Quin," she said in an attempt to bond with him.

"I'm finishing the last of this pot of tea," he said, walking back to the refrigerator. "I've got spring water or Diet Coke."

"Diet Coke, thanks."

He returned with drinks and his own mug of tea, sitting in a leather chair alongside the couch where they sat. "Well?" he said to Christopher.

"Candace thinks Ben won't go to trial, that he'll cut a deal," Christopher said.

"How do you know that?" he asked her.

"Ben told me."

"Hmmm," Quin said.

"What? That's good news, right?" Christopher said to Quin. "No long, drawn-out trial, no need for me to take the stand and testify against him. And Ben goes to prison."

Quin nodded, but Candace could see he was skeptical. "Why would he tell you that?" he asked her.

"He originally hired me six months ago to do public relations stories about him. But as you know, he was arrested. Still, he seems to trust me. He wants me to explain his side of the story."

"Have you?" Quin asked.

"No, I'm waiting."

"For what?"

"Ben wants me to wait, and he'll give the go-ahead for me to publish his story," she explained.

Quin sipped. "Hmmm."

"What are you thinking?" she asked Quin.

"A wolf doesn't howl now to be heard later," Quin said. "What's he waiting for?"

"He told me detailed information about death brokers, how they operate, but he wanted me to sit on the information until he was ready. I recorded him on video."

"Let's see it," Quin said.

"Well, he's holding onto the video," she said. "Until he's ready for me to release it."

"Sounds like he's using you," Quin said. "If he's confessing, he should hand the video over to the FBI."

"But you're the FBI," she replied, frustrated.

"I'm a bounty hunter working for a *division* of the FBI. Search and retrieve, not investigations."

His detached reaction surprised her. She had come all this way, waited months for a meeting with Quin, and he didn't even care about the case. "What should I do with this information?"

"Contact the FBI," he said.

She looked at Christopher and he shrugged, and the three sat quietly for an awkward moment, the curtains from the open deck door blowing in the breeze. "You doing a lot of laundry?" she joked, pointing at the duffel bag.

"Traveling to Arizona."

"Arizona?"

"You on a bounty assignment?" Christopher asked.

Quin turned his gaze from the deck back to his old colleague. "Sort of."

"Who are you after?"

"A family member," Quin said.

"Wait a minute," said Candace, confused. "You have a relative out on bail?"

"My sister isn't a fugitive, she's a missing person."

"Since when?" she asked.

"A long time ago, a cold case."

"Now *that* would be an amazing story," she said. "A bounty hunter in search of his sister."

She knew he had no interest in her stories. He was slipping out of her grasp again, so she took a shot and asked him, "Mind if I tag along?"

He smiled at the absurdity of it.

"I won't get in the way. I'll carry my own weight. You'll hardly notice I'm there."

"It's not safe," he said. "Things happen in the field that most people wouldn't understand."

"What kind of things?" Christopher asked, beating her to it.

"Most people don't like the idea of hunting wolves. A wolf's life is sacred, like a human life. But sometimes you need to hunt humans, just like the wolf," Quin said.

"I'd like to see that. I won't judge you," she promised. "I can do background research for you and help find her."

"I have my raven spirit guides for that."

For a second she thought he was joking, so she played along. "Raven guides, huh?"

"For thousands of years ravens have followed humans, kept close. And after the great flood, the first bird sent out to find dry land wasn't a dove, but a raven. My totem name is Raven," Quin said, standing up from his chair and walking out onto the deck.

She and Christopher exchanged confused glances, wondering what to do next. Quin's body language relayed the message; he was done talking, his thoughts suddenly a million miles away. He hummed a low groaning tone before his voice rose higher into a chant as he stretched out his arms like wings, his hair blowing off his neck as if he were in flight.

Of course she knew of several great flood myths that were passed along from different ancient cultures. The Noah story, how he sent out a dove, but only after the raven that was sent first had not returned. Was that what Quin meant? That he was leaving and had no intention of returning? She felt disappointed and cheated out of an opportunity to spend time with him because all she wanted to do at that moment was follow the raven.

Since Hawk and Slim Jim were driving to Arizona instead of flying, Quin had offered them his truck for the journey. The vehicle could haul gear and handle the rugged terrain of the desert better than Hawk's Cadillac. Quin's plan was to meet up with them at the reservation and have them drop him off at the airport before they began their road trip.

He was outside his apartment, all packed and ready to go when a woman called out, "Good morning!" It was Candace, who stood in front of the truck with a backpack strapped to her shoulders, her blond hair tucked under a cowboy hat.

"Sure is," he said. "Where *you* headed?"

"With you," she said, setting the overstuffed pack on the ground. "Last night you said I could tag along."

The previous night was like a thick fog that wouldn't burn off. He remembered the ravens and receiving the knife from her, but that was all. "I said that?"

She dragged the pack across the pavement to the back of the truck. "You were high or buzzed on something. You said you're searching for your sister."

"I did?"

"Yes, and I said that would make an interesting article...a bounty hunter searching for his sister. Frankly, that's a better story than Ben's."

"I don't need you writing a story about me, Candace."

"Really? Because I was up late last night doing research on you and you've got a PR problem. You're a bad-ass dude. You've hurt people while bounty hunting."

"Goes with the job," he said. "Some people are just—"

"What? Wild animals? Look, I'm not judging you, but I want to know what it is that makes Quin Lighthorn unique."

"Don't you have a real job?"

"This *is* my job. I'll even let you approve of anything I write before it's published, and I *never* do that with other people I write about. And if you can't stand me, I'll catch the first flight home."

She was persistent, even had some bravado. And he figured she was probably a better driver than Hawk. She and Slim Jim could share the driving duties.

"I'm dropping this truck off with two friends who are planning to meet me in Arizona," he explained. "I'm flying, courtesy of the bureau."

"Oh," she said with disappointment.

"If my friends are cool with you playing paparazzi, then you can ride along with them," he said. "Still interested?"

"Yes!"

"Follow me in your car to the reservation. If they don't want you along for the ride, your trip ends there. Agreed?"

"Okay, cool," she said, trying to lift the backpack.

Quin took it from her arms. "Here, let me." He tossed it into the truck's bed.

"Thanks," she said with a smile as she adjusted her hat. "I'll follow you then?"

Inside the truck, he adjusted his jeans over his boots, felt the knife strapped to his right leg, and thought about his meeting with Candace last night. She could've kept the knife or used it to barter for a story, but instead she'd simply given it back to him. He pulled out of the parking lot onto the street and adjusted his side mirror to watch her following in her car. This could be a short trip for her. He wasn't sure if Hawk would let a complete stranger hitch a ride with them across the country.

When he arrived at Hawk's house, Quin slowed the truck as it bounced up the curb onto the driveway. Hawk was seated in a pine rocking chair on the front porch of his log home. Next to him was a backpack, too large for him to carry, and two hunting rifles in canvas bags leaning against the log wall behind him.

Quin climbed out of the truck as Candace parked on the curb along the street. He realized Hawk was asleep, so he left him there while he loaded the old man's bag into the truck.

"Can I help?" Candace asked, walking up the driveway.

"Shhh," Quin said, motioning at Hawk.

"He's the friend who needs to give his approval?" she asked.

"His name is Hawk," he said. "Take my advice, you don't wake an old sleeping dog."

"Nonsense, it's how you do it that's important."

Quin watched Candace walk up to the porch and step on it, her boots creaking the boards. Hawk opened his eyes at the woman in the cowboy hat holding out her hand. He accepted it and after she helped him up to his feet, they talked for several minutes. Quin couldn't hear a word, but there was an outpouring of laughter from both of them before she returned with some of Hawk's gear.

"I got approval," she said, handing Quin the rifles.

"What? How?"

"We just hit it off. I have to get a few things from my car," she said, walking down the driveway whistling.

"If you get in the way, I'll put you on the first bus ride home."

"Bus? You wouldn't even fly me back?"

Hawk approached him, eyes still on Candace. "She's beautiful. Where did you find her?"

"She's been following me for months. What did she say to you?"

"She said 'Good morning' and I saw an angel. You know how long it's been since I awoke to the sound of a woman's voice?"

"What did she say after that?"

"She agreed to do a story about our people if I let her ride with us."

Hawk was always a vocal champion for the Sioux and other tribes. He had once run for city council and lost by fewer than a hundred votes. He considered it a victory.

"Reporters are your friend until they publish their stories," Quin warned him. "They can twist the truth."

"She said she brought you back your knife last night. True?"

"True."

"That's a good sign. Our journey has already begun."

"Hurry up, Jimmy," Hawk said. "Let's go!"

Slim Jim emerged from the house, shielding his eyes from the morning sun, stumbling down from the deck. When he reached the truck, he pulled out his earbuds, rap music blasting. "Who's she?"

"I'm Candace," she said with a wave of her hand.

"She's a reporter doing a story on us. This is my grandson, Jimmy."

Slim Jim turned to Quin with a look of *What the hell is she doing here?*

"She's another driver," Quin whispered. "You've got a long trip ahead of you."

"Whatever. She takes the first shift," Slim Jim said, climbing into the truck. Hawk followed, sitting next to his grandson on the bench seat behind Candace and Quin.

She accelerated in reverse down the driveway, the truck's bumper scraping the curb, and Quin smiled to himself. Hawk had been sitting on that porch for God knows how long, meditating for a sign. And the first thing he sees when he opens his eyes is Candace, the "angel" in a cowboy hat.

"So we drop you off at the airport," Candace said to Quin, "and then where?"

"Lakota country," Quin said.

"Where exactly? I'll plug the address into my phone."

"Hawk knows where to go," he said. "He'll be your GPS."

CHAPTER 4

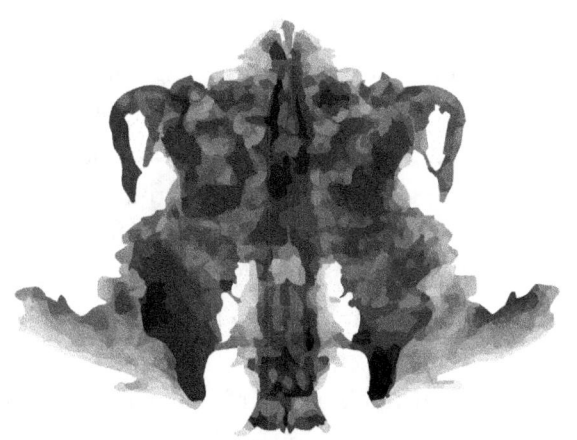

After an hour and a half of driving through south-western Minnesota heading toward South Dakota, Candace realized that Hawk and his grandson were in no hurry to get to Arizona. Hawk pored over an ever-evolving bucket list of sites he wanted to see, and sites he definitely wanted to avoid, while Jimmy just listened to music, staring out the window. Mount Rushmore was a *no* because Hawk considered it an insult that white people—or *Wasicu* as Hawk called them—would etch their faces into sacred Sioux mountains. As to the Crazy Horse Memorial, he was undecided, because while some tribes wanted the memorial, Crazy Horse's own family had never given their permission. The World's Only Corn Palace was a *yes*, and when she had questioned whether the Corn Palace had been built on sacred Sioux land, Hawk's only response was, "Who doesn't like corn?"

Harney Peak, the tallest point east of the Rocky Mountains, was a *maybe*, depending on whether Hawk could climb the trail. He thumbed through his journal, earmarking pages and newspaper clippings of South Dakota landmarks. The handwriting in the margins wasn't Hawk's; the script was too perfect, too feminine.

"Whose notes are those?"

"My wife, Lily. This was our homemade travel log."

"You two made this trip together?"

"Many times," Hawk said, nodding. "Lily was born in South Dakota, an Oglala Sioux. We'd stop at places on our trips back and forth."

"How old is that?"

He fanned through the book and said, "1979."

"That's one old travel diary."

"I'm an old man," he responded, smiling with stained teeth.

"I could download an app for my phone and get the latest information. I'm sure there are new attractions to see."

Hawk shook his head. "What's wrong with *old* things? Those who don't know their history—"

"Are doomed to repeat it," she said.

"Yeah, something like that," he said, still paging through his log.

Puffs of white and gray cotton clouds drifted overhead, casting shadows onto the paved ribbon of Interstate 90. Candace watched Hawk in the driver's seat, his eyes locked on the road as he drove, barely going sixty. Trucks hauling campers and boats passed in blasts of wind, rattling the truck. Soon the sun would set and she was concerned he would slow down even more when the sun shone in his eyes.

"You want me or Jimmy to drive?" she asked from the back seat, nudging Jimmy, who road shotgun.

"Nope."

"At least wear sunglasses," Jimmy said.

"Why? I'm sun gazing," Hawk joked. "Staring into the sun for knowledge."

"You'll burn your eyes and kill us all," Jimmy said.

"Hand me some shades," he said, holding out his hand.

Jimmy dug through the glove box, through zip ties and bungee cords, where he found a pair of sunglasses that he slid onto Hawk's face.

"Once the sun sets, we'd better pull over and rest for the night," Candace suggested.

"We'll go to The Corn Palace first, then we'll stop in Chamberlain. I've got a friend there. You ever been to The Corn Palace?" Hawk asked.

"Too many times," Jimmy said.

"No," she said. "This is my first time in South Dakota."

"It's the next exit," Hawk said.

Mitchell, South Dakota, is the home of "The World's Only Corn Palace," a Moorish revival building of spires, flags, and inlaid crop art murals along the side of the building. Each year the corn art is replaced with new murals with a new theme, but Candace couldn't figure out why Hawk cared about this tourist trap. "What's so special about this place?"

"Hawk always stops here for corn," Jimmy said.

He parked the truck, handing Jimmy the keys. "You don't like it? Lily and I always stopped here," he said, stepping out of the truck and slamming the door.

He was halfway across the lot when Candace and Jimmy caught up to him as they passed some trinket shops. "Explain, Hawk," Candace said.

"The palace closes in fifteen minutes. Hurry up."

They crossed the street, passing tourists, and walked along the building, where she examined the corn murals of pioneers and Native Americans, a mosaic display of the Dakotas' history. Candace shot photos with her phone, the air carrying a buttery flavor of corn, and Hawk picked up his shuffling pace as they stepped inside the palace. It was nothing more than a gymnasium with wood floors and basketball hoops raised high to the ceiling. Below them were aisles of souvenirs, books, and crafts. Tourists lined up at the cash registers with Dakota souvenirs that were probably made in China.

"This is on your list of places we had to see?" she questioned.

"Tourist trash," Jimmy whispered to her.

"Oh, that's all crap. I'm here for the caramel corn." Hawk led them down a hallway to a kiosk selling bags of popcorn. He bought a bag and immediately tore it open.

"We could've bought this at any convenience store," Jimmy said.

"Try it," Hawk said, holding the bag in front of Candace. "Ladies first."

She popped a few kernels into her mouth, the caramel and salt melting on her tongue. "Yum!"

Jimmy took a handful. "Yeah, that's good."

"C'mon, I want to show you something," Hawk said, leading them out of The Corn Palace and into the warm twilight air in the parking lot. "A few years ago, the Department of Homeland Security gave money to the Corn Palace."

"Why?" Candace asked.

He pointed up at the building. "They installed those."

She saw small cameras mounted on streetlights. "What terrorist would bother attacking this building?"

"There's tight security at Mount Rushmore, too," Hawk said. "Let me show you something."

They crossed the street and entered a gift shop where an elderly woman was folding t-shirts. Hawk ignored her and lifted a shirt up to his chest. It was an old photo of four Indian warriors holding rifles. The headline said: "*Homeland Security, Fighting Terrorism Since 1492.*"

"I get that one," Jimmy said, amused.

"This t-shirt became popular after 9/11," Hawk told her. "The guy who invented it? He's Navajo, like Quin."

"Quin isn't Dakota?"

"Does he look Dakota?" Hawk said.

"You think all Indians look alike?" Jimmy pestered.

"I don't know," she said, embarrassed. "I assumed Quin was from the same tribe."

"You want one, Candace?" Hawk asked, holding the shirt.

"Ah, no thanks," she said, shaking her head because the t-shirt's message had an obvious bite to it: "*Now you know how it feels to be attacked.*"

Chamberlain, a small community on the east bank of the Missouri River, was an area Hawk called *Makha-thipi*, a Lakota word for "dirt house." He kept breathing down Candace's neck from the back seat as he gave directions. Jimmy slowed the truck in the dark, the glow from his phone filling the cab. "I lost my GPS signal," he complained.

"Me too," Candace said, looking at the small homes with boats and campers in the driveways.

"Joe's house is up on the left, slow down," Hawk said. "That one on the corner."

Jimmy turned left and parked on the street in front of a white house with a porch light swarmed by moths. "Looks quiet."

"You sure Joe is still awake?" she asked.

"Let me talk to him. Wait here," Hawk said.

He stepped out of the truck and walked up the driveway alongside a Cadillac Escalade, climbing the steps of the porch and knocking on the door. He swatted at a moth as the door opened and a pudgy man with silver hair like Hawk's answered and let him in. She watched them talking in the doorway as Hawk occasionally pointed back at the truck.

"Who's Joe?" she asked Jimmy.

"Family friend."

"I'm curious, how do you know Quin?"

"Are you interviewing me now?"

"Just curious."

"Quin is a friend of my Aunt Helene."

"How come she didn't come along?"

"She's in prison."

"Oh…"

Jimmy laughed at her. "You'll probably say that a lot on this trip."

Hawk stepped off the porch and along the driveway back to the truck. "Joe's gonna give us some groceries. Grab the cooler so we can restock on ice."

Jimmy got out of the truck and opened the topper to retrieve the cooler while Hawk opened the passenger door for one of the t-shirts and said, "I told Joe you're writing a book about Sioux Indians. Don't mention you're a reporter."

"How come?" she asked, stepping onto the driveway with them.

"Joe lived in Minneapolis with me in the 1970s. We were both into AIM."

"What's that?" she asked.

"The American Indian Movement. We marched on Washington. You know, Martin Luther King, Jr. kind of stuff. Joe's mellowed, but he's suspicious of new people he meets, especially people like you."

Hawk led them onto the porch and opened the door as they stepped inside the small house with the cooler. Joe squinted at her, his belly rising with each breath. She nodded with respect and stepped inside when he motioned them to the kitchen.

"Set it on the floor in there, Jimmy," Joe said.

Walking past him into the narrow doorway between the living room and kitchen, Jimmy set the cooler on the linoleum floor.

"Aren't you a pretty thing?" Joe said to her.

"Hi, I'm Candace," she said, shaking his calloused hand.

"Writing a book about Oglala?"

"Well, researching at this point."

"Where you headed?"

"Arizona," Jimmy said. "Quin's home."

"Navajo country?" Joe said. "Where's Quin?"

"He flew, thanks to the FBI," Jimmy said, and Candace noticed Hawk giving his grandson an angry stare.

"FBI? Shit, don't tell me he's a fed," Joe said.

"No, it's not like that," Hawk said.

"The hell it's not."

"He's a bounty. We're joining him on a hunt."

"You just proved my point, Hawk," Joe said.

Candace had no idea what they were sparring about but she took a chance and asked Joe, "Why are you concerned about Quin's work with the FBI?"

Joe turned to her and crossed his arms. "The bureau rules over tribal lands. They're corrupt. First they lean on you, make you an informant, and then they recruit you to become one of them. Been happening for a long time."

"That reminds me, we brought you a gift," Hawk said, tossing the t-shirt.

Joe caught it and held it up, smiling with yellowed teeth. "Homeland security, God! Yeah, I already got one of these."

"But you're fatter now," Hawk said. "Bought you an extra-large."

Joe pulled the shirt over his already tight t-shirt. He lumbered back into the kitchen and opened the freezer door, where he pulled out a bag of ice. He tore it with his teeth, opened the cooler, and poured it on top of the bottles of water and cans of beer. "Need food?"

"We have hamburger," Jimmy said.

"How about a couple of steaks for tonight?" Hawk asked, reaching into the back of the freezer before tossing a bag of frozen meat into the cooler.

"You remember how to get to the spot?" Joe asked.

Hawk nodded. "Yep."

"What spot?" Candace asked.

"I own land along the river," Joe said.

"He's been buying back pieces of the Dakotas for years," Hawk said.

"Where you headed in the morning?" Joe asked Hawk.

"Badlands."

"Badlands, huh?" Joe said. "You stopping at Pine Ridge, Hawk?"

He shook his head. "No, we've got a tight schedule."

Tight schedule? In Candace's opinion, Hawk was in no hurry at all, traveling like a vagabond. And here he was, insisting he didn't have time to visit an Indian reservation. He seemed nervous around his old friend.

"You got family at Pine Ridge," Joe said, pointing a finger at Hawk.

"Lily's family."

"But still, you should stop by."

"On the return trip. I want Candace and Jimmy to see Crazy Horse Memorial."

Joe set his hand on his belt buckle. "Crazy Horse? You never stopped there back in the day."

"They should see it," Hawk said. "The *spirit* of Crazy Horse is what's important."

Joe shook his head as if that made no sense at all. "I took my kids there once," he admitted. "Wasn't much to look at."

Jimmy lifted the cooler and walked out of the kitchen to the front door with Joe, Candace, and Hawk following.

"Why is Quin bringing old Hawk on a bounty hunt?" Joe asked Jimmy.

"A chance for Hawk to go on one last hunt."

"Well, Hawk was always good at finding things… mostly trouble, though." Joe closed the door.

"What did Joe mean by that?" she asked Hawk, following them out to the truck.

"We got into trouble back in the '70s," Hawk whispered.

"I thought you were doing Martin Luther King, Jr. stuff," she said. "That implies non-violent protests."

"People die all the time in the name of peace," Hawk said. "Like King…and Crazy Horse."

Candace realized this slow journey through the Dakota country was as much for her benefit as it was for

Hawk's and Jimmy's. He wanted her to see, smell, and even taste the land they called home. He wanted her, an outsider, to understand the struggles and hardships that his people had endured.

Their campsite was a high ridge of pine trees above where a rising moon shimmered off the flowing surface of the Missouri River. Candace picked up sticks and branches while Jimmy and Hawk prepared the evening dinner. They insisted that she rest by the fire while they unpacked the truck, which they did in silence. There was no banter, no tasteless jokes, just a man and his grandson unpacking as if they'd done it a hundred times. Occasionally one of them would hear a sound in the trees or along the river and they'd look at one another with a nod and return to their tasks.

"You sure you don't want help?" she asked. Hawk shook his head. She pulled out her phone and checked for texts.

"Pssst," Hawk said, pointing up at the night sky.

Above her was a sea of stars piercing through the blue-black canopy of sky, the most stars she'd ever seen. It was the same feeling she got when she entered a cathedral, where she felt the presence of something greater than herself. In awe, she was suddenly aware of how small she was in this great universe.

"Steak and beans all right?" Jimmy asked. "You're not a vegan, are you?"

"Steak and beans sound great," she said, trying not to come off as defensive.

"Tonight you're a guest on sacred land," Hawk said. "What would you like to drink? Water, beer, or wine?"

"Glass of wine," she said, surprised that they'd brought it along.

"Red or white?"

The smoky aroma and the sound of steaks sizzling above the fire triggered her response. "Red."

Hawk opened a bottle and poured a single glass for her to taste, as if they were in some posh restaurant. She sniffed the fruity bouquet and sipped the cherry and vanilla overtones. "It's perfect, Hawk."

He poured two more glasses, handing one to Jimmy, and they sat with her on the log, Hawk to her left and Jimmy to her right. "This is Joe's land?" she asked.

"For thousands of years it was everyone's land," Hawk said. "But the Europeans arrived and asked us who owned it. Nobody owned it."

"But Joe owns it now?"

"He's buying back the land from ranchers and farmers," Hawk said. "Tribal members who have money sometimes do that."

"What will he do with the land?"

"He's not doing anything with it. He's setting the prairie free again," Jimmy said, sipping wine.

"Preserving it," she said. "Like the land the government purchased for national parks?"

"The government stole the land from the Sioux, Cheyenne, Arapaho, and Kiowa, who all consider it sacred." Hawk recounted the numerous treaties broken by the US government since 1850. When the Europeans asked to pass through this territory on their way to California gold, the Indians allowed it. When the government asked if the railroad could pass through, the Indians agreed, but then settlers began encroaching on the land, ignoring treaties to find gold in the Black Hills. "And they just kept coming like waves of a great ocean, one generation after another," Hawk said. "And our people fled to our small islands in the ocean, reservations that kept shrinking."

She knew some of this from her US History classes, but only as dates to memorize for tests. It was all part of the birth of a nation, a melting pot that would one day make America better than any other country the world had ever known. Now here she sat among indigenous people, feeling the sorrow in Hawk's voice to her left and Jimmy's quiet frustration to her right—two generations cheated out of their freedom like their ancestors before them.

"Isn't there a way to get your land back?" she asked.

"Some tribal members sued the government in the 1980s," said Hawk, "and the Sioux were awarded $105 million. Largest sum ever awarded to Indians for illegally seized property."

"We refused to accept the money. Lots of different opinions among tribal members about that," Jimmy said.

"Money for land isn't the answer," Hawk said.

"Then why do you want the land back?" she asked.

"To protect it," Jimmy said.

"And set it free again," Hawk added. "The Wasicu thirst for gold and other minerals has never been our way."

This was a refreshing outlook given the recent mortgage crisis, a modern-day land grab where too many people were sold mortgages they couldn't afford. Hawk and Jimmy didn't want land they could sell to somebody; they wanted to return the land to its natural state.

"The t-shirts you bought in the gift shop…" she said. "Do you still think of us as terrorists?"

"Better the devil you know than the devil you don't." Jimmy shrugged.

"But Indians from many tribes have fought for this land," Hawk said. "You know the Iroquois also declared war on Germany and Japan, right?"

"No."

"And Navajo soldiers used their native tongue to defeat Japanese code breakers in the South Pacific," Hawk said.

Candace was aware of that fact, but it wasn't until now that she saw the great irony and the gift the Navajo nation had given the United States. After years of losing their language and culture, they used it to help the government defend the homeland.

"Terrorism is different today. We're in this together," Hawk assured her. "That's what the shirt means to me."

After dinner she crawled into the tent alone, Hawk insisting that he and Jimmy sleep outside by the fire, under the stars. She watched the flicker of fire on the nylon tent, a guest on Sioux land, and felt remorse for what had happened to them and all the other tribes that had been marginalized. The remorse wasn't something Hawk or Jimmy had forced on her; it was self-imposed, an awakening that left her anxious. She turned to her phone; she had a good enough connection to go online. She learned from her online research that more than 40,000 Indians had fought in Vietnam, some to protect their sovereign nations, and others because it was the only career they could find off the reservation. Either way, they were always protecting their motherland, and for that she was thankful.

By eight o'clock the next morning, they had refilled the truck's tank with fuel and the cooler with ice at Al's Oasis and were on the road again. Candace sat in the back seat, eating a granola bar and watching Hawk page through his travel diary, talking with his grandson about possible stops along the way. At times they would chatter and joke in Lakota and she'd stare out the window, wondering what they were talking about.

The landscape west of the Missouri River was made up of soft, rolling hillsides of green prairie grass speckled with yellow wildflowers. As they drove further into South Dakota, weathered billboards hailed to them from the roadside with messages like: *"Free Ice," "Wild West Show," "WALL DRUG."*

Candace thought about what Hawk had said, how early settlers passing through the Dakota territories with dreams of finding gold in California eventually settled there instead. And they sold supplies, lodging, and entertainment to the next wave of travelers hoping to make it to the West Coast. For some traveling by horse, this journey must've been the proverbial road to hell, paved with the good intentions of prosperity.

"Where are the towns, Hawk?" she asked, looking out at the hillsides and slopes.

"Closer to the train tracks. We're going there now."

"Where?"

"Badlands," Hawk said. "Homesteaders tried to settle there but they failed."

"How come?"

"It's not fertile like this," Jimmy said, nodding to the prairie.

Hawk turned a page in his travel log. "Indians thrived in that area and could hunt and find water, but home-steaders couldn't. Too bad," he joked.

Less than two hours later they arrived at the entrance of Badlands National Park, stopping at a ranger's station. Jimmy bought a day pass and set it on the dashboard as they drove into the park.

"The Oglala Lakota live near here," Hawk said. "The tribe my wife was from."

"You want to stop and say hello to anybody?" Jimmy asked.

"No."

"You sure? Joe thought you should."

Hawk waved his hand. "Keep driving."

They drove across the flat grassland toward outcrops of rock and towers of gray clay that reminded Candace of the moon's dry, white surface. Jimmy parked the truck at the first lot and they stepped out into arid, 90-degree heat as tourists in the distance climbed their way up and around rock formations.

"Are they allowed to crawl around on it?" she asked.

"Only in a few places," Hawk said.

"Let's climb it," Jimmy said.

She followed them up a narrow trail to an incline, where Jimmy helped his grandfather and Candace up. Candace followed them higher up along a ridge and rocks of dry, hardened mud. "What created this?"

"Erosion, wind, and water," Hawk said.

"And ice," Jimmy added. "Took millions of years to form this."

She looked between two spires of mud at a valley of rock towers as if she were looking down onto an ancient city. "It's like a desert, so lonely."

"That's why it's sacred," Hawk said. "Barren places are where you find yourself."

"I see why the homesteaders couldn't make it here," she said.

"Oh, this isn't the place where they tried to settle," Hawk said. "That's a few miles away. Let's go."

They climbed back down the rock, sweating in the day's blinding sun, then Jimmy drove them through the park, winding down into the valley between rock formations wrapped in colored stripes of sediment before they climbed higher again and reached another small parking lot.

"Pull in there," Hawk said.

They got out of the truck and walked to a grassy, windy cliff that looked down onto flat land.

Hawk pointed. "That's where the homesteaders tried to live."

"Farming down there?" she said.

"Yep, they sold them small parcels of land," Hawk said. "In good seasons they could've made it, but the dust bowl drove them out of here."

"I suppose there was some relief that they had left your sacred land?"

Hawk shrugged. "By then we were already on reservations…" he said, his voice dropping off as he gazed out into the Badlands, the wind blowing through his silvered hair.

Jimmy rested a hand on his grandfather's shoulder. "You sure you don't want to stop at the Pine Ridge Indian Reservation?"

Hawk ignored Jimmy's question, still gazing out on the horizon, and Candace felt an undercurrent of tension. Whatever it was they weren't saying, it made her uncomfortable. "Am I the reason you won't stop there?"

"It's not only you, Candace," Hawk said. "It's Quin."

"Quin?"

"We stopped by Joe's last night out of respect for Joe," Hawk said. "But he's got a big mouth, and he's probably already told everybody he knows at Pine Ridge that we're passing through."

"What does Joe have against Quin?"

"He suspects he's a fed," Hawk said.

"Well that was pretty obvious," she said. "What did Joe mean when he said the FBI recruits tribal members?"

Hawk sighed into the wind. "The FBI works with tribal police, but the bureau's track record hasn't been a good one."

"And the bureau recruits tribal members to be informants, to spy on other tribal members," Jimmy said.

"But not Quin," Hawk insisted. "They haven't gotten to him yet."

"How do you know?" Jimmy said. "Quin's official title is *informant*, yeah?"

"Quin wouldn't spy on us," Hawk said.

"Even if they're fighting terrorism? What happened at Pine Ridge could happen again on a bigger scale," Jimmy warned.

"What happened at Pine Ridge?" Candace asked.

"Goes back to a long time ago," Hawk said. "Some tribes began to unite because of the Prophet Wovoka's vision. God showed him how to live peacefully among other tribes along with white settlers. In his vision, he learned the Ghost Dance that he taught to the people, and we began to unite and celebrate together. But US soldiers got nervous and misunderstood our celebrations and they chased the Miniconjou Lakota and Hunkpapa Sioux, who sought refuge near Pine Ridge. That was the Wounded Knee Massacre in the winter of 1890. More than 150 Indians died that day."

"I'm sorry, Hawk."

"And they carved up the reservation land into smaller reservations, dividing us," Jimmy said.

"What does that have to do with the feds today?" she asked. "It was so long ago."

"Was it?" Hawk said. "In '73, members of the American Indian Movement protested with the Oglala at Pine Ridge. Government had us surrounded. Both sides exchanged gunfire; they killed a tribal member barely older than either of you."

Hawk described to her the Wounded Knee Incident: a stand-off that lasted seventy-one days. An FBI agent was mortally wounded and a US Marshall paralyzed by a bullet. The Oglala Lakota man who was killed was Buddy Lamont, a thirty-one-year-old who had served his country in Vietnam. He was shot by a government sniper and buried on site by tribal members. It was his tragic death that eventually brought an end to the occupation.

"You were there, Hawk?" she asked.

"Me and Joe were with AIM. After that, we went our separate ways. Now you understand why I can't parade you around Pine Ridge? Why Joe is so suspicious of Quin?"

"But you trust Quin," she noted. "Why?"

"I've lived with him and I know his spirit. He's the raven."

Jimmy shook his head. "They had him locked in a hospital for a while. Quin's kind of crazy."

"What do you mean, Jimmy?"

"Sees things, hears things," he said, pointing to his head.

"Jimmy!" Hawk said, grabbing his grandson by the arm. "He has his demons just like anybody else."

"Why would the FBI work with somebody who has a condition like schizophrenia?" she asked.

"He doesn't have a condition," Hawk said. "He has a gift. Quin is a Windwalker."

"That's why the bureau wants him," Jimmy said. "And what Joe meant is they've been recruiting tribal members for many years, searching for those who have the gift."

Quin had instructions from Agent Kruse to check in with the bureau's office within twenty-four hours of landing in Phoenix. They would provide transportation to his home; but Kruse never mentioned that the bureau would also provide a support person, who was really a chaperone. Agent Maria Lopez was a short, talkative, fifteen-year veteran agent who treated Quin as if they were life-long partners. On the drive from Phoenix to Tucson, she complained about her life in too much detail, which included her divorce and two sons living with her ex-husband in a golf community with his new wife. Her story wasn't unique among the bureau's 15,000 special agents who served their country, sometimes at the expense of their own personal lives. Job stress and the need to keep everything confidential and bottled up eventually tore families apart.

Quin steered the black Suburban off the highway onto a dirt road and changed the subject. "Why are you really here, Agent Lopez? I know where my family home is."

"It's not yours anymore. It went into foreclosure after the murders. And guess who bought it. The bureau," she said.

"Why would the bureau want it?"

"For forensic training purposes. And, it's conveniently located near the border. DEA camp out there once in a while."

"You've been there?"

"It's practically my second home," she said. "All the nights I spent there gave my ex plenty of time to find a new honey."

He steered around a pothole on a road covered in sand drifts. "You've spent nights there?"

"They don't got a Ritz Carlton in Santa Cruz county. And if they did, the government wouldn't pay for it. I got a friend who works for the service. They stay in places like that, but not us," she said, shaking her head. "Take a left at that tall cactus and follow the dry creek bed and you'll save us a good ten minutes."

She knew the area as well as he did, even better, and he followed the creek bed, the truck bobbing over rocks as he reacquainted himself with the red outcrops in the distance. The desert, with its orange haze and rocky hills, was familiar terrain to him, like déjà vu. Above him in the distance, two ravens soared along updrafts higher and higher, like kites that he and Autumn would fly in the late afternoon sun on days when they knew their father would return from his travels.

Quin's boyhood home looked the same as he remembered it—a small cracker box house with a swing set in the front and no neighbors in sight. The nearest town, ten miles away, was Nogales, Arizona's largest international border town, which borders Sonora, Mexico. The highways meeting there comprised a major intersection in the CANAMEX Corridor, connecting Canada, the United States, and Mexico. Quin's father, a long-haul trucker, made his living on that highway, crossing back and forth from the US to Mexico and sometimes up to the Canadian border.

"What do you think of it?" Lopez asked.

"Looks the same," Quin said, parking the truck on the dirt driveway.

"I'll unlock it." She stepped out of the truck. She and Quin walked to the front door. "Welcome home! I'll give you a few minutes," she said, lighting a cigarette.

He stepped onto the sand, a wave of heat engulfing him as he walked up the stone path for the first time in a dozen years. He'd left as a frightened boy and now returned as a man on a journey that had come full circle. There was a dream catcher twisting in the wind above the door, just like in his truck. Stepping through the doorway was like going back in time. The family room looked the same; thick brown carpet, a threadbare couch, a coffee table, and a TV that were all too big for the room. The kitchen was the same, too, except the bureau had replaced the round table with a rectangular one and bench seats. He crossed into the back hallway to his parents' bedroom and it was empty except for a single chair and lights on tripods. The floor was hardwood, with no carpet. This room had been made into a makeshift interrogation room, something the DEA and the bureau used when they needed more information before dragging thugs off to jail. He turned and walked to the room he had once shared with Autumn. Turning the knob on the closed door, he heard the hinge creak as he entered and he saw their two beds in the exact same position as he had left them, his near the door, and Autumn's near the window. He wondered if Agent Lopez slept here in his old room.

It was like slipping into a dream world, with some memories that were happy, like dinners with his family, and others that were dark, like the alcohol-inspired arguments his parents would start after he and his sister went to bed. He walked to the window and pulled back the curtains. The white light of day filled the room and he squinted toward the desert, searching for her. If Dillan and Susan could spot this place with their remote viewing, could they also spot Autumn somewhere out there?

"Sorry we had to rearrange the furniture," Lopez said. "The carpet had blood stains and we replaced the mattresses and bedding."

"Otherwise, it looks no different," Quin said.

"There's food in the fridge."

"Thanks." He didn't feel hungry.

"You look kind of shaken up," she said. "You want company tonight?"

"No, I'll be fine. I've got friends stopping by in a couple of days."

"At least let me buy you dinner in town tonight," she said. "We'll talk about the case before you get started. There are a few things you need to know."

For the next hour and a half, Candace drove with Hawk seated up front and Jimmy resting on the seat behind them. As they entered Custer State Park, they discussed the *Paha Sapa,* the Lakota word for the Black Hills. Hawk was eager to climb *Hinhan Kaga Paha,* or what was known as Harney Peak, the highest summit east of the Rocky Mountains at 7,200 feet.

"You sure you can climb that high?" she asked him.

"Black Elk climbed it when he was only nine years old," Hawk said. "I've done it before and I'll do it again today."

"Who is Black Elk?"

"A shaman," Hawk said. "One who had a great vision on Hinhan Kaga Paha."

"What was the vision?"

"He was taken into the clouds and shown how the world really is," Hawk explained, "how we are all inter-connected like a great hoop."

"Like the medicine wheel," Jimmy said from the back seat.

"Medicine wheel?"

"A circle that connects all things; north, south, east and west," Hawk said. "Tribes have their own interpretations of it, but each direction has its own philosophy, animal, and color. East is the beginning because the sun rises from the east. Its color is gold. The animal is the golden eagle, who sees the world as it is, without illusion. South is green; its animal is the mouse that is curious, ever exploring. West is black, where we see the setting sun, and it's the hibernating bear, where one goes for reflection. North is winter; its color is white and its animals are the wolf and the buffalo, who represent intelligence and insight that comes later in life."

He was describing the interconnected nature of all things. Candace once had a class in World Religions where she learned that Hinduism has a mandala, a circle with four colored gates. And of course, in Chinese philosophy the yin and yang incorporates a circle of black and white, representing opposing and complementary forces. "It's a beautiful concept."

"All directions meet at the center," Jimmy added. "If you live a balanced life, you live in the center."

"In Quin's Navajo nation, they believe a criminal isn't bad or evil, but somebody who is sick and out of balance," Hawk said.

She wondered what Quin thought of Ben Moretti, a man accused of murdering people for money. That would certainly be a life out of balance, a very sick person.

"When we pulling over?" Jimmy asked,

"First we stop at the Crazy Horse Memorial," Hawk said. "We'll rent a cabin at Sylvan Lake tonight. It's at the base of Hinhan Kaga Paha."

"This is tourist season," Jimmy said. "Did you make a reservation?"

"Nope."

"How do you know we'll get a room?"

"Got a feeling we will."

"He always gets a feeling," Jimmy said to her.

"Call the lodge if it makes you feel better," Hawk said.

"Oh, now you're okay with me using my phone?" Jimmy laughed.

"You're a wise ass when you haven't eaten," Hawk replied.

They were a perfect fit for each other, old Hawk with his grandson, a man of wisdom and a young man of the digital age. They knew each other's hot buttons, yet they respected their boundaries as well. She drove along a highway bordered by pine trees, many of them a dead gray. All it would take would be one cigarette to set the entire mountain ablaze. As they climbed a hill, she saw the carving of Crazy Horse jutting out of the rock, his face in profile, his long arm pointing to the horizon. She had seen it in photographs, but it was far more spectacular in person as they drove up to the entrance to pay the park fee. Hawk gave her money and she handed it to a teenager with spiked black hair. Hawk said something in Lakota and the young man nodded as they drove forward into a full parking lot.

"He's Oglala," Hawk said. "They run this exhibit."

"Are there security cameras here that we should be concerned about, Hawk?" Jimmy asked.

"Any cameras they have here belong to the Oglala, not the feds."

She parked the truck and stepped out onto the hot pavement, stretching her stiff muscles. Most of the people in the lot were tourists—families with children, grandparents, and couples on motorcycles arriving to see Crazy Horse.

"How close can we get?" she asked Hawk.

"I dunno, never been here before. I've always seen it from the road."

They followed tourists to a visitors' center that had a movie theater, a gift shop, and displays of tribal art. Hawk immediately recognized a gentleman he knew and walked over to him with Jimmy. Candace, on the other hand, wandered into the theater and sat in the cool darkness with other tourists to watch a movie about the making of the Crazy Horse Memorial.

Korczak Ziolkowski, a sculptor who'd worked briefly on Mount Rushmore, had received a letter from Chief Henry Standing Bear asking for assistance in creating a memorial to honor the traditions of North American Indians. The letter stated: "My fellow chiefs and I would like the white man to know that the red man has great heroes, too." Ziolkowski was inspired by the tribe's vision for the project and he understood why the Oglala, one of the last tribes corralled onto reservations by the United States Calvary, needed to carve their image onto the American landscape.

It was destined to be the largest man-made sculpture in the world. All four of the sixty-foot-tall presidential heads of Mount Rushmore could fit inside the head of the Crazy Horse monument. It is larger than the pyramids of Giza and it stands proudly like America's version of the Sphinx. Ziolkowski died in 1982, but most of his ten children are still working on it, a project that is privately funded. The Oglala have been offered government funding to finish the memorial, but the tribe has refused to accept it. They had already learned that lesson; whenever they accepted money from the government, it came at a steep price. This time they were doing it at their own pace, in their own way. And Crazy Horse points across the *Paha Sapa*, reminding everyone that he once declared, "My lands are where my dead lie buried."

After the short video, she followed the other tourists out of the theater into the visitors' center, carrying the guilt and burden of history on her shoulders. Why did westward expansion have to be so hard on indigenous people? And what could be done about it today?

She found Jimmy and Hawk talking near the gift shop. "This place is amazing," she said respectfully.

"Not everyone thinks so," Hawk said. "The family of Crazy Horse never wanted this." He pointed at the trinkets in the shop, the images of Crazy Horse on t-shirts.

"He never allowed his photo to be taken," Jimmy said. "Now people take pictures of *this* Crazy Horse and post them online, every day."

"What do *you two* think of that?"

"Can't stop it now," Hawk said. "It's the *spirit* of Crazy Horse that's important."

He left the gift shop, so she and Jimmy joined him outside on an observation deck with a clear view of the memorial in the background. Hawk stopped at the edge of the deck and leaned on the railing.

"Who was Crazy Horse?"

"A cousin to Black Elk," Hawk said.

"The shaman with the visions on Hinhan Kaga Paha?"

"Yes."

"Crazy Horse was a great warrior," Jimmy said. Together they explained how Crazy Horse had led the Lakota in wars with tribes such as the Crow, Shoshone, Arikara, Blackfeet, and Pawnee before uniting with enemies to fight the US Calvary across the Great Plains.

Because of his bravery and ability to unite the tribes in 1865, Crazy Horse became known as *Ogle Tanka Un,* Shirt Wearer or War Leader.

"He was a spiritual leader, too," Hawk said. "He had visions at Lake Sylvan."

"Isn't that where we're staying tonight?" she asked.

"Yep. In his vision he traveled south into the spirit world, where he received a medicine bundle to protect him, and where he was shown his war paint markings for battle: a yellow lightning bolt on his left cheek and white powder, like hailstones, on his body."

Hawk went on to say that despite Crazy Horse's success in battle, the warrior couldn't turn the tide and the oncoming waves of soldiers who killed most of the buffalo and effectively starved the tribes, forcing them to live on reservations. And at Fort Robinson in 1877, during a scuffle and an exchange of misunderstood words, a soldier stabbed Crazy Horse with a bayonet, killing the Lakota War Leader.

Behind Hawk and Jimmy, the statue of Crazy Horse shone white in the sun. Candace imagined the war paint on his face and skin, and how this heroic leader had united warring tribes in a shared struggle to preserve their way of life.

"Quin has the spirit of Crazy Horse. That's why I believe him," Hawk said.

"The spirit of Crazy Horse?"

"Quin is a great warrior, wild, with a fighting spirit," Hawk said. "A time is coming when we'll need to defend our homeland again, all of us together. It's people like Quin who will lead the way."

A gust of wind rose up, carrying Hawk's words across to the monument as Candace felt a shiver, the hair on her arms prickling. While terrorism wasn't new to this part of the world, she sensed that Hawk was bracing for something bigger than the tragedy of 9/11. That must be why Homeland Security had mounted cameras at places like the Corn Palace and Mount Rushmore. What intrigued her even more was the FBI's interest in psychic gifts like wind walking. Were they once again relying on Native Americans in a new world war?

Dinner conversation with Agent Lopez was more of a rattling monologue. Quin drank his home-brewed tea and ate tacos while listening to her. She had opinions about everything from the drug trade in Nogales to the lack of napkins at their wobbly table in the Border Line Bar, her favorite after-hours watering hole. All Quin had to do was feed her a question and she was off talking again, her burrito getting colder by the minute. He actually liked her, though, because Lopez was a bubbling font of knowledge about the Phoenix bureau and its gossip.

"A lot of agents talk about your division these days," she said, cutting her burrito with a fork and knife.

"Because of the paranormal aspect?"

"Well, that's certainly part of it," she said. "But some agents are suspicious of you, Quin. They think you know what happened to your family. They say you and Autumn conspired to murder your parents, but I don't think so. There's no motive; your mom and dad were dirt-poor, with no life insurance or assets for you and

Autumn to share. And if you had committed the perfect crime and got away with it, why return now? What I've learned over the years is that life is messy, and sometimes you can't trust even your own family members. I bet you don't know what happened to your family, but you're wondering if Autumn knows. You think she's alive and she knows why all that happened."

She was good. Quin realized he had underestimated Agent Lopez. "Doesn't bother you that I'm here on your turf?"

"Not a bit," she said. "Why wouldn't the bureau let you assist in the search for your own sister? Makes sense. Where you gonna start?"

"Wherever my team points me."

"I hope you brought your passport."

"You think the men who took my sister crossed the border?" The bureau had dropped that theory early on, searching instead near Tucson and Phoenix.

Chewing a piece of burrito, she said, "Tunnels."

"Tunnels?"

"Underground roadways all over this place," she said. "Mules transporting drugs, money, and people back and forth, under our feet. One tunnel is the length of three football fields and they use battery-powered golf carts to carry their supplies. Smart, huh?"

He knew of small tunnels under the border fencing that people would use to crawl under to get to freedom. His father had talked about them often, how easy it was to cross back and forth. But the idea that there was a labyrinth that large surprised Quin. "When did the bureau discover them?"

"Not the bureau, the DEA. Pissed off the bureau agents. The DEA guys got such egos."

"How long ago?" he asked again.

"Three years."

"How long would it take to dig those tunnels?"

"Some of them have been there for ten or fifteen years."

"So it's possible that whoever grabbed Autumn fled through one of the tunnels."

She nodded, chewing. "If they did, they went south. All the tunnels end just outside of Nogales on the Mexico side."

"The men who grabbed Autumn spoke good Spanish, too," Quin said, remembering their haunting, barking cheers as they chased his sister. "Why didn't the bureau focus their efforts across the border to search for her?"

"A lack of resources and a change in priorities," she said. "The new Office of Homeland Security changed everyone's workload. We focused on terrorists, not a girl who might be a runaway."

"She wasn't a runaway."

"Then somebody murdered your parents, cut you up pretty good, and kidnapped your sister. Who hated your parents that much?"

"I told investigators I didn't know. It was their job to figure it out and they let the case go cold."

"Autumn and those men weren't terrorists," Lopez said. "Our new priority at that time was battling the drug cartels. Now it's the jihadists."

"And that's still the priority," he said. "This is nothing but a practice mission. Agent Kruse has his sights set on chasing terrorists."

"In the good old days we contained *organized* crime," she said. "Today it's like the wild, Wild West. Every country has its specialty; China and Russia are hackers, in the Middle East you got religious zealots, and south of the border the cartels pump drugs into the USA like Americans are on an IV drip."

"Can you show me one of those tunnels?"

"Sure, there's one right by the house. I'll show you in the morning."

"Why wait for daylight? We're going underground and I've got plenty of flashlights. Let's go now."

Agent Lopez parked the truck in the driveway and Quin ran inside to fetch two flashlights and a GPS. Back outside, she was standing in the yard smoking, checking messages on her phone.

He shined a light on her. "Those smokes will kill you."

"I'd quit but you know what they say, nobody likes a quitter," she said, stepping out of the light, walking into the dark desert.

"What about the truck?"

"Leave it, we can walk to the tunnel. I told you it was close to here. Why do you think we bought your old house?"

They walked side by side, each of them holding a flashlight toward the ground in front of them. When Quin was a boy he never went out into the desert at night. His parents warned him and his sister of bandits, deadly snakes, and scorpions. Whenever Quin questioned these warnings, his father would tell them stories of an even more frightening beast, the chupacabra, a wild animal that feeds off the blood of goats. And when Quin reminded his father that there were no goats near their home, he would say, "There are young boys and girls who taste every bit as good. Stay inside." They did as they were told, except for the night Autumn climbed out their bedroom window into the hands of wild men who might as well have been living chupacabras.

Lopez swung her light toward an object in the sand. "We're close."

"Car battery?"

"Golf cart battery. Battery-powered golf carts transport people and drugs faster without asphyxiating everyone in the tunnels."

CHAPTER 5

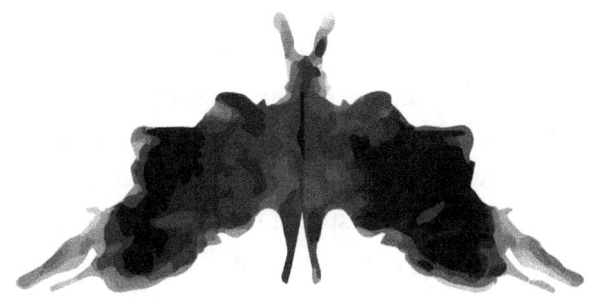

Candace helped Hawk and Jimmy unload bags from the truck, carrying the gear into a log cabin above Lake Sylvan. This was tourist season, yet somehow Hawk had secured a cabin without any prior reservations.

"You got lucky this time, Papa." Jimmy tossed the bags onto one of the two queen beds.

"Not luck. I've got intuition." Hawk turned to Candace. "You ready for a hike?"

"I suppose I could stretch my legs. Where to?"

"To the top of Hinhan Kaga Paha."

"How far a climb is that?"

"A couple hours each way," Jimmy said, collapsing onto the bed. "If we do it we'll be up half the night, and we've got to get up early to make it through Arizona tomorrow. Forget it."

Through the dusty windowpanes she saw the late-afternoon sun illuminating the pine trees in a wash of yellow light. They'd have to leave soon if they wanted any daylight on the walk down. "I'm up for it if you are, Hawk."

"Good. Jimmy, get up and pack a ceremonial bag."

He did as his grandfather told him, quietly unpacking one bag into a smaller one.

"Should I bring anything?" she asked.

"Hiking boots, a jacket, and an open mind."

They hiked a stone path along Lake Sylvan where a group of children splashed in the water, their voices echoing off the rock walls on the north side. From the lake, Hinhan Kaga Paha didn't look challenging to her; it seemed more like a pine-covered bluff. But as they walked the trail, she realized that was just a foothill blocking her view of the real journey in front of them.

Hawk led the way with Jimmy right behind him, traversing a series of rocky switchbacks along the mountainside. The higher they climbed, the more tree stumps and boulders she tripped on, yet her guides seemed to glide over the ground without losing their footing. She wondered how an old man could out-hike her on this mountain. After forty minutes of climbing, the men waited for her at the top of a steep trail, talking to one another under their breath.

"Sorry," she said between breaths. "Thought I was in better shape."

"It's not your body that fails you," Hawk said. "It's your mind. Meditate as you walk."

"Meditate? About rocks?"

"No, about your life's journey."

She bent over, hands on knees, sweat cooling her body in the evening air. "Okay, I'll clear my mind and ignore the rocks, but tell me again, why are we climbing this mountain?"

"To make a sacrifice, to unite all of humanity."

She stood up, her legs aching. "You're not throwing me over the edge, are you? Because that would be really cruel and unfair to drag me up here only to throw me off Hinhan Kaga Paha!" she shouted.

Hawk whispered something in Lakota to his grandson.

"What did he say, Jimmy? Tell me right now what Hawk just said or I'm turning around!"

"He said you watch too many movies."

Angry and frustrated, she reached for a rock and threw it at their feet, where it bounced and skidded off the cliff. The two men walked to the edge, listening to the rock tumbling down the mountain.

"Don't tell me that was a sacred rock," she said.

"Everything's sacred," Hawk replied.

"Yeah, you better go down and get it." Jimmy laughed at her.

"Oh God!"

"No, we're messin' with you," Jimmy said. "C'mon, catch up."

She closed the gap, still trailing behind them. "You guys are terrible at sarcasm, you know that?"

She hiked with them in the twilight that soon bled into darkness, her sense of hearing and smell compensating for the night blindness. In the air, she tasted the dust from the rocks, her lips dry. Overhead, she heard an owl calling out into the night.

"That's a sign," Hawk said, pointing in the owl's direction, toward a pine tree.

"Good or bad?"

"Good."

"Jimmy, can I have some of your water?" she asked.

He pulled a bottle out of his pack. "Here, keep it."

It wasn't cold, but the water soothed her throat as she followed them up the mountain, clearing her mind, going with the rhythm of the hike. She hoped they were near the summit as she fought for each breath in the thinner air.

"What happens when we get to the top?" she asked between breaths.

"We'll have a ceremony," Hawk said.

"Like a vision quest?"

Hawk and Jimmy stopped on the trail and turned to her.

"What do you know about vision quests?" Jimmy said.

In the darkness, she couldn't read their expressions. She decided it was time to stop asking so many questions. "Nothing. Like you said, I watch a lot of movies."

"There it is," she said, pointing her flashlight into the darkness at a rock formation. She stood her ground and lit another cigarette as Quin walked toward the rock wall.

"Are agents allowed to smoke on duty?" he asked.

"I'm on a smoke break; been trying to quit for months. The door is right in front of you," she said, blowing smoke upward. "It's hard to see in the daylight and even harder at night."

He searched the crevices and wiped away the red desert clay, feeling cool metal under his fingertips. "Who covered it up?"

"DEA."

He stepped back and marveled at the door; it must have been ten feet wide and ten feet high. "I want to see it. How do we get in?"

"If you got your passport, there's no reason to go down there to cross the border," she said.

"But this might be how they escaped with Autumn," he said. "I want to see it."

"It's a dark tunnel, not much to see. Mules don't even use it anymore."

"Homeland Security uses it, right? That's why they haven't filled them in," he suggested. She said nothing and he continued, "Open the door, Agent Lopez."

She jingled her keys as she approached him, cigarette smoke trailing her. Along the left edge of the door, she searched for and found a handle; below it was a keyhole. She inserted the key and the door rattled from the other side. "Help me pull."

He stood next to her and gripped the rusted handle. They heaved and the door slid to the side along a track, with a rush of musty wind and dust whipping past them.

"What's that odor?" Quin asked.

"If you're an illegal crossing the border? It's the aroma of freedom."

"That's a musty kind of freedom."

"Mother Earth, she's like wine. She needs time to breathe," Lopez said. "And if you're down there long enough, you get used to it."

The tunnel sloped downward into the rock and earth. A ramp could easily fit a couple of golf carts, as Lopez had said. Quin walked into the blackness with his flashlight illuminating the floor, walls, and ceiling.

"What are you waiting for?" he asked. "Let's see how far this goes."

"It connects to other tunnels," she said, without moving forward.

"How far is the intersection to the next tunnel?"

"Fifty or a hundred yards," she said. "If you go, you're on your own."

After hours of constant chatter, Lopez was finally quiet. He sensed her fear, her resolve to go no further. He walked without her deeper into the tunnel and reached for his phone to see if he could get a signal as he descended into the earth. His phone lit up like a second flashlight, but he couldn't access a cell tower this deep underground. The tunnel narrowed as he waved his light across the clay floor in front of him. There were tire tracks and footprints along with garbage, empty water bottles, beer cans, and more batteries. He paced what felt like fifty yards and turned the light to the left and right walls, searching for an opening.

Nothing.

He knelt and felt for a rock and threw it in front of him, listening. It bounced off a wall in front of him, so a turn must be ahead. He walked another thirty yards and felt a change in air pressure, a breeze to his right, and there was the next tunnel.

"Found it!" he shouted, waiting for her response. "Lopez, how long is the next tunnel?"

No answer from her. He wouldn't proceed further without knowing where it would lead. He satisfied himself that this was worth exploring, but not tonight. He turned and backtracked to the dirt ramp where he'd left Lopez. The air pressure changed again, then he heard a clanking sound.

She'd left him and was closing the door. Quin sprinted up the long ramp, his feet slipping on sand and dirt, his flashlight like a baton in his hand.

"Lopez!"

He reached the metal door and searched for a handle. In the dark he was disoriented; was the handle on the right or left? He searched the right side first, feeling the edge of the metal against the rock. There had to be a handle on the inside; unless, of course, the DEA never intended this to be a two-way passage. With all his weight, he pulled on the edge of the metal, trying to walk it back, and it moved only a couple of inches, but it moved! He pulled again and the door rolled another three inches, grinding over sand caught in its path. He gave it another tug and it opened enough for him to slide through into the cool air outside. There she stood, talking on her phone.

He walked over to her, wiping sweat from his brow. "What the hell are you doing?"

Lopez turned with the phone to her ear. "Shhh," she said, motioning to the phone. "Talking to my boss."

This explanation better be good.

She ended the call and stuffed the phone in her back pocket. "Sorry about that," she said, pointing at the tunnel door. "I closed it because you kept calling my name and I was afraid my boss would overhear."

"Oh, I thought you—"

"You didn't think I would leave you in there?"

"It crossed my mind, Lopez."

"I didn't lock it. Besides, if I wanted to kill you, I would've shot you in the tunnel, then closed the door."

"That's very comforting. Thanks for your reassurance."

"You got trust issues, Quin."

"Why was your boss calling you so late?" Quin asked.

"He said Agent Kruse has been trying to reach you."

He checked his phone and he had missed two calls from Kruse in the past hour. "I'll call him in the morning."

"I better lock up and make my way into town, find a place to sleep," she said.

"Can you leave the door to the tunnel unlocked?"

"You're going back down there?"

"I need to see how far it goes, where it surfaces."

"The DEA has already mapped it. Those tunnels go for miles."

"Can you get a copy of the map?"

"I suppose, but even with a map, it's dangerous down there; walls collapse when we get flash floods."

"Get me a map."

"I'll see what I can do," she said. "Hey, you don't have to stay at the safe house. It's a spooky place at night. We can get a hotel room in town."

"I'd rather stay at the house."

"I meant separate hotel rooms, of course," she said.

"It's important for me to stay there. I hope you understand."

She nodded and started walking back toward his old house, scanning the ground with her flashlight. "If you go down into those tunnels, you might want to buy yourself a golf cart, but you didn't hear that from me," she said.

The view from the top of Hinhan Kaga Paha was worth the two-hour climb. Candace caught the last rays of the setting sun on the horizon to the west. To the east, she saw hills of pine painted black on the dark blue of twilight. She breathed in the clean air as Hawk and Jimmy gathered sticks for a fire. This felt like sacred ground to her and she understood how this isolated place could inspire visions.

"What happens in the ceremony?"

"We drink tea," Hawk said.

She felt a chill in the air. "A warm cup of tea sounds good right about now."

"Not for you, Candace. For me and Jimmy."

"What will I drink?"

"Water," Jimmy said, using a lighter to ignite a birch log.

"You're a writer," Hawk said. "You'll record our visions. Sit here," he said, patting a rock by the small fire.

She sat, watching as Hawk stuffed a large tea kettle with leaves and roots that he pulled from his ceremonial bag. He opened a water bottle and poured it on top and then rested the kettle on the fire.

"What kind of tea is that?" she asked.

"Ayahuasca," Hawk said. "Medicine."

She'd never heard of it. "Is it like marijuana?"

"Stronger, more like peyote," Jimmy said.

"You're getting high?" she said.

"No, we're seeking truth, as our fathers before us did," Hawk said.

For an hour she sat across from Hawk and Jimmy as the men stared into the fire, Hawk occasionally stirring the leaves in the tea. They conversed in Lakota, and only once in a while did she pick up on English words like Quin's or her own name. Hawk eventually poured a cup for Jimmy and one for himself, and they both sipped the hot brew a few times before drinking the entire cup in one swallow. Within a few minutes Jimmy slumped over, his head in his hands, moaning, as Hawk patted his grandson's back.

"What's with Jimmy?"

"He's entering the spirit world. It's harder for young warriors."

"Are you there in the spirit world, Hawk?" she asked.

He closed his eyes. "I am."

"What's it like? Describe what you see."

"Jimmy is with me, we are running with wolves."

"You're chasing?"

"We're among them, running *with* them," Hawk whispered.

"What are you and the wolves running from?"

"From nothing. We are searching for prey, following ravens in the sky."

"Ravens?"

"Ravens see the prey and wolves follow the ravens."

She remembered Quin mentioning ravens before he left town. "Hawk, do you see Quin?"

"He is here."

"What's he doing?"

"He's a raven in flight. Chasing evil spirits." Hawk's head bowed into his knees like his grandson's.

The men were silent, physical forms; she could detect no movements or breathing in them. They were so still their bodies could have been empty cocoons, left behind as their spirits took flight. Was there another world out there she couldn't see? She felt alone there, and the evening winds at seven thousand feet left her shivering, even next to the fire. She decided she'd pour herself a cup of tea, something warm to hold onto until they awoke. She grabbed Hawk's cup, stood over the fire, and poured the dark, steaming tea into the ceramic cup. She sat down again, clutching the warmth as the winds increased and the tree branches behind her creaked and moaned.

Hawk raised his head. "This medicine isn't for you, Candace. Go to sleep."

Quin knew he could never really go home again, because when he returned, it would be a different place. Or maybe he had changed and was the stranger seated with a cup of Ayahuasca on the floor in the family room, remembering his life here. During the holidays, a Christmas tree filled a corner of the room, a tradition his father had instilled in them. And on many nights his mother would help Quin and Autumn build a *Hogan*, the Navajo word for house, using wool blankets and cushions from the couch. They had so many happy memories that were swept away, like tumbleweeds scattered across the sands.

Yes, his parents sometimes argued, but his father never raised a hand to his mother, never threatened to harm her or his children. Quin always felt there was a rift between his parents that always boiled over into an argument that they took to the bedroom. He and Autumn would listen to their parents' muffled conversations down the hall and the next day, they would be happy again. The family would ride in his father's big-rig truck into Nogales for ice cream and a fresh supply of water and beer. And after two or three days, his father would drive off in his rig and not return for a week or more. He was gone for longer stretches of time than he was home.

Quin drank more tea, his head lighter, and he rocked back and forth to the rhythm of the wind that tossed a rusty swing into the night. He used to push Autumn on that very swing as she pumped her legs in squeals of excitement.

"I want to fly, Quin!" she'd shout. "Push me higher!"

And with one more running shove he'd push Autumn with all of his strength and she'd soar off the swing, her arms outstretched.

She caught an updraft, lifting her into the sky, and he chased her, afraid he'd lose her forever.

"Autumn! Come back!"

"Fly with me!" she shouted, her voice small and distant.

He ran, stumbling on the sand, gasping the dry air as he followed Autumn, flapping her wings. What would his mother and father think of him? How could he have pushed her so hard that the winds would carry her away? He ran faster, sprinting, pumping his arms, and he lifted off the ground, too. It was only a few feet, but, elated, he sprinted again and he flew farther this time. Then with one final kick of his feet, he was aloft! His arms stretched out like wings, the wind whipping through his hair like the tail of a great kite. He circled higher with each updraft of heat but he couldn't find her. Autumn was gone. His house below grew smaller as he rode the winds, and he feared he would never find his way home again.

"Caw! Caw!" Above him were two ravens gliding across the sky, and he followed them with no effort at all. He thought of it and it happened. They led him across the desert, gliding along the currents when they slowed and landed on the desert's floor on the edge of a small bubbling arroyo. Quin joined them as the ravens hopped along the edge.

"Caw...*drink*," one of the ravens said to him.

Kneeling onto the sand, he cupped the tepid water with his hands and sipped. It was as bittersweet as his tea.

The birds drank it, too, dipping their silky black heads and raising their beaks to swallow. They fluttered before resting on each of his shoulders. He felt comforted until he saw two shadows emerge from the desert heat. He blinked but they were still there as he focused on them, the spirits of a woman and a man standing before him.

"Am I in danger?" Quin asked the ravens.

"Fear nothing," the raven on his left said.

"Love," the raven on his right whispered.

"Mother? Father?"

The shadows remained on the other side of the water, lurking, as if they were afraid to approach him. Quin stood up as the ravens remained on his shoulders, balancing themselves, and the shadows stepped back. He sensed the shadows' curiosity; they wanted to know why he'd returned after so long.

"Is there another among you?" he asked.

They remained still.

"I don't see Autumn," he said, stepping forward, one foot landing in the bubbling brook.

The shadows stepped back even further.

"Where is she?" he said, wading through the water toward them.

They moved back again.

"If you won't answer me, then go away!"

With that, the ravens took flight in pursuit of the spirits across the sand until the *chindi* (the Navajo word for ghost) vanished into a dust devil shooting up into the sky. Quin remained there, feeling the presence of somebody or something still watching him.

He stepped out of the water and spotted a lobo, a Mexican gray wolf, peeking at him from behind a thick cactus. Mexican grays once ranged from central Mexico up through the southeastern United States until they were over-hunted and pushed into the borderlands between Arizona and Mexico. The wolf was smaller than its ancestors to the north, and appeared scrawny to Quin. His mother had taught him and Autumn that to see El

Lobo was good luck, but to never approach it or your luck would suddenly change. Quin knew in this moment that he had no choice; he had to approach the wolf, to move toward danger, if he wanted to find Autumn.

Quin awoke to his phone vibrating next to him on the floor. *What time is it?* He had no idea, but his wake-up call was from Agent Kruse, who no doubt wanted to know what he was up to. He picked up the phone and teapot and brought them to the kitchen.

"Good morning," he said in a groggy voice.

"You're just waking up?" Kruse asked.

"I'm in a different time zone. It's earlier here."

"It's noon where you are."

Quin pulled the phone from his ear and read the display. "Actually it's only 11:50 a.m., don't exaggerate. I'm not a total slacker."

"You're settled in?"

"How come you didn't tell me the Phoenix office would assign an agent to shadow me?"

"You would've gone straight to Nogales. You had to check in, it's office politics. But sometimes you have to play by the bureau's rules. How is Agent Lopez?"

"She knows the area but so do I," he said, without admitting that she'd revealed the tunnels. He opened the fridge. Inside were bottles of water and Diet Coke. No milk, eggs, or bagels. *What do agents eat around here?*

"We've been busy remote viewing this morning," Kruse said. "Dillan and Rachel have some interesting leads to share with you."

"What about Susan?"

"We've already covered this, Quin. She's done."

"I know, but how is she doing?" There was a long pause at the other end. "How's her health?"

"Fine."

"Well enough to go home?"

"Very soon," he said. "Can we focus on the case?"

Quin reached for a bottle of water, closed the refrigerator door, and leaned against the center island. "What have you got?"

"Dillan, Rachel, and Dr. Hayden are here with me." His voice was now on speakerphone. Everyone gave a quick hello.

"Good morning, or should I say 'good afternoon,' team?" Quin said with a yawn. "Ready when you are."

"We're coming up with a series of buildings. I'm e-mailing you the drawings as we speak," Kruse said. Quin found the documents in his e-mail and opened them. "They could be warehouses. Do you see them?"

Quin scrolled and zoomed in on the sketches. "Very impressive warehouse-like buildings," he said with a touch of sarcasm.

"I knew you'd appreciate my work!" Dillan shouted.

"Your shading and the way you captured the light is pure genius. And Rachel, might I say your detail is exquisite as well."

Rachel burst into laughter. "Takes an artist to know an artist."

"Can we move on from the ass-kissing?" Kruse said. "Quin, you have to trust the process."

"These could be any of a hundred warehouses in and around Nogales," he said. "This is a gateway to Mexico, with container trucks loading and unloading all the time. You really want me to start investigating warehouses?"

"Check your e-mail. I sent you more drawings," Kruse said.

He opened the next document and it was a depiction of a woman. "Who is this?"

"I saw her there," Rachel said.

The woman in Rachel's sketch had shoulder-length hair. She was wearing a t-shirt, ripped jeans, and cow-boy boots. She looked Indian, or at least a mix, and Quin couldn't deny the resemblance to himself. Was this his sister?

"I've seen her near those buildings several times now. She's walked right by me," Rachel said.

"Walked by *you*?"

"In a deep state, a remote viewer can see the location as if he or she were actually there," Kruse said. "I'm send-ing you another sketch, this one from Dillan's separate viewing of the same location."

Quin opened the document and zoomed in on the incredible details. The woman had a thin nose and a scar above her left eyebrow, possibly from a piercing. What stuck out the most was her earring: a dream catcher with a feather hanging from it.

Quin wore a similar earring to his sister's. He might've told Dillan that in the past, but he wasn't sure. There's no way, though, that Dillan and Rachel would collaborate pulling a hoax on him, but he had to ask anyway. "How do we know they haven't copied each other's work?"

"They drew those from separate viewings," Kruse said.

"I observed them," Dr. Hayden said, speaking up for the first time.

"This might be Autumn or somebody who looks like her," Quin said. "But again, there are warehouses all over this part of the country."

"I just sent you the GPS location," Kruse said.

"After twelve years of my sister missing, the three of you in a matter of a couple of days pinpointed her location? You're shitting me."

"No, we're not," Kruse said. "That's the power of RV."

Quin opened his e-mail and clicked on the GPS link, then launched his mapping software. The warehouses were across the border, roughly ten miles from the kitchen where he was standing. Was it possible Autumn was really only ten miles from home? Had she been there all along?

"I'll call Agent Lopez and we'll drive there to check it out this afternoon," he said.

"Give us thirty minutes' notice before you cross the border," Kruse said. "And I want you wearing the glasses and earpiece we provided you. We want to see and hear everything as it happens."

Quin couldn't even remember where he'd packed that gear. He agreed and then asked, "Dr. Hayden, do you have a few minutes to talk?"

"Sure, what's on your mind?" she asked.

"It would be a private conversation, my weekly check-in with you."

By the time Dr. Hayden called back, Quin was outside drinking another bottle of water. The sun felt warm on his back as he watched a scorpion run across the hot sand. He was reflecting on last night's dream, how he would describe it to Dr. Hayden when she finally called.

"Good afternoon," he said. "You alone?"

"Yes, I'm in my office," she replied. "How are things?"

"Glad I'm here. I should've come sooner."

"It's not always easy to face one's past."

He walked across the property in his bare feet and stood next to the old swing. "I had a dream last night that I pushed Autumn on our swing and she flew away."

"How did that make you feel?"

"Responsible."

"Because you pushed her?" Dr. Hayden suggested.

"She asked me to push her higher."

"So you were only responding to what she asked you to do. You didn't shove her out of the swing against her will?"

"No, she told me to push higher."

"You complied with her request and for that you feel responsible?"

He looked at the house with a new understanding of his past. "The night my family was attacked, I told Autumn to go out the window," he said. "I should've gone with her."

"And you woke up with a false sense of guilt, Quin. Dreams are very powerful. They can evoke real emotions. But they are the mind's way of dealing with the pain. You can't blame yourself for what happened to Autumn."

"After that, my dream became a vision."

"How do you mean?"

"The ravens arrived and flew with me."

"The ravens are your shadow-self, your darkest fears," she said. "And medication has suppressed those fears."

"You reduced my meds; the ravens are back."

"Were you taking any recreational drugs?"

"Ayahuasca tea last night."

"You know how I feel about that substance. It causes hallucinations."

"Call it what you want. It was a vision."

"I understand. What happened when you saw the ravens?"

"They led me to the end of earth and time, where waters separate the living from the dead," he said, looking out onto the horizon that shimmered in a wave of heat, beads of sweat sliding down his back. He drank the last of his water and again spotted a lobo across the desert.

"What happened when you and the ravens reached the water?"

"The ravens showed me chindi."

"I'm not familiar with that term, Quin."

He explained to Dr. Hayden that chindi are evil spirits left behind from the dead. His mother had warned him to never approach a dead animal because good spirits depart while evil spirits remain on Earth. Evil spirits can make a person sick. When his parents were stabbed to death, Quin entered their bedroom and knelt over them to stop the bleeding. It was too late; their spirits had departed.

"Is it possible that on the night my parents died, their chindi entered my body?"

"In a metaphorical sense that would be a good way to describe a childhood trauma," she said. "You've carried them with you all these years. You said they were on the other side of a river?"

"Yes, and the ravens chased them back into the spirit world."

"Then possibly your parents' chindi are gone now. You've set them free."

He breathed a sigh of relief. "I hope so."

"Are the ravens gone too?"

"My ravens are not chindi," he said. "They're my spirit guides, protecting me."

"Do you see the ravens now?"

He looked up into the sky at them circling high overhead. "They're here."

"Are you drinking tea now?"

"No, not since last night."

He noticed her long pause—*is she taking notes?*

"Well, you seem to be making some progress. Now prepare yourself for what might happen when you learn the truth about Autumn. You must let go of any self-imposed responsibility you're carrying."

He heard the hum of a truck approaching. It was Agent Lopez in her FBI-issued SUV, bobbing and weaving the vehicle across the dunes. She honked twice and the wolf ran off, bounding and darting across the sand.

"I have to go," he said. He didn't want Lopez to hear any of this conversation.

"Good session," she said. "We'll talk again in a few days?"

"Yeah, sure," he said, hanging up on Dr. Hayden.

Lopez parked the truck and lowered the passenger-side window. "Did you see the coyote?"

He walked up to the truck and leaned through the window. "It's a wolf, and it means we're in luck."

Her headache lifted as Candace gazed out at the northern desert sun in the distance. She had been up most of the previous night, shivering at the top of the mountain while Hawk and Jimmy slept motionless until dawn. Then they all packed up and started their jog down the trail. Her toes were bruised and her feet, swollen.

They had been driving for sixteen hours, pushing to arrive at Window Rock, Arizona, before dark. Hawk wanted to meet somebody there, somebody from the Navajo Nation who knew Quin. From the back seat she listened to their Native American music, flutes and pipes with the occasional drumbeat that soothed her as they rode along in silence until Jimmy said to Hawk, "We can go there, if you want."

"Where?" Candace asked.

"Navajo Nation." He turned his head to her.

"Quin's home?"

"His mother's home," Hawk said. "Quin never lived on that rez."

"How come?"

"Indian women who marry white guys move off the rez."

"Why would we go there?" she asked.

"Number one rule in bounty hunting: You start with the family of the missing," Hawk said. "I taught Quin that."

"Family always knows something," Jimmy added.

"Does Quin know we're stopping there?" she asked.

"No," Hawk said.

"Then how did you get this person's name?"

"Joe knows of her," he explained. "That's why we stopped at his house. Joe knows lots of people, some Navajo, Hopi, Cocopah people."

"We're pretty tight these days," Jimmy said to Candace. "Tribes meet, share ideas."

Hawk slid a torn magazine page from his travel journal. It was a picture of a casino. "Can you find this?"

Jimmy read the address and with his free hand he tapped it into his phone. "It's only two exits away."

"Where are we?" Candace asked.

"Fire Rock," Jimmy said.

Fire Rock Casino is off Route 66, nestled in Red Rock State Park. Unlike Vegas-style casinos that tower above busy streets, Fire Rock is more of a boutique establishment. To Candace, it looked like an expensive restaurant with stone pillars and a drive-up valet service.

"Tell me we're not here to gamble," she said.

"This is where we meet Quin's relative," Hawk said.

"He works at the casino?"

"Not he, *she*, and she's one of the owners," Hawk said.

Jimmy set the truck in park and stretched his back, waiting for the valet. "I'll play a couple hands of black jack while you talk to her."

"Don't go broke," Hawk said.

"What about me?" she asked as they all stepped out of the truck and Jimmy handed the keys to a valet.

"You play cards?" Hawk asked.

"A little, but I don't gamble. I'd rather go with you to meet Quin's family."

Jimmy shook his head with a laugh and walked off to the casino by himself. She looked toward Hawk, who must have been debating whether or not he should let her into this meeting.

"You want me to write this story?" she said. "I have to have access to meetings like this."

"Let me do the talking," Hawk said as he turned and followed his grandson.

She caught up with Hawk as he shuffled past tourists leaving the casino. "I appreciate that you trust me enough to be in this meeting. It could be helpful background information—"

"I do the talking."

"Of course. I'll observe, and then we can discuss the meeting afterwards—"

"Stop talking."

"We're not inside yet."

"I gotta think about what I'm gonna say."

They entered the casino through revolving doors and she was overwhelmed by the cold air and darkness inside the building. It was as if they had stepped out of the desert heat into a cave, except this cave had slot machines, music, and waitresses carrying drinks on trays high above their heads. She and Hawk walked to an information desk where he asked a young man for a woman named Nizhoni. The man made a phone call and then told Hawk to wait.

"How is she related to Quin?" Candace asked.

"She's his mother's cousin."

"Second aunt?"

"Family," Hawk said.

"What did Joe say about her?" she asked.

"She was married to one of the Lighthorns. Now divorced."

"And she's agreed to meet you?"

"Nope."

"So you showed up anyway."

"Yep."

"What will you say to her?"

"Don't know yet."

"Hawk, she'll be here any minute. What's the purpose of this meeting?"

"Not sure yet."

"Not sure?"

"I'll know as soon as I see her."

They waited in silence as casino tourists walked by with drinks and plastic cups filled with coins from slot machines. An elevator opened to their right and Candace saw a slender woman in her early sixties with gray hair pulled back in braids. She walked quickly toward them, scanning faces, smiling, and waving at the staff as she walked.

"That's her," Hawk said.

"How do you know?"

"Walks like she owns the place. Now stop talking."

The woman approached with a confused expression on her face. "Hawk?"

"That's me," he said, shaking her hand with both of his. "This is Candace."

"Hello, I'm Nizhoni," she said, shaking Candace's hand. "How can I help you?"

He looked up at her. She was a good four inches taller. Clearing his throat he said, "I'm from the Prairie Sun Casino in Shakopee, Minnesota."

"Joe had great things to say about you. Welcome."

"I'm not here about business," he said. "I'm here about family."

"Whose family?" Nizhoni asked.

"The Lighthorns."

"I'm not a member of that family now," she said, looking away across the casino. Candace wondered if she was searching for security, or some other excuse to exit this conversation.

"But you know them," Hawk said.

"Not anymore. They've all left."

"Was it because of the murders?"

"Why do you ask?"

"The information might be helpful to Quin," Hawk said.

Nizhoni seemed suddenly more interested. "You know Quin?"

"He lived with me in Minnesota."

Nizhoni turned to Candace. "Are you a friend of Quin's?"

"Yes," she said, unsure of how else to put it.

"He's back in Nogales searching for Autumn," Hawk said.

"The feds gave up on that case years ago," Nizhoni said.

"That's why I wanted to meet with you," Hawk replied. "What happened?"

"I already told tribal police and the FBI what little I knew."

"Can you tell us? It might help Quin in the long run," Candace asked.

The woman sighed. "The FBI took over the investigation from tribal police and focused on Jack, her real husband."

"How do you mean?" Hawk said.

"Quin's mother, Lina, married a man here on the reservation but they had troubles right away. After a couple of years of not conceiving children, he blamed her. She said he'd become abusive, so she left the clan and the reservation. She was gone for five or six years, nobody knew where she went. One day she returned with a white man named Derek to visit her parents and he had two children with her. And it's as plain as day that her children are not just Navajo but also white. Turns out she could conceive after all. I was happy for her and that she'd returned."

"But her husband was angry?" Candace asked.

"Jack? He didn't care at all," she said. "He liked the single life and was no threat to her or the children. It was her father who was disgraced, who couldn't allow her back. So they left, went back to Nogales where her husband worked in trucking. He tried stopping here during his travels to mend the rift between his wife and her father, but her father only argued with Derek."

"About what?" Candace asked.

"Everything, but mostly smuggling," Nizhoni said. "He wasn't always hauling auto parts in those trucks. He made extra money as a mule."

"Carrying drugs?" Hawk asked.

She shook her head. "Unfortunately, no."

Candace noticed Hawk seemed troubled by this response. He looked up at the ceiling, closing his eyes as if he were sending up a prayer.

"What's wrong, Hawk?" Candace asked him.

"He transported people across the border?" he asked Nizhoni, who nodded.

155

"And that's worse than smuggling drugs?" Candace asked.

"More dangerous," Hawk said. "More at stake."

"The men who broke into their home were sending a message," Nizhoni said.

"It wasn't random," Hawk said.

"No, they knew who they were killing," she said, "and spared the children."

"Quin was stabbed, though," he said.

"Superficial wounds only," she said. "The men left him and kidnapped his sister instead."

These were details Candace hadn't heard before and she felt sickened by how tragically Quin's family had been brutalized. "Why would somebody do this?"

"To send a message to the DEA or FBI. There're a lot of bad people struggling in the borderlands," Nizhoni said.

"And the FBI swept it under the rug?" Hawk said.

"Pretty much. You're the only people in the past twelve years who have even asked about the case."

CHAPTER 6

Each keystroke that Dr. Hayden tapped on her keyboard felt more ominous than the last. She was reluctantly authorizing Susan Johnson's request to exit the paranormal program, to leave the hospital on an outpatient basis, which for some paranormals amounted to a death sentence. Former paranormals rarely complied with the required outpatient checkups. While suicide rates were higher among them than among the general population, they were no higher than among soldiers returning from the battlefield, so there was no reason to deny Susan's request. Dr. Hayden handed the letter to Kruse as he sat in a chair across from her desk.

He stared at it in disbelief. "She's not ready to leave."

"She's within her rights to do so."

"Make sure she does the outpatient therapy," he said.

"I always follow up with them," she said, as if she had to deflect his accusation. "If they don't walk through those doors, what else can I do?"

He signed the letter and handed it to her. "I can recruit more."

"That's your solution? Recruit more. How many psychic warriors have to suffer or die before you stop recruiting people for this program? I care about these young people."

"We both do, Dr. Hayden."

"Then show it."

"We need more funding to do this right, but I have to show the bureau successes in the field," he said. "How did your call with Quin go?"

"He's using ayahuasca again."

"We knew he would."

"In the call I noticed something about his behavior," she said. Kruse pulled the chair closer to her desk and she continued, "He hallucinates while on the tea, of course, but he still sees ravens long after the effects of the tea should've worn off."

"They're like his spirit friends," Kruse said.

"Yes. I think the tea helps him slip into an altered state of mind, but after the tea's effects wear off, he's able to remain in that altered state for longer periods of time. He's reverting to totemic beliefs, a worldview that draws upon nature, a kinship with animals where he sees them as protectors or helpers, possibly because of his heritage."

"In my previous assignments with the bureau, I've seen that belief many times on reservations. Totemism is not unique to the tribes of North America. Most tribes and clans around the world share in a similar belief system."

"It's a way to explain the natural world around them," she said.

"Certainly, but isn't it interesting that an aboriginal tribe in Australia could have a totemic belief system similar to that of a tribe in North America? They also created similar tools, legends, and myths, with no contact with one another. It's as if they drew this belief from the same source."

"What source?"

"The interconnectedness of all things."

"A collective unconsciousness?"

"It's what indigenous tribes tapped into, and it's what a remote viewer accesses today."

She resisted the urge to roll her eyes. "You're still pushing that New Age theory?"

"It's not New Age. The point I'm making is that it's very old and very real."

She couldn't back Agent Kruse into a corner. He was too confident in his own theories, and good enough to convince the FBI that his ideas were worth testing. But their recruits weren't lab rats, they were people.

"None of the other paranormals describe their experiences quite like Quin," she said. "When they meditate and focus on seeing distant objects, locations, and people, what else do they see?"

"Sometimes they'll go to a location in their mind, as if they're there, but only briefly," Kruse said. "Usually they're seeing locations in a void."

"And for those few minutes they reach that heightened state, and they come out of it exhausted and weaker, like Susan did," Dr. Hayden said.

"When Quin enters that state of mind, he's able to live in it much longer," he said. "That's why I have such high expectations of him."

"Is it possible that at times he's sleepwalking, interacting with the physical world that we see and the non-physical at the same time?" she asked.

"I've never thought about it that way." Kruse folded his hands in his lap.

"Is it possible Quin is tapping into a totemic belief to make sense of an uncertain world? He's overriding the analytical side of his consciousness and delving into the spiritual realm."

"There's nothing wrong with that," Kruse said.

"Except how does he know what's real and what's imagined? What if trafficking in this source is like…free diving? With enough practice, deep breathing, and relaxation, one can go further and further underwater with a single breath before returning to the surface for more air. Quin is proving to be the best diver; he can go longer into the deeper state of mind before he needs to return again—"

"Are you suggesting we give Dillan and Rachel ayahuasca to enhance their remote viewing?"

"No, of course not. I'm suggesting there's a downside to this altered state of consciousness." She paused for a moment, realizing Kruse had baited her into this conversation. How long had he been thinking about this?

"It will be a simple test to see if Dillan and Rachel can go deeper," he said.

"You'll never get approval."

"Bet I will."

"You'd still need Dillan and Rachel's approval," she reminded him.

"They'll give it to me."

Step by step, he was backing her into a corner. He would win; he'd get his way once again.

"We need to know the capabilities and also the limitations of this herb," she said. "We definitely have to monitor Quin's vitals. He must wear the equipment we sent along with him into the field. What time is he investigating those leads Rachel and Dillan uncovered?"

"Within the hour. We're setting up in the auditorium." Kruse reached across the desk and shook her hand. "This is exciting."

"Yes, but the health and safety of the team is important," she said. "Remember, Quin crashed once before when he entered Safe Haven. He's your best free diver, but he can only be submerged for so long. Eventually, he must come up for air, to return to this physical world, or he could drown somewhere out there in the depths of his own mind."

Nogales is a city straddling two countries, the United States and Mexico, separated by a rusted iron fence that today towers eighteen feet above the rocky ground. The government that once corralled indigenous people onto reservations has begun fencing itself off from the rest of the world.

The barrier stretched as far as Quin's eyes could see in either direction, draping the rising hills and ridges of the desert. This side of the border was actually higher than the US side, giving bandits and illegals an advantage over US Border Patrol agents.

Agent Lopez drove up a two-lane highway as Quin looked out the window at the desert of freedom, littered with water bottles, blankets, stuffed animals, and even a few makeshift crosses. Looking at all that, it was obvious to Quin why people dug tunnels; the afternoon heat and the frigid evening temperatures could kill people.

"Did you send me the tunnel map?" he asked.

"Check your e-mail," Agent Lopez said.

He opened it on his phone and its attachment. It was a black line connected to a green one intersected by a red one. "It's like a subway map."

"Seriously, though, that's miles of underground roads, parts of it very narrow," she said. "There's some natural caves in there, too. The black line is the tunnel near your house."

"What's more dangerous, running across the desert or under it?" he asked.

"Up top we got surveillance, you know, things like night vision, planes, even drones. If they use tunnels, they can get pinched at the exit points. And they still have to pay for a guide to take them across and they could be robbed, raped, or killed along the way," she said matter-of-factly.

Quin's phone vibrated. It was Agent Kruse. "Almost there," he reported.

"Good, you need to pull over and wait for my instructions before entering the warehouse."

"Affirmative," Quin said before hanging up. "Are any of these tunnels near the location where we're headed right now?" he asked Lopez.

"The green line on the map stops about a mile from there. Why?"

"Just curious."

The GPS coordinates brought them to a small village on the outskirts of Nogales and just as promised, there was a series of warehouses, garages, and semi-trailers parked side by side. Lopez pulled into a dirt lot and drove past the buildings painted with blue and orange graffiti. Whoever Jesus Coolio was, he was prolific.

"This can't be the place," Quin said.

"I'm just following the coordinates Agent Kruse gave us," she said, slowing the SUV, setting it in park.

He called Kruse. "Hey, we're here, wherever here is."

"Put on the glasses and pair your Bluetooth earpiece," Kruse said. "I'm in the auditorium with Dillan, Rachel, and Dr. Hayden."

"Good afternoon, everyone," Quin said.

"We'll hang up and you'll call us once you're connected."

Quin reached for a box in the seat behind him where he kept the bureau-issued sunglasses. He put them on and the world outside transformed into a rose-colored glow. He inserted the earpiece and turned both devices on. In the upper right corner of the right lens he could see his heart rate, which was climbing.

"Testing, one, two, three."

"We hear you," Kruse confirmed in Quin's ear. "And we see the location as well."

Quin turned toward to his new partner. "Everyone, this is Agent Lopez."

She half-smiled. "Hello."

"Is she authorized to wear the other gear?" Quin asked Kruse.

"Yes, get her set up."

Quin reached for the second pair of sunglasses and the earpiece and handed them to Lopez. "Join the party."

Lopez seemed genuinely excited about the gear as she tried it on.

"This is like a Tom Clancy novel." She looked at herself in the rearview mirror.

"I prefer Vince Flynn's work myself," Quin said.

Kruse ignored their banter and went right into his instructions. "You are presently on land patrolled by a drug cartel named—"

"Sinaloa," Agent Lopez said, adjusting her glasses.

"Correct," Kruse said. "And they know you're there. They're watching you right now."

Quin knew of the cartel; he'd heard of them when he was a boy. He looked out the window up at the hills, his pulse climbing higher. He felt it, but to see it in the lens only made him more anxious. "How many are watching?"

"Could be two or three, could be twenty for all I know," Kruse said. "They think you're there to retrieve a man on the FBI's Most Wanted list."

"Why didn't you tell them we're looking for a woman?" Quin said.

"There's no women listed on our Top Ten Most Wanted," Kruse said.

"Why would this drug cartel give us permission to walk around here searching?"

"We made a deal with them," Kruse said.

"What kind of deal?"

"You're not authorized to know. Now hurry up. You only have thirty minutes."

"What happens after that?" Lopez asked.

"Get started!" Kruse said.

She adjusted her shoulder strap where she kept her Glock 23 pistol. Then she opened the glove box and handed Quin an inferior gun.

"Why do I get a 17 and you carry a 23?" he said.

"Pistol envy, Quin? You don't meet the qualifications for a 23" she joked.

"That sucks."

"Sucks for me because you're supposed to be my backup," she said.

He stepped out of the SUV into a wave of heat. The sunglasses darkened, adjusting for the bright sunlight. *Not bad.* They both walked to the front of the vehicle and studied the buildings with garage doors coated in sun-dried graffiti.

"Dillan and Rachel, do you see her?" Quin asked.

"Hey, Quin, it's me," Dillan said.

"I know it's you, stop wasting time," he said.

"Yeah, cool, all right. Of the five storage buildings in front of you, I feel like the one on the left has a stronger presence," Dillan said.

Quin was already in motion and Lopez followed off his right shoulder as they walked toward the buildings. The place was so quiet—almost dead in the late afternoon heat.

"Rachel, are you getting the same signal as Dillan?" Quin asked.

"Yes, but I think she's in the building next to the one Dillan is seeing," she said. "I mean, we could be splitting hairs. The buildings could all be connected from the inside."

He went with Dillan's hunch first. There was a metal door open slightly where Quin caught a whiff of something familiar. It was the irritating sting of ammonia seeping through the doorway. He pulled the door open and walked inside, with Lopez following. Meth labs come in all shapes and sizes, but what usually gives them away is their stench. He had his weapon drawn, walking into a dark hallway. He peered around a corner to his right. The room was filled with silver vats, pots boiling, five people working, sweating with bandanas covering their mouths. A flat-screen TV hung from one wall by a chain, the sound turned up so they could follow a soccer game.

"Trouble?" Lopez whispered.

Quin nodded.

"This isn't a drug bust," Kruse said into Quin's earpiece. "You're off target. Get out of there."

Desperate for fresh air, Quin turned and motioned to Lopez to move out and they exited the building, back into the bright sunlight. They jogged back fifty yards, gasping for air. He thought of Gino Baxter hauling meth through Minnesota to Canada. How many mules like him did the cartel use to spread their drug through American towns? He tucked the gun in his waistband. "What's our status with Sinaloa?" he asked Kruse.

"US Intelligence considers them the world's most powerful drug trafficking organization," Kruse said. "That meth lab is not your target. Leave it for the DEA."

What a dead end. Here they were, standing in front of a meth lab in the hills of Mexico. "How often are the remote viewers wrong?" he asked, without calling out Dillan and Rachel by name.

"Autumn must be somewhere nearby," Kruse said.

"Where?"

"Your job is to pinpoint her exact location. Follow your instincts," Kruse said.

He was studying the buildings again when Lopez said, "We have visitors."

A white Chevy Tahoe pulled off the dirt road and drove a complete circle around Quin and Lopez, surrounding them in a cloud of dust before the truck skidded to a stop. She set her hand on her gun. Quin did the same and as the dust settled, he spotted two men in the truck watching them.

"They're from the cartel," Lopez said.

"How do you know?" he asked.

"Bad guys don't wear black hats anymore. They drive white trucks."

The men climbed out of the truck. One man in his thirties was tall. The younger, in his twenties, had acne scars and a semi-automatic.

"Don't engage with them," Kruse warned.

"We're out-gunned," Quin said. "Nobody is engaging in anything other than polite conversation."

Quin's Spanish was good but Lopez's was better, and she greeted the men with her own brand of machismo. But Quin could see she was nervous in their presence.

"Who you looking for?" the tall man asked while his partner stood silently with his weapon at his side.

"A fugitive from the States," Quin said.

"Who?"

"A gringo," Quin responded.

"Find anybody in there?" the younger man asked, pointing at the warehouse.

Quin shook his head. "Just some guys cooking tamales."

The younger man smiled at Quin's sarcasm. "Tamales?"

"Not interested in tamales," Quin said.

"Another dead end," Lopez added.

Quin saw the flashes of raven shadows on the ground. He looked up as the two birds circled the men's truck.

"Jefe!" a woman called from the truck.

The young man turned and looked back at her without answering.

Quin's mind was tripping, his heart racing. There was a tone, a note in the woman's voice that sounded familiar.

"Who's she?" he asked, motioning to the truck.

"Ella es de la familia." *She's family.*

"Sister?" Quin asked.

"Mi esposa." *My wife*, he said, disinterested in her.

Quin, however, was very interested. He walked past the men through the waves of heat toward their truck.

"What are you doing?" Kruse said into his earpiece.

"You told me to follow my instincts."

"Do not engage the cartel," Kruse said. "Get out of there!"

He turned off the earpiece, ignoring Kruse and the commotion behind him; Lopez was arguing with the men as they followed Quin. When he reached the truck he saw a woman in the passenger seat with long black hair and a young girl, maybe five years old, in her lap. The woman was staring back at him intensely through the waves of heat rising from the desert ground. Was that Autumn? Or was his mind playing tricks on him?

A crack of gunfire brought Quin to a halt. He turned to see young Jefe holding the semi-automatic skyward before he lowered it, pointing it at Lopez's chest. Quin looked back at the woman and girl, now hiding in shadow inside the truck, but they were watching him. He knew it.

"I could kill your partner," Jefe threatened.

"Or we can all go our separate ways. Nobody gets hurt," Quin said, slowly moving away from the Tahoe.

"Leave," Jefe said, shoving Lopez forward. She walked quickly toward the Suburban and Quin joined her, never taking his eyes off the men until he was in the driver's seat. He started the engine.

"What was that all about?!" Lopez asked. "Kruse is screaming in my ear."

"Disconnect your gear," Quin said, accelerating toward the road. They both removed their sunglasses and earpieces, tossing them in the back seat.

"They're following us," Lopez said, looking out the side mirror.

Quin had noticed it too, the white truck trailing them as he increased his speed to 80 MPH. But they never caught up, instead turning right off the highway. Quin slowed and looked back to see the truck heading south before he pulled over and parked on the side of the road. He opened the glove box and grabbed a pair of binoculars. The Tahoe turned toward a walled compound with six buildings.

"What are you doing?" Lopez asked.

"We need to know where they're going."

"Why?"

He watched the ravens soaring in the distance, above the compound. "Autumn was in that truck."

Lopez sighed. "The heat is getting to you, Quin."

"Dillon and Rachel said she was nearby. They were right."

"That woman who Jefe said was his wife, she's Autumn?" she asked.

He nodded, still observing the ravens soaring over the compound.

"How could you make a positive ID so quickly?"

"Got a feeling," he said.

"A feeling?"

"There was something in her voice, and the girl in her lap looks a lot like Autumn did at that age."

"You realize how bad this is? Jefe works for Sinaloa, he's married to a woman who you think is your sister and they have a child. And now you show up to say 'Hey, sis, it's time to come home.' What if it's not her?"

"It must be her. I'm bringing her back."

"Now? What if she doesn't want to leave?"

That was something he hadn't considered. He'd always assumed that if she were alive, she'd want to be rescued. But what if Autumn now considered this place home?

"I have to find out if it's her," he said.

"Maybe I can call in a drone to fly overhead," she said.

"We're not waiting. We're going there now."

"They stiff-armed us off their land and you want to go back for more?" she said.

He put the truck in gear and maneuvered it further off the road behind a dune. "We'll leave the truck here and approach the compound by foot."

"And if they see us we're supposed to outrun them back to the truck?"

He thought about the distance, the heat, and terrain. Lopez would only slow him down. "Stay here and I'll check it out. If I'm not back in thirty minutes, leave."

"No, that's not a good plan."

He stepped out of the truck, ignoring her list of reasons why this was such a bad idea. He left her, jogging on the hard ground, his gun tucked behind his back. The terrain was small rolling hills and cacti, the perfect golf course—if it were only on the other side of the border. Was this what it was like to cross the border, to flee from one danger possibly toward another? Was the freedom of a better life the biggest mirage of all?

He walked up a small dune. Looking back, he couldn't see the truck or Lopez anymore, and that could be a problem when navigating his return. He used his boot to draw a line in the sand, pointing in the general direction back. Ahead of him, a hundred yards in the distance, he saw the compound surrounded by a white cinderblock wall that couldn't be more than seven feet tall. The buildings beyond the wall were houses with red tile roofs—a suburban oasis in the middle of nowhere.

He heard tires crunching on gravel and he kneeled low into the dune. It was the white Tahoe leaving the compound. He wasn't sure if Autumn was in the truck but it looked like Jefe driving again, his skinny elbow sticking out the open window.

Caw!

Quin turned to the sound of the ravens circling over one of the houses. He walked toward them along the compound wall until he reached what had to be the back of the house in question. He listened but heard no voices, no TV coming from the house. Reaching up, he grabbed the top of the wall and used his boots as leverage to peek over it. On both sides of the yard were wood fences separating this yard from the neighbors'. He scaled the wall, checking for dogs. There were none so he leapt onto the other side. The backyard had a brick patio, teakwood furniture, and fruit trees. Life with Sinaloa couldn't be all that bad.

He drew his weapon and walked toward a sliding-glass door, keeping his eye on the ravens as they hopped and fluttered along the roof. He reached for the handle but it was locked, as he'd expected. The ravens were calm, perched on the edge, but Quin's heart pounded in his chest as beads of sweat dripped from his brow. He wasn't chasing a skip on the run this time and there was no bounty at stake. If Autumn was inside this building, he was about to be reunited with this sister. Of all the doors he'd kicked in over the years, this one was different. It required a more civil approach. He did something he'd never done on any bounty assignment.

He knocked.

He heard voices and the shuffling of feet. His gun was low and to his side, pointed upward if he needed to drop someone. The voice behind the door was louder now, filled with excitement. It was the girl.

He quickly shoved the gun under his shirt behind his back.

The glass door slid open. Inside, the girl shielded her eyes from the late afternoon sun.

"¿Habla Inglés?" Quin asked.

She stared in confusion.

He smiled at her. "¿Dónde esta tú madre?" *Where is your mother?*

Before she answered, a woman stepped into the light and the girl blanketed herself in the safety of the woman's dirt-stained white dress. She made a step forward with the girl. Both of them had sun-bleached auburn highlights and tan-freckled skin. They had to be mother and daughter. The woman in front of him was similar to the one in Dillan and Rachel's sketches. What the sketches couldn't capture, of course, was the woman's state of mind, how she'd react when a stranger came knocking at her door. There was anger and suspicion in her eyes. He was having second thoughts; maybe this wasn't her after all.

"Who are you? What do you want?" she said in perfect English.

"I'm looking for somebody."

"Why not come to my front door?"

"I'm a bounty hunter. We don't usually go to the front door."

"You're arresting this person?"

"No, I need to speak with her." He soaked in her every detail, including the small scar above her eyebrow.

"What's her name?"

He could see the fabric of her dress quivering, her knees weakening. She held her daughter closer.

"Autumn," he said softly, studying the expression on her face. She had a prolonged look of surprise, something the human eye cannot disguise.

"What did you say?"

"Autumn."

Her eyes locked onto his, as if she finally saw this stranger in a new light. He held his arms open, offering a welcoming hug. Instead, she stepped back with her daughter. There was no hugging Autumn; she acted cornered and frightened.

She whispered and the girl ran down to a bedroom at the end of a hallway. But she left the door open enough to peek out at them.

"It's me, Quin."

"My God, what are you doing here?" she said, without any hint of relief or appreciation.

"I was about to ask you the same thing."

"How did you find me?"

He thought about the months of mind-bending training with Agent Kruse back in Minnesota to reach this place in the foothills of Mexico. He remembered his promise to Rebecca Baron, that he'd look for his sister, and how it was really a promise he had made to himself. "It's a long story, but we found you."

"To bring me back to the States?" she said. "You're a fed," she said accusingly.

This isn't the reaction of somebody who's been held prisoner for twelve years. It was more akin to Stockholm Syndrome, where the captive bonds emotionally with the captor.

"How do you know I'm a fed?"

"We have Internet here. I've read about you."

"And you never contacted me?"

"I wanted to many times but…" She looked down the hallway at her daughter. "I have a life here."

Quin glanced around at the house. It was small, no more than two bedrooms, but it was clean. The furniture looked new, the view out her front window was of hills and saguaro cacti.

"You live here?" he asked.

"It's not much, but we make enough."

"You're married?"

"No."

"That man Jefe I met out by the meth lab, he said you were family."

"He's Marta's father but we're not married. Why does it matter?" Autumn said.

It didn't matter. He was picking away at simple questions, making small talk to make sense of this bittersweet reunion, so utterly unlike the scene he'd always imagined. How could she have a life here and not have made contact with him?

"You're taller than I had imagined," she said, reaching out to touch his earring. It was the first sign of tenderness from her. "But you have to go. Jefe is coming back any moment," she said.

"Come with me."

"I can't."

"Why not?"

"Jefe works for Sinaloa. He'd never let her go, and I'm not leaving without her."

"Do you love him?"

"Jefe? No—"

"Forget him," Quin said, imagining what this guy must be like.

"Jefe is a decent man. He got work through the cartel to provide for Marta and me. Sinaloa has jobs, security from bandits, healthcare when we need it."

This was more complicated than Quin had expected—a hostage situation, and the hostages weren't ready to leave.

"Do you work for Sinaloa too?" he asked.

She nodded, looking away. "In the meth lab. I clean it at night."

"Who watches Marta while you're working?"

"Jefe or a neighbor," she said. "Or sometimes I bring her and she naps on a cot while I work."

"Are you happy here?"

She sighed without answering.

"You don't look happy, Autumn."

"I have responsibilities…"

"How did you end up in this place?"

Up on the roof, he heard the squawking from the ravens. He looked up at a skylight and they were circling in flight, agitated. He knew there was a chance that if he left Autumn here, he might never see her again. She seemed nervous about returning to the States and when in doubt, most people on the run are more comfortable on the run. He was approaching his thirty-minute time limit when Lopez was supposed to give up on him.

"How often do you work at the meth lab?" he asked.

"Every evening around seven, until ten or eleven."

"If I return later this week, will you come back with me?"

She hesitated, her eyes darting around the room at the life she'd have to leave behind. "Not without my daughter."

"Bring Marta to the lab every night you work," he said. "I'll meet you there."

The sun had set behind the hills as Quin and Agent Lopez crossed the border back to the United States. She drove, peppering him with questions about his sister. What was Autumn like? How had she ended up with the cartel? He had very few answers for Lopez because his reunion with Autumn was so brief. They finally arrived back at the house, where he recognized Hawk's truck in the driveway. They'd made the trip in good time. The old man must not have been driving.

"You expecting anyone?" Lopez asked with suspicion.

"Some friends from home," he said, parking next to the truck.

"Did you clear this with the bureau?"

"No."

"Where are they?" she questioned, stepping out of the truck.

"Probably inside. I left them a key and texted them."

"That's not your house anymore; it's government property."

Government property. How many times had he heard that phrase? The government seizes land, seizes property, and for what? To build walls, to protect its interests. He wasn't about to argue about it with Lopez, though; she was just doing her job.

He opened the door and found Slim Jim snoozing on the couch and Hawk sitting at the kitchen table with Candace. She was eyeing him pretty good, as if she were relieved to finally see him again.

"We made it," Candace said.

"Ahead of schedule," he said.

"Jimmy has a lead foot." Hawk smiled.

Quin stepped inside. "This is Agent Maria Lopez."

Candace and Hawk stood and introduced themselves. Lopez walked over and shook their hands and Slim Jim continued his snoring.

"You drove all the way from Minnesota?" Lopez asked.

Hawk nodded. "Yep."

"That's a long drive," Lopez said.

"Yep," Hawk said, stretching his lower back.

"There are lots of direct flights from Minneapolis to Phoenix," Lopez said.

"Are you interrogating them, Agent Lopez?" Quin asked.

She turned to him and the serious expression on her face softened. "Sorry, it's a bad habit. I wasn't expecting visitors other than you, Quin."

"I had places I wanted to see, people to meet," Hawk said to Lopez. "And I can't fly. Gotta inner-ear problem."

She nodded, smiling at him. "Well, there's room enough here for you all to sleep. Be mindful that this belongs to the bureau. I'll call you in the morning, Quin."

Lopez turned and left, closing the door behind her. He waited for the sound of her SUV engine to come to life before he joined Candace and Hawk in the kitchen. "You two look worn out."

Candace rubbed her eyes. "It was a long drive."

"Rest up tonight because we've got a lot of work to do in the morning," Quin said, checking his phone. He had three texts from Agent Kruse. He figured this was as bad a time as any to call him.

Kruse answered on the second ring. "What the hell happened down there?"

"Lost our connection in the field."

"How?"

"We must've been between cell towers," Quin said. "A gap in the signal."

"The bureau doesn't use cell towers. You were on an encrypted satellite feed."

"Maybe I bumped the off switch?"

"You *turned off* the connection and Agent Lopez did, too. Everyone here is worried about you."

"Tell Dillan and Rachel they did a great job getting me this far. How are they?" he asked Kruse.

"Rachel is fine. Dillan is…struggling. He's losing confidence."

"Don't cut him from the team. Give him some time off."

"What happened down there?" Kruse said.

Quin described every detail as Candace and Hawk listened; what the compound looked like, how the woman and her daughter lived together in a small home there.

"Was it her?" Kruse interrupted.

"Possibly," he said.

"Possibly? You'd know your own sister!"

"I haven't seen her or spoken to her in twelve years," Quin said. His biggest concern was that Kruse would call in more FBI agents to swoop in and take over once he made a positive ID. Quin didn't want anybody to jeopardize the mission. "I didn't have a lot of time with her. Call Lopez, she'll back me up on this."

Kruse sighed heavily into the phone. "Go back there, keep the video rolling, and make a positive ID."

"All right, play this out for me. If it ends up being her and we get an ID on video, then what?"

"Then we have a monumental success for remote viewing," Kruse said. "We'll have demonstrated that we can find not only locations, but people."

"But if she is Autumn, how do we bring her daughter across the border?"

"That would involve legal paperwork. We have a department for that end of it, but our part would be done."

"Search and retrieve, mission accomplished?" Quin said sarcastically.

"Granted, the kid complicates it."

"That kid could be my niece and I'm not leaving her behind without her mother. You hear what I'm saying? They're a package deal. They travel together or they don't travel at all."

"Return and capture her on video. Make a positive ID and we'll make a plan from that point."

"Doesn't anybody care about the case? Who killed my parents? Why did somebody take Autumn?"

"Of course, but it'll be handed to another department to pursue, probably the Phoenix office," Kruse said.

The Phoenix office had botched the investigation twelve years earlier. *Why hand it back to them again?* This was his case and he wasn't about to hand it off. He needed to know what happened, and he knew Autumn could give him more information than anybody in Phoenix.

"I'll interview her myself," he said.

"You have to go back there this week," Kruse said.

"Give me a couple of days to prepare. And I need at least one day to rest up. This is a vacation, after all."

"Very well, but I need to know exactly what day and time you're returning to the site. I want Agents Clark and Backstrom from HQ here to witness it."

That's what this is all about for Agent Kruse, a big show for the home office. It reminded Quin of Ben Moretti's flashy presentation to Rebecca Baron. He sold the dream while distracting her from the dark side of her decision. And he felt Kruse might be doing the same thing, selectively showing the good results from the paranormal team, but ignoring the downside, the trainees who'd flamed out searching for the unseen—desperately seeking results or seeking a way out of the paranormal research.

There were times when Quin thought he'd heard a sound, a pebble bouncing off the hardwood floor, screams in the distance, or the call of ravens. This was one of those moments as he awoke in his childhood bedroom on a black leather couch, probably hand-picked by an FBI-authorized interior decorator. Black, they always went with black, a covert color that easily conceals sweat and blood.

He heard voices outside his window whispering, even laughing, and he stood up and walked barefoot to the window. He opened the blinds just a quarter of an inch. It was morning, nearly seven, but he saw nobody. The voices stopped as if the speakers had seen him first. Stepping back, he listened and there it was again, a hushed conversation somewhere outside. He tugged on the cord, lifting the blinds, filling the room with morning light, and the voices were gone again. *A dream*, he thought. He was working too hard, not getting enough sleep.

He felt a presence behind him and turned to see Hawk standing there with two steaming mugs. "See something?"

Quin rubbed the sleep from his eyes. "Thought I heard somebody."

"It's only us out here," Hawk said. "Coffee?"

He accepted the hot mug, feeling more awake already after a couple of sips. "How was your trip through Dakota country?"

Hawk closed the door. "We must talk."

"Oh yeah, I can tell you more about yesterday—"

"You have a relative named Nizhoni?"

Quin hadn't heard her name since he was a child. "Yes, how did you know?"

"We stopped along the way and spoke to her about the case."

"Nobody on the rez talks about it."

"Given enough time, people come around, Quin."

"And?"

"Your father traveled across the border."

"Yes, I went with him often," Quin said. "Autumn did, too."

"What was in the truck?" Hawk asked.

"Sometimes he hauled sheet metal into Mexico, other times it was auto parts into the States." He thought back on those day trips with his father, riding shotgun with Autumn, the panoramic view through the truck's windshield.

"Was he a…?" Hawk asked, his voice dropping low.

"A mule? Carrying drugs? He would never…did Nizhoni say that?"

"No, not mule; a coyote moving immigrants, laborers, families."

Quin had never considered that possibility. How many children question what their parents say they do for a living? "I never saw him loading people into his semi."

"Maybe you weren't there on those trips?" Hawk suggested.

The tunnels would make it much easier to load people into that truck.

"God, she could be right," he said. He reached for his phone and showed Hawk the map. "Tunnels run underneath us and the entrance to one of them is within walking distance. People could travel underground and surface right here." He zoomed the map in.

"Then your father could've driven them further north."

"A modern-day underground railroad," Quin said. He'd never thought of his father as anything other than a long-haul trucker. A reclusive man who drank too much on his days off and did God knows what while he was on the road. He chuckled.

"What's so funny?"

"My parents argued so often," Quin said. "I never figured out what was the cause of all their tension. Was it money, booze, or women? Could've been any or all of those things—or was it their secret business of smuggling people?"

"They must've needed the money," Hawk said, defending him.

Quin knew the bureau statistics on human trafficking. It was a $100 billion industry. Some bounty hunters made a lucrative living freeing people from forced labor, but other bounties in that line of work disappeared, never to be heard from again.

"If Nizhoni is right, if my father was involved in human trafficking, that could explain the attack on my family."

"How will you get her back?"

Quin had been up most of the night wondering the same thing: *what's the best way to rescue Autumn and Marta?* He wouldn't settle for a positive ID; he needed *time* with her to learn what had happened. And to do that, he'd have to bring her back here, to the bureau field office that had once been their home.

"I'm meeting Autumn and her daughter. And I'll need your help and Jimmy's to bring them across the border," Quin said.

"When? How?"

"Later this week. But you and Jimmy need to find us two golf carts."

Hawk's eyebrows rose. "We have time for golf?"

"Carts will be the getaway vehicles, Hawk."

"Gas engine carts go the fastest."

"Battery-powered are quieter." He spared Hawk the minor detail that they'd drive the carts underground.

CHAPTER 7

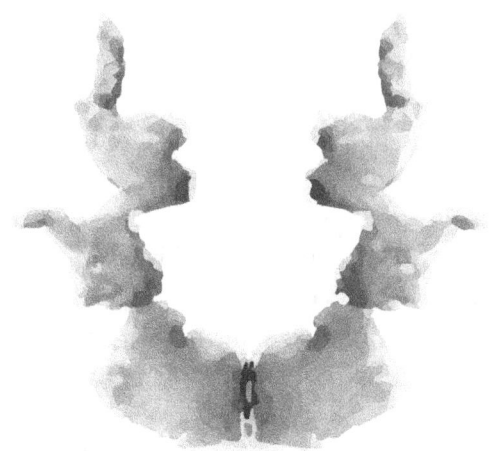

Hawk and Jimmy drove off into the morning heat in search of golf carts in Nogales while Candace sat outside with Quin on the front step holding a warm mug of coffee. She was uneasy with him as she nervously stared out at the desert horizon. He was one of those entrancing people whose presence had a powerful gravitational pull. He was seated next to her in blue jeans and dirty bare feet, sipping tea, hardly saying a word.

"So this was your home?"

He glanced back at the house behind them. "Years ago, not anymore."

"Of course, but in a symbolic way, you've returned home."

"The prodigal son has returned," he wisecracked. "Is that the theme of the story you're working on?"

"No, and why would you label yourself that way? You've done nothing wrong."

"I left Autumn out there."

"You were a boy, you couldn't live here alone searching for her."

"I should've returned sooner," he said. "I waited too long. I only returned because I had nothing better to do."

She knew this wasn't entirely true. Hawk had shared with her stories of Quin's accomplishments, how he'd recaptured people skipping out on bail and partnered with the FBI to track fugitives, even dangerous escaped convicts.

"You returned here when you were ready."

"There's something you might help me with," he said. "It's why I let you come down here."

She thought about the morning when she'd talked her way into his truck, expecting to tag along. She'd thought she was so persuasive, and now she realized Quin had had a plan of his own all along.

"What do you want me to do?"

"Research."

"The case? Certainly; I'd like to review the files with you and then—"

"No, something more pressing."

"Okay, what?"

"It's confidential. You can't tell anybody about what I'm asking."

He reached out his hand and she shook it.

"You have my word. Tell me," she said, begging.

"Have you heard of remote viewing?"

She thought for a moment. "No."

"Do you believe in a third eye? That the mind can see beyond?"

"Intuition? Sure, there are some people who are very intuitive."

"More than intuition. I'm talking about seeing and traveling with your mind to faraway places."

"ESP?" she asked in disbelief.

"A form of ESP," he said, describing how remote viewers entered a hyper-conscious state to retrieve information about objects or people. "The deeper a viewer goes into his or her mind, the more detailed information they can bring back," he said. "All of this is done by tapping into the collective unconsciousness, something everybody has the ability to do to some extent, but very few people take the time to practice."

He described the months of training and testing the recruits endured, how Kruse gave them targets to search for with their minds, how little time they had off, and how they were kept cloistered away at the state security hospital, away from bureau agents. Quin told her how he would bounty hunt on weekends to get a break, but how the other recruits rarely strayed from the hospital grounds.

She was skeptical, unsure if he was exaggerating or possibly high on his tea. "Agent Kruse taught you this method?"

He shrugged. "I have my own way, different from what Kruse teaches the remote viewers."

"Your method is better?" she asked.

"That's what I need you to find out. I'm concerned about them. Before I left, a team member, Susan Johnson, had a breakdown. Kruse removed her from the program. It's possible that Dillan, one of the other remote viewers, is suffering from side effects, too."

"Is his technique dangerous?"

"Something is happening to the recruits. Can you find out what and research it?"

"I'm happy to help," she said, but asked, "If you knew back in Minnesota that you wanted me to research remote viewing and its effects, how come you had me drive all the way down here with Hawk and Jimmy?"

"You needed to see the miles and miles of Indian land, what we'd all given up," he said. "I knew Hawk would show you. And I hoped that once you saw it, smelled it, and tasted the journey, you'd be committed to the rest of it. What you saw on your journey should also be in your story."

"Hawk bought a t-shirt at the Corn Palace that said, '*Fighting Terrorism Since 1492.*' He acts like you're all on a mission. He thinks very highly of you."

Quin smiled. "Did he show you the security cameras?"

"Yes."

"Homeland Security has everything under surveillance. The threat of terrorism from abroad or homegrown is on their radar. Agent Kruse received more funding for RV after the 9/11 attacks. Now he's got to prove it works."

"Oh, I thought Hawk was just acting paranoid."

"He's aware of his surroundings. When a person sees things that others miss, that doesn't necessarily make him paranoid," Quin said.

"No, of course not," she said apologetically. "It's just that Hawk seems to have a lot riding on you. On our night on Hinhan Kaga Paha he compared you to Crazy Horse."

Quin nodded and sipped.

"Does that mean anything to you?"

"I'll ask you the same question."

"Crazy Horse was a great leader," she said. "He embodied the spirit of independence, and you do as well, correct?"

"Some would agree."

"What are you breaking away from, Quin? What does Hawk mean?"

"Crazy Horse died only after he'd given himself up to the government. He surrendered to save his people," he said. "Hawk is saddened that I work with the FBI because the government has never been fair to our people."

"But you trust the bureau, right? They're helping you find Autumn."

"The bureau has a reputation for coming onto reservations and causing trouble, dragging people off to prison, covering things up."

"Nizhoni said the bureau abandoned your family's case."

He nodded.

Is it possible that Quin joined with the FBI for this one purpose, to find his sister? She wanted to ask him, toss the idea out into the conversation, but she felt he might pull away, deny it. Instead, she offered him encouragement. "I hope you find every answer you're searching for."

"This won't be an easy story for you, Candace."

"What do you mean?"

"It's hard to distinguish between good and evil. When a wolf kills a deer, is that wolf evil?"

"No, it's the natural order of things," she said.

"When a wolf kills cattle, is that evil?"

"Well no, the wolf doesn't know that a rancher owns the cattle."

"And when the rancher kills the wolf to prevent it from hunting his herd, what is that?"

"It's a dilemma, I suppose."

"When I return to Mexico to save Autumn and my niece, I have the same dilemma," he said.

"They're your *family*."

"But Marta has a father. He would claim the same thing; they're his family, too. Hawk is right; my work with the FBI forces me to enter another man's land, to tear apart his family."

"You and the FBI are wolves," she said. "There are many cases of the FBI paying informants, creating sting operations that are nothing more than entrapment."

He didn't accept or deny it, but she could see he was considering the possibility.

She sipped her coffee as he sipped his tea. Was he high or comfortably numb? He seemed uneasy here, preferring to sit outside rather than in the house, constantly looking out at the horizon, rarely making eye contact with her as he spoke. *Pensive* was the word she would use to describe Quin's personality. Sometimes he was deeply present and at other times, his mind seemed aloft, floating away.

"While you're working on Autumn and Marta's rescue, I'll research remote viewing," she said.

He stood up and stretched like a cat after a long nap. "And find out what's happening to Dillan Mercer, while you're at it."

Hawk, Jimmy, and Quin devoted a full day in experimenting with the golf carts to prepare them for their subterranean journey. By the end of the day, Quin wondered whether all of Jimmy's tinkering would make much of a difference. The kid insisted he could make the vehicles go over their standard top speed of twenty-five miles per hour to forty, and he wouldn't rest until he could prove it. Puffed up by his experience working summer jobs at a private golf club, he lectured Quin about electric golf cart motors. There were two basic kinds; motors optimized for torque, and those optimized for speed. Most of this Quin already knew. He watched Jimmy bend the rod that governs a golf cart's speed so he could easily increase it by five miles per hour.

"We need to go faster," Quin said.

"I can give you speed or torque, not both," Jimmy said, wiping his sweaty brow with his forearm.

"What difference does it make?" Hawk asked.

"Torque motors give us more pull, carry heavier loads, and are better on inclines," Quin said. It was why he always drove a truck, so he could haul heavy loads without burning out his engine.

"But they're slower," Jimmy added. "We've invested in speed, and I'm gonna increase the voltage and RPMs to go faster. Comes at a price, though: we can't carry as much weight."

"We have two carts to distribute the weight," Quin said.

"How much weight we talkin' about?" Jimmy asked.

"Yeah, what's the plan?" Hawk said.

He was still formulating a rough, ad hoc strategy. "Agent Lopez and I will return to the Mexico side, where we found Autumn and Marta. Rather than bring them through customs at the border crossing, we'll meet you and Jimmy at one of the tunnel entrances nearby. My sister, niece, and I will ride with you underground back here."

Jimmy scratched his sweaty scalp. "We drive the get-away cars?"

"Four adults and a child on two carts?" Hawk said. "That's a lot of weight."

"Plus the back-up batteries," Quin said.

"Why do we need back-ups? How far are we going?" Jimmy asked.

"I don't know yet, the maps don't show distance," Quin replied. "But there are a lot of dead batteries down there."

"Any inclines in those tunnels? Do we have to climb?" Jimmy asked.

Quin wiped his hand on his jeans, took his phone out of his pocket, and called the only person who might know.

"Yeah?" she said, half-shouting over what sounded like talk radio.

"Lopez?" he asked, putting her on speakerphone.

"Hold on," she said, lowering the volume on her stereo. "Sorry, I listen to books on CD while I drive."

"What book, dare I ask?" Quin said.

"Nothing you'd be interested in."

"A romance novel or something smutty?" he asked, looking up at Jimmy and Hawk smiling.

"It's a self-help book, okay?"

"A quit-smoking meditation?" he teased.

"No, *How to Quit Loving Your Ex-husband*," she said. "Once I do that, then I'll focus on the smoking thing."

"Sorry, Lopez," he said, kicking himself.

"No, it's all right."

"Where are you?"

"Phoenix, with my kids," she said. "On my way back down to Nogales."

"We need to know about the tunnels. Are there inclines down there?"

"God, you're really planning to use the underground highway, huh? It's like the world's longest gravesite. People get lost down there, go crazy, and many die. The locals say the tunnels are haunted."

Quin suddenly regretted that he had her on speakerphone. He could see the doubt on Jimmy's face and the angst in Hawk's eyes.

"We're not afraid of chindi," Quin said, bolstering his men.

"As for inclines, you have to descend into them and ascend on the way out," she said.

"Besides that, do you have any elevation info on your maps?" Quin asked.

"They're tunnels; who would build hills inside tunnels?" she said. "Should be a smooth ride except for debris and garbage."

"Thanks, we'll see you tomorrow." He hung up on Lopez.

Jimmy and Hawk agreed that made sense; the tunnels should be relatively flat, so giving up torque for speed should be an easy trade-off. He gave Jimmy the go-ahead to make the necessary adjustments before they would drag race the carts alongside Quin's truck. He went around to the front of the house and started his vehicle, cranking the air-conditioning to high and waiting for the cab to cool. He remembered sitting in his father's truck as a boy, holding his hands over the vents, cooling his underarms as his father steered out of the driveway to take him on a delivery run.

"You hot?" his father would ask.

He would nod. "Yeah."

"Out there it's a hundred degrees...in the shade," his father said, shifting gears, staring through the dusty windshield. "Imagine if you had to walk across that sand today. Heat like that can kill a man, much less a kid."

And then he'd turn on his radio, singing along to country music. Quin's job was to monitor the radio, punch the dial anytime a station went to a commercial break, and find the next song. He never questioned what was in the trailer behind them and he never saw it unloaded, either.

He parked his truck next to the golf carts, revving his engine as Jimmy and Hawk each drove circles around Quin, testing the tight turning radius of the carts. Jimmy pulled up to Quin's left and Hawk to the right side of the truck. Through his side window, he spotted Candace standing on the front step of the house. She was drinking a bottle of water, ready to see what came of all their hard work. This drag race would show the top speed of each cart and he would lead them up an incline to a butte to see how the carts handled the relative lack of torque. He revved his engine again and waved to Candace.

She raised her arm into the sky as if she were the starter. When she dropped her arm he punched the gas, racing forward too fast, leaving Hawk and Jimmy in a cloud of dust behind him. He eased off the accelerator until he saw both golf carts emerging through the dust storm, Hawk slightly ahead of Jimmy, both of them squinting and bouncing in their seats. They caught up to him and they drove three abreast, with Quin in the middle, over a dry riverbed, weaving around cacti and boulders. Jimmy was a reckless driver, plowing over sand dunes that tossed him out of his seat. Hawk, on the other hand, kept his skinny elbows locked, his hands clinging to the steering wheel. He was winning, not by much, but his cart was either faster or he was the more efficient driver. Their top speed was an impressive forty-eight miles per hour on the flats. So Quin led them up a red clay slope, an incline of possibly ten percent grade. The carts slowed, Jimmy's more than Hawk's, and it was obvious that their speed deteriorated rapidly on an incline. He had to test them in the real environment so he led them to the tunnel entrance that Agent Lopez had shown him. Walls of rock stood before him, casting long shadows on the sand. He parked and stepped into the shade as Hawk and Jimmy pulled up.

"Congrats, Hawk," he said. "You're the better driver after all."

"It's not the driver, it's the motor," Jimmy protested.

"Or maybe you're heavier," Quin said to Jimmy. "Hawk really pulled ahead on the incline."

"Go on a diet, would ya?" Hawk teased.

"Let's test these vehicles in the tunnel." Quin walked to the backside of the rock as they followed in their golf carts. He found the metal door and pushed it back, a burst of musty air emerging from underground.

"Gentlemen, whenever you're ready."

"Cool," Jimmy said, driving ahead of Hawk into the tunnel, which was barely tall enough to fit the cart.

Quin sat in the passenger seat of Hawk's cart and Hawk drove into the darkness, more cautious than his grandson.

"What's wrong?" Quin asked.

"It's haunted," Hawk said. "Lopez said it's a mass grave."

"Ah, she's exaggerating."

"Since when does a bureau agent exaggerate about stuff like that?"

Quin hadn't considered that Hawk would have so much fear of the tunnels. He was counting on Hawk and Jimmy to bring the carts through. "You want to wait here while Jimmy and I explore?"

Hawk nodded, got out of the cart, and walked out of the tunnel entrance. Quin slid into the driver's seat. He drove forward and parked next to Jimmy at the top of the ramp that seemed to vanish into darkness. They sat there for a moment waiting for their eyes to adjust, relaxing in the cool air. They turned on their cart headlights, illuminating the narrow and low ceiling.

"Where's Hawk?" Jimmy asked.

"He's taking a break. Let's see how these vehicles handle the ramp."

Quin drove forward and Jimmy trailed him down the dirt ramp, swerving around tires and a pile of wool blankets. At the bottom, they turned around and faced the ramp and the halo of daylight. Quin used his phone to set a timer. "You go first."

Jimmy impressed Quin by stepping on the accelerator and leaping into a jackrabbit start. Halfway up the cart slowed, and two-thirds of the way it almost stalled and had trouble holding traction in the sand. He made it to the top in one minute thirty seconds. Quin reset the timer and raced up the ramp, slowing earlier than Jimmy had, plodding to the top in almost two minutes.

"Hawk's cart is faster on the flats and yours is stronger on the inclines," Quin confirmed. "We have to equip the vehicles with brighter lights so we can make a practice run."

"When?"

"Tonight, if possible," he said. "But you have to talk with your grandfather, give him the courage to do this."

"He's afraid, huh?"

"Extremely. I've never seen him like that before."

Jimmy sighed. "He's been on edge the entire trip, always talkin'..."

"About what?"

"Old days and old ways. We can do it without him, leave him back at the house."

"We need two drivers, one for each cart," Quin said.

Jimmy got out of his cart and stretched. "What about Candace? Heck, she drove most of the way down here."

Quin had thought of her, too, but he had other plans for her. He needed Candace to figure out what was happening to the remote viewers who were removed from the program. "I want Hawk with us on the entire journey. Whatever you can say to him to ease his fears, I'd really appreciate it."

Everything Candace needed to know about remote viewing was already on Quin's laptop. He'd given her the password to open files he'd collected over the past six months. He was meticulous, if not obsessive-compulsive in gathering background data. It was obvious to her that he had invested his free time in gathering files to share with somebody. Agent Kruse had given him training materials on remote viewing. And Quin had downloaded hundreds of pages from the web.

She learned that during the Cold War, the Soviet Union pioneered the field and during the 1970s, the United States caught on and began experimenting with it as well, launching Project Stargate. The CIA and the Defense Intelligence Agency (DIA) spent more than twenty years testing and perfecting remote viewing. The Pentagon considered an army officer and Vietnam War veteran named Joe McMoneagle to be one of its best remote viewers; he had uncovered hidden Soviet submarines and underground nuclear test sites. The military's early success in Project Stargate allowed it to invest as much as $25 million in psychic warfare with the Soviet Union and the People's Republic of China.

According to scientists in the field, everyone has some ability to remote view, to see beyond, but most people are unaware of it. With enough practice, a person could hone his or her sixth sense, but researchers discovered that certain people could reach a deeper level of viewing. In a common entry-level RV test, a soldier would watch images appear on a video screen while researchers measured his heart rate and overall anxiety level. Some of the images were pleasant, such as a beach scene or a puppy, while others were more traumatic, such as a car wreck or a corpse in a battlefield. Naturally, the most unpleasant images evoked the most anxiety, a rapid heart rate, and increased perspiration. What surprised researchers, however, was that some test participants actually displayed anxiety even before the computer had randomly selected the traumatic image. A small percentage of test subjects could actually see into the future, reacting emotionally before a traumatic photo was selected. In other words, they were seeing across time and space, and those soldiers were the best remote viewers, the most successful spies.

Candace remained at the kitchen table, poring over online documents, clicking on websites, copying and pasting blocks of text into her own notes. There was plenty of historical information through the 1990s, but she found very little after that period. Project Stargate had lost funding. The CIA and DIA had seemingly scuttled remote viewing research, thanked the soldiers, and moved on.

That was when former military remote viewers began writing. David Moorehouse wrote *Psychic Warrior* and Russell Targ wrote *Limitless Mind*, among many more. Quin had found that one remote viewer nicknamed PsychicChic had blogged about her post-traumatic stress from her years of remote viewing work. Her symptoms included:

- Changes in circadian rhythm
- Insomnia
- Unexpected visions or images of target locations or people she had never met
- Waking nightmares of traumatic events
- Paralyzing daydreams

Her blog updates ended in 1999 when a family member posted that she had sadly taken her own life.

The military officially now labeled remote viewing as junk science, not as reliable as the National Security Agency (NSA) tactics of eavesdropping on global phone calls and later hacking over the sprawling Internet highway. But Candace wondered if the claims by the military that remote viewing had been abandoned were actually an exaggeration. Obviously, Agent Kruse was still actively training Quin and others using the same technique. And, according to Quin's notes, Kruse did it within the walls of a hospital psychiatric ward. How interesting.

She heard the front door open. Quin stepped in and removed his boots. "Almost ready. Hawk and Jimmy are adding lights, and then we can explore the tunnels… what's wrong?" he asked, staring at her.

"Is all this real?" She pointed at the screen.

He joined her in the kitchen and opened the refrigerator. "Ah, the research, it's very real. A lot to take in, I know."

"The military uses psychics?"

"Did at one time, maybe still does," Quin said. "Homeland Security is testing us now."

"How many psychics are there?"

"In Minnesota? Only three left that I know of. Dillan, Rachel, and me."

"You're one of them? You can do it?"

"Not the way they do," he said. "Traditional remote viewers spend hours sitting in dark rooms, sketching. I can't hunt like that, I need to move around."

"From your notes, Agent Kruse seems intense. Do you like working for him?"

Quin nodded. "Even though he and I have our issues, he and the team helped me find my sister."

"If you're not like the other viewers, what's your method?"

He sat with her at the table, twisting the cap off his water and guzzling it down. She could see that he was tired and there was still much work to do.

"I view into the other side even while I'm mobile."

"Other viewers can't do that?"

He shook his head, his feathered earring swaying. "No, they establish the location or the objects while sitting in a quiet place. I'm better in the field, and sometimes view while I'm mobile."

"Even after reading all your research, I still don't understand how it works."

He nodded with patience. "There are obviously other dimensions we don't see, but our subconscious minds are able to tap into one of those spaces. Kruse calls it a 'matrix' where all information is stored. And while we have brains to process information, our minds are made of thoughts, emotions, and memories that exist outside our bodies. By focusing your mind on something, you bring it forward into your present reality, just like a memory. You see it; you know where it is."

"Like a dream world?"

"Similar, yes. Have you ever had a dream where you knew that you were dreaming? That's when you're pushing through to the other side."

"Why do the remote viewers sketch?" she asked.

"Makes it easier to bring the details forward, to literally 'draw' them out of their subconscious mind. And it's how they document the location as it comes into focus."

"Wow, this isn't bullshit?"

"Agent Kruse found my sister using RV," he said. "That's proof enough for me."

She nodded and sighed, still trying to make sense of it.

"What's wrong, Candace?"

"It's not what I was expecting. I came down here to interview you, a bounty hunter searching for his sister, and now you're handing me a totally different story."

"You're disappointed?"

"You could've told me what this was all about back in Minnesota."

"I haven't lied to you."

"You withheld information."

"You wouldn't be here now if I had told you a week ago."

"How do you know? Oh, that's right, you're psychic," she said with irritation in her voice. No need to disguise it.

"Very funny—"

"If you can see into other dimensions, you could see into the future."

"Remote viewers see in the present, across great distances, and sometimes they can revisit locations from the past. As for seeing into the future, I have done it, but the information is very unreliable. The past has already happened, the present is happening now, and the future is affected by too many possibilities until it enters the present, where remote viewers capture it."

She rubbed her stiff neck, reflecting on their conversation; it was strange, so unexpected. "What now?"

"Fly back to Minnesota and find out what's happening to the remote viewers at St. Francis," he said. "Find Dillan."

"Wait a minute; is there any chance I'll get in some kind of trouble? Hawk has nothing good to say about the bureau."

"Use caution. Avoid Agent Kruse, which should be easy, because right now he's focused on me and Autumn."

Agent Kruse paced the small, dimly lit conference room behind Dillan, watching him draw on a tattered sketchpad. Kruse knew his recruit was exhausted because he kept circling the target coordinates on the page, 7545Q202, yawning before sketching again. This session was a blend of Coordinate Remote Viewing (CRV) and Extended Remote Viewing (ERV), which can last two or more hours, or sometimes through multiple sessions. They had been at it for almost sixty minutes, the meaty edge of Dillan's left hand black from the lead pencil. Kruse had moved him through the first three levels of RV quickly, pushing him to formulate images faster than usual. He looked down at Dillan's sketch of a rock structure in the desert hills. Dillan had drawn a tall rectangular box, and now he was shading it in.

"What is it?" he asked Dillan. "Give me the gestalt again, your impressions, descriptors."

"The tall one, metal, steal, rust."

"Describe the smaller boxes."

"Heavy." He licked his lips. "Acidic, like battery acid."

That made no sense to Kruse. Batteries in the desert? Maybe Dillan was tired and going off on a tangent.

"Get closer to the large rectangle. Walk up to it."

Dillan shaded the rectangular box for another two minutes and said, "Height eight or ten feet."

"What's on the other side of it?"

"I can't pass through." Dillan scratched the back of his right hand nervously.

"Why not?" Kruse asked.

"It's locked."

To Kruse's frustration, some remote viewers were literal in their spatial perceptions. Despite the fact that they could use their minds to travel across the world, some viewers couldn't easily pass through walls or locked doors, at least not without coaching.

"Dillan, take a breath."

"I'm tired, man. How about a break?"

"Touch the metal, Dillan."

"It's warm," he said, gripping the pencil tighter.

"Is there a heat source on the other side?" Kruse paced with his arms behind his back.

"No, it's warm from the sun," Dillan replied. "The other side is cold, damp."

"Relax and move through the heat to the cold."

Dillan breathed deeper and dropped his pencil on the floor. "I need a break. Isn't it Rachel's turn?"

"We'll switch in a minute. First, tell me what's on the other side of that metal structure."

Dillan stood up. "What difference does it make? I give you all these drawings and you never tell me if I'm on target or not."

That was the hard reality of remote viewing. Agent Kruse had to keep his viewers in the dark about the targets they were searching for. Strict protocols prevented him from front-loading them with information or clues about what they were searching for. And he wouldn't share the results of their sessions because the viewers might talk and share them with each other.

Kruse would document everything for his files and he'd forward the information onto the upper echelons of whatever client had hired him, whether that was the CIA, the NSA, or the FBI. Sometimes they acted on his team's reports, but most of the time the information slipped into a black hole. The only way Kruse knew he was succeeding, making some progress in the war on terror, was thanks to repeat requests from the bureau or Homeland Security to search for a target, such as a sleeper cell of terrorists or dirty bombs. Tonight's session was all about Quin and what he was up to. This was a case where Kruse was determined to see the outcome for himself. He might even break with protocol and share the information with his team.

"When Quin found Autumn, I shared that with you," he reminded Dillan. "Tell me what's on the other side of that metal, and then we'll finish," he said, bargaining.

"It's dark in there, I can't see anything," Dillan said. "Smells like a cave, though."

A cave? Again, it made no sense to Kruse. That didn't mean the viewing was wrong; sometimes they needed more than one session to collect a full picture.

"Well, how did I do?" Dillan asked.

"How do you think you did?"

"The target is in the desert, and it has something to do with finding Autumn. Am I right?"

"We're done, get a good night's rest."

Dillan mumbled under his breath and opened the door, where Rachel stood in the hallway.

"How did it go?" she asked them.

"You know he can't talk about it," Kruse reminded her.

"Same old shit, just a different day," Dillan said.

Rachel entered with a sketchpad under her arm and sat at the desk with perfect posture. Unlike Dillan, who slouched over the desk, Rachel sat poised like a model student, ready to begin. She made no small talk with Kruse, no jokes or complaints about how warm the room was. She was in her ready position with an charcoal black drawing pencil in hand. He dimmed the lights because she preferred the room darker than Dillan.

Kruse wanted to know more about Autumn's location, where Quin had briefly reunited with his sister, and where he would likely retrieve her.

Instead, he showed her a card with the same coordinates that Dillan had viewed only moments earlier. He wanted to know if she'd see the same details in her session. "Coordinate 7545Q202," he said.

She wrote them on her sketchpad and repeated the coordinates, "7545Q202," then her pencil glided across the page in an upward arc. The first sketched line was the subconscious mind tapping into the signal. The coordinates were arbitrary, something Kruse had randomly assigned to what he was searching for somewhere out in the vast universe of the matrix. She was working off his intentions, where he thought she needed to go, and her mind was chasing after it like a search dog following an invisible scent. He watched over her shoulder as she drew lines and shades of black that she smeared with her fingers to create shadows of gray. Dillan was more like a police sketch artist, fast and efficient, but Rachel's approach was like that of those artists who stand along the Seine River in Paris, capturing details on the horizon that you didn't even know were there.

After twelve minutes, he spoke to her in a low, calm voice. "The gestalt, first impressions?"

"Rock and sand," she said without lifting her eyes from her pad.

To Kruse it looked similar to Dillan's drawing, a wall with jagged rocks. There was no way Dillan could've passed this information to her when they'd met in the hallway. And the room was soundproof. She was sketching the exact location with more detail, more enthusiasm. She drew boxes, larger than the ones Dillan had viewed.

"What's your impression of those?" he asked, sitting next to her at the table. "What kind of proportions?"

"Pretty big, you could climb inside them."

She drew a circle inside each box.

"Stay with that, describe it," he guided her.

"Solid, has grooves or grips for fingers, like a…may I label it?"

The problem with labeling an object early in a session was that if the viewer was wrong, the entire session could go off on a tangent. But she was close enough to what Dillan had sketched. "Go ahead."

"A wheel, feels like a steering wheel," she said.

"Hmmm, are those vehicles, possibly Jeeps?"

She shook her head. "Smaller…golf carts."

"Golf carts?" he said with disappointment.

"There are batteries or power cells on the ground," she said, pointing to the smaller boxes she'd drawn.

Dillan had mentioned the batteries, so maybe they weren't off target after all.

"They're beneath an overhang," she said.

"Is there a door?"

She nodded. "Steel door is on the left side, the carts are parked near it inside."

"The carts are inside what?"

"A passageway."

"A garage or cave?"

She looked up at him. "Are you labeling objects?" she asked.

"Sorry, continue."

"Two carts at a cave entrance."

"Good, what else—"

"People are here, men."

"How many?"

"Three."

He rarely asked them to draw people. It was too time-consuming and too difficult for viewers to capture accurately.

"Give me your impressions of the men."

"An elderly man and a young one, they seem related and…" She dropped her pencil.

"What about the third person?"

She rested her elbows on the sketchpad, rubbing her temples. "Oh, God."

"What?"

"He sees me! The others don't, but he's looking at me." She pushed the sketchpad away, toward Kruse.

"Who?"

She turned to him. He couldn't ignore the smoldering anger in her eyes.

"You know who, it's Quin!"

Cornered. There was no way he could deny to Rachel that today's target was indeed Quin. "I only want to know his whereabouts."

"We're spying on him?"

"No, we have his back," Kruse said in a calming voice, "making sure he's safe. Nogales is a dangerous place, Rachel. We want Quin to succeed, correct?"

She dog-eared a corner of the page, creasing it with her fingers. "Correct."

"We gave him all the training, the support, and gear to bring Autumn home, remember?"

She nodded, staring at the drawing. "Yeah."

"I would've told you and Dillan everything if I could," he said. "But the protocols of RV don't allow that."

"You've told us that a million times," she said. A small tremor in her legs rose up to her chest and her face as a tear splashed onto the page.

"How big is the cave?"

"I can't see it anymore," she said with a sniffle.

"Take a breath."

"I can't do it!"

"Can't, or...*won't?*"

"Pick up your phone and ask him yourself," she said.

"That's enough for today," he said.

"Not exactly ending this session on a high note." She stood, tore the drawing out of her sketchpad, handed it to him, and left him alone.

"Damn it!" he shouted, his words deadened by the soundproof panels on the walls.

He was too hard on them, and he knew it. In the early days of RV research he had given military recruits more time to practice their craft. His funding and assignments came from the slow-moving Defense Intelligence Agency (DIA), an agency with a growing $4 billion budget that officially has 17,000 employees, two-thirds of whom are civilians. The talent pool Kruse had to work with was minuscule: ten or twelve people at a time. But he had to give them plenty of rest and time off between RV assignments so doctors could evaluate the health of each recruit. It was unnecessary, in Kruse's opinion. *There's nothing dangerous about RV; it's as natural as meditating.*

His assignments reflected the times and the branch of the military requesting intelligence. In the 1980s, the navy needed intel on Russian submarines. Then in the early 1990s, the CIA requested intel on Iran's nuclear ambitions. Kruse would task his viewers with assignments, then he'd return detailed reports and drawings to the appropriate branch. By the late 1990s, most of the assignments focused on the Middle East and the plague of religious fanatics that eventually slammed two airplanes into the Twin Towers, one into the Pentagon, and a fourth into a Pennsylvania field.

Kruse was asked why his team hadn't predicted an imminent attack. He had explained the complexities of seeing and predicting future events.

"Isn't that what you're paid to do, see into the future?" one congressman had asked him in a private meeting.

Kruse had given him the abrupt answer, "We see the now. It's the military's job to respond to it."

That comment was the reason Kruse and his research were jettisoned from the DIA's 450,000-square-foot building in Washington to a state security hospital in Minnesota. The National Institutes of Health (NIH) had learned of Kruse's work in parapsychology and it fit with their research in neuroscience. They wanted to know if he could give "meaningful work to psychiatric patients," some of whom had already displayed "talents in intuition."

Kruse had politely declined the offer; he was in the twilight of his career and had no interest in lab rat research.

But then he received a call from the director of Homeland Security, who convinced him to accept the new assignment. Kruse would build a paranormal team to locate terrorists. The funding would flow from the NIH, and he'd train recruits from within the cloistered halls of the hospital.

Remote viewing didn't prevent 9/11, but Kruse had helped the Department of Homeland Security find and degrade terrorist cells on American soil in the years since. Even though it was more challenging to train psychiatric patients, if he could speed them through the learning curve, they were more reliable remote viewers than the general population. Outbursts like Rachel's were common, and usually a sign he had brought them to a new level.

What was Quin up to? Kruse reached into his pocket and considered Rachel's suggestion: call him.

He sent a text instead: *We'd better get started soon. Time is running out.*

At the tunnel entrance, Quin was sitting in the driver's seat of the golf cart with Hawk next to him. Moments earlier, Quin had felt a presence, as if somebody were watching him. He looked over his shoulder again onto the desert hills that met a blue-black sky punctured with pinholes for stars. Nothing. Whatever it was, it had moved on.

Jimmy was in the other cart, pouring his grandfather another cup of tea, for courage and strength. Quin took only two sips; he needed his focus for what lay ahead of them. The test run would take them through the underground corridors littered with man-made debris and nature's own surprises—and who knows what else.

"This is a good thing," Hawk said.

"What do you mean?" Quin asked.

"You're doing all of this to reunite what's left of your family. I'm proud of you. Four years ago when Helene brought you home, all I saw in you was a lost spirit. You've changed, you've grown."

"Thanks, Hawk." Those were the exact words Quin needed to hear.

"You're a good influence on Jimmy, too," Hawk said, lowering his voice. "He respects you."

He looked over at Hawk's grandson seated in the other golf cart, gazing into the glow of his phone.

"If anything happens to me, check on him once in a while."

"Nothing will happen to you."

"I'll die before you, that's for sure," Hawk said. "And when it happens, make sure my daughters don't waste money on a big funeral. Have my ashes mixed with Lily's. Her urn is a clay pot on my mantel. Spread our ashes to the winds on Hinhan Kaga Paha. Jimmy knows the place."

"Stay by my side, Hawk, and nothing will happen to you."

"You suppose there's bats down there?" Hawk asked, pointing into the blackness of the cave.

Quin laughed.

"What's so funny?" Jimmy said.

"Could be bats down there," Quin said. "Keep your head low."

"And snakes, too?" Hawk said.

"Keep your feet up," Quin teased.

Jimmy looked up from his phone. "How can we drive with heads down and feet up?"

"And then, of course, there's chupacabra," Quin said.

"Chupa-what?"

"Blood-sucking dog, or something like that," Quin said as he described the warnings his parents had given him as a boy. He was teasing Jimmy for the same reason his parents had done it to him—to keep him close and prevent him from wandering.

"Bullshit," Jimmy said.

"I'm ready, let's go," Hawk said, finishing his tea.

"I'll lead, you stay close," Quin said to Jimmy.

He stepped on the pedal and the cart leapt forward into the tunnel, down the shifting sands of the ramp, their headlights bouncing up and down as they rode. He heard Jimmy following close behind. Hawk acted as the navigator, holding Quin's phone with the map lit up on the screen. There were so many side tunnels not even shown on the map, it was important to have Hawk checking the map often.

If everything went well, they should make it to the exit tunnel within thirty minutes. Lopez would be waiting there to ensure they could actually get out. Then they would clock themselves on the return journey. In theory, once they were in the tunnels, they would be safe. Quin's experience in bounty hunting, however, had taught him that once you had possession of a fugitive, you had to move quickly.

The sand on the flats had softer sand than the ramps and the walls were narrower than Quin had expected. He hit a rut and the cart leaned on Hawk's side, scraping sand off the wall. Jimmy cursed and slowed, then speeded up to close the distance. This routine of surging and fading continued for ten minutes until they came to a sudden stop. Something was blocking their path. Quin got out of the cart with Hawk and inspected it.

"What?" Jimmy called out.

"Dirt pile," Hawk said, kicking it with his boot.

"Drive over it," Jimmy said.

"We have to clear it," Quin said.

Jimmy moaned and joined them as they used their hands, scooping away the sand, flattening the pile along the floor of the tunnel.

"Why would somebody leave a heap of sand here?" Jimmy asked as they worked.

"It came from there," Quin said, pointing to the low ceiling.

Jimmy and Hawk looked up at a gaping crevice.

"Is this tunnel collapsing?" Jimmy asked.

"Looks like it," Quin said, masking his own anxiety.

Jimmy went into panic mode. "Let's go back. You don't want to be down here either," he said to Hawk.

"Quin decides."

He considered the possibility of turning back; they were still closer to the entrance ramp than the exit. But there was one problem. "We can't turn the carts around, it's too narrow," Quin said.

"Drive in reverse," Jimmy said.

"No tail lights. We couldn't see where we're going."

"We got flashlights."

"The carts are too slow in reverse."

"We'll walk back."

Quin ended the debate. "We're continuing forward."

He and Hawk got back into their cart and drove twenty yards as Jimmy sat in his without following. Quin knew he was contemplating an exit. Rather than slow down, Quin sped up, leaving Jimmy alone in the darkness, taking a risk that he'd back up and leave. Moments later, the headlights from Jimmy's cart grew brighter as he closed the gap.

Hawk set his hand on Quin's knee. "See? He's following because he trusts you."

Quin drove faster into the haze of bouncing headlights and dust. He was in a rhythm, only scraping the walls occasionally. The narrow passageway and rock walls whizzed by, making their speed of 45 miles an hour feel more like 80. He squinted ahead at what looked like a dead end and then realized this tunnel turned to the right. He slowed to make the turn; the new tunnel was wider, with a higher ceiling, too. He stopped and waited for Jimmy to pull up alongside them.

"Where are we on the map?" he asked Hawk.

Hawk zoomed in with his callused fingers. "This is the first turn. One more coming up."

Jimmy skidded to a stop. "Whoa, now we got head room."

Quin realized this manmade tunnel interested a natural cave. It felt cooler and musty, and Quin heard dripping from the ceiling. He stepped out of the cart and shone a flashlight at the walls. There were cave drawings, painted in red, over ten feet above them: an image of an eagle and a herd of animals with horns.

"I wonder who drew that," Jimmy said in awe.

"Could've been a tribe," Hawk said.

"Most likely the Hohokam," Quin said. "They were the only tribe to build canals and irrigation systems for their crops. They knew how to find water," he said, remembering a story his mother had told him about life in the desert. He walked forward onto a rock ledge and shone his light onto a bubbling stream that was cutting its way through the rock. Around him were signs of modern visitors: empty water bottles, propane tanks, a rusted camp stove. Above him, he spotted bats hanging from the ceiling, fluttering their wings and waking up. Other bats were dropping from the ceiling and flying; a river of bats headed into the darkness.

"Whoa, that's crazy!" Jimmy aimed his flashlight up.

"It's a sign," Hawk said.

"Good or bad?" Quin asked.

"Good, there's another way out of here if we need it." Hawk pointed to an uneven path that twisted along the banks of the stream.

Quin joined Hawk back at the golf cart, grabbing his phone off the seat. He was curious to see if he could get a cell phone signal in here. Upon entering the tunnel, he had set his phone in airplane mode to save power. He changed it back now and his phone chirped.

"What was that?" Jimmy asked.

"I have a text," he said, realizing it was from Agent Kruse: *We'd better get started soon. Time is running out.*

Quin couldn't agree more. Instead of responding to Kruse, he texted: *Lopez: Are you there?*

A moment later his phone chirped: *Yes. What's taking so long?*

Quin thumbed his reply: *Blazing a trail down here. Should be there soon.*

He opened the map again and handed the phone back to Hawk. "Let's go. Agent Lopez is waiting for us on the other side."

After thirty minutes of driving, he turned into the connecting tunnel driving at top speed, threading the needle, with Jimmy right behind them. They were climbing an incline and Quin felt the cart's wheels slipping. He eased off the accelerator. Jimmy's headlights grew brighter and without warning, he rear-ended them.

"Damn it! Tell me when you're braking!"

"We're sliding backwards," Quin said.

"That's cuz I got the torque," Jimmy said, and he nosed his cart to the back of theirs. "Go, I'll push you."

Impressed with the idea, Quin continued up the incline as Jimmy prevented them from sliding backwards. They were working as a team, ascending slowly as one subterranean vehicle. The path ahead was littered with more remnants of past journeys: a bandana, a teddy bear, a broken two-way radio, and they rode right over them like stones in a river.

The path finally leveled out and Quin accelerated away from Jimmy's cart for fifty yards, where the path rose higher again. They continued their routine of Jimmy pushing as Quin drove. *At least this portion will be a fast and easy descent on our return trip.* He felt a change in air pressure, his ears popping as a gust of fresh air enveloped them.

"We made it!" Hawk said, calling back to his grandson.

They cheered as the ramp leveled again into a flat, sandy area. Quin spotted a three-foot opening in the metal door covering the mouth of the cave. He smelled cigarette smoke. "Lopez! Open the door!" he called out.

She stuck her head into the narrow opening. "Stay in your carts."

"Why?"

"Look at the ground."

The cave floor moved beneath them in swirls and s-curves. There had to be a hundred or more snakes slithering under their vehicles.

"Oh God!" Jimmy said, kicking one out of his cart.

"Can you walk the door back?" Quin said to Lopez.

"Trying, but it's heavy."

"Tell me this is a good sign, Hawk," Quin said.

The old man lifted his boots up onto the dashboard. "I never liked snakes. The Hopi tribes might take this as a good sign, but it's just spooky to me."

As a native of Arizona, Quin wasn't turned off by snakes. Non-venomous snakes outnumber venomous snakes three to one, so he knew his odds here were pretty good. If the tail came to a point, the snake was harmless. He illuminated the specimens, which were black and white common king snakes. Nothing to worry about.

He stepped out of the cart, lifted a snake out of the way with the toe of his boot, and helped Lopez tug and pull on the door. It opened gradually, as if the cave were waking from a long sleep, the cool night air rushing in like an inhalation. Hawk slid into the driver's seat and drove straight out of the cave, with his grandson right behind him.

"How was it down there?" Lopez asked.

"Bats, snakes, and lots of trash," Jimmy said.

"But no bodies," Hawk said. "That we know of."

Quin reached out to shake Lopez's hand. "The return trip should go faster."

She smiled, her cigarette balancing on her lower lip. "Let's hope so."

Lopez and Quin left Hawk and Jimmy at the tunnel entrance and drove to the two-lane highway that would lead them to Autumn. Lopez had driven only one and a half miles after she had turned off the highway to the warehouse-meth lab they'd visited a couple of days ago. She set the Suburban in park and turned off the engine and lights.

"Here it is," Lopez said.

"It's close to the tunnel."

"I told you so," she said.

He looked out the side window into the darkness at the warehouse, where he saw a glow through a skylight on the roof. "Somebody's in there."

"Could be anybody."

"It's her," he said. He had a feeling. "And Marta's there, too. It's showtime."

"What if we're not ready?"

Quin turned to Lopez and saw the concern on her face. "Hawk and Jimmy are at the tunnel. You and I are here. Autumn and Marta are in there. How much more ready can we be?"

"What about Agent Kruse?" she said. "He wants to record it on the live feed."

"Have you spoken to him recently?" he asked.

"He called because he couldn't reach you."

"What did you tell him?"

"We're making a practice run tonight. Why? Is that bad?"

He took in a calming breath. "It's all right, Lopez. This isn't like chasing any old skip. I'm here to rescue my family. And while I appreciate Kruse's help so far, I need to do this without him watching me."

"Then this is it, huh?"

He felt his chest tightening, the hair on his forearms rising. Outside on the warehouse roof his ravens had landed, silently hopping across it with wings outstretched.

"What are you looking at?" Lopez asked.

He breathed as he meditated on the building. Dillan or Rachel could do it; they could simply see through these walls. Quin could only sense danger, get an impression, and react to it. He slid his phone out of his pocket and called Dillan. It rang and rang.

"Yeah?" Dillan said with a sluggish grumble.

"It's me. You awake?"

"Hey, Quin. Sleepless as usual."

"How you feeling these days?"

"Shitty. I had a marathon session with Kruse tonight."

"Tell him you need time off. It's not healthy to work non-stop."

"He won't let up until we find Autumn."

Quin felt guilty about that. He wanted to help his team members even while he was in the field. "Dillan, there's a reporter named Candace Johnson who's agreed to research the long-term effects of RV. I want you to speak with her."

"Cool, whatever."

"If you're up for it, I could use your help."

"Sure, anything."

"I need you to Remote View into a structure."

"For real? You mean without Kruse?" The guy was in disbelief.

"I'm outside the building in Mexico."

"Don't front-load it. Just give me coordinates."

Quin held the phone to his chest and said to Lopez, "Give me some random numbers."

"What kind of numbers?"

"Doesn't matter. What's your date of birth?"

"October 12, 1975."

Quin turned the speakerphone on and told Dillan, "One. Zero. One. Two. One. Nine. Seven. Five."

Dillan repeated the number and Quin heard him rustling paper and scribbling. Five minutes later, he had the target. "This is easy, you're at the warehouse."

"Who's inside of it?" Quin asked.

"Several people; a woman who must be Autumn, and a young girl."

"Good," Quin said. "As expected."

Lopez stared at Quin in surprise, experiencing how RV worked in the field.

"Wait, there's another person," Dillan said. "A man."

"Tell me about him."

"He's upset."

"Angry, sad, or what?"

"Stop labeling it, Quin. I don't know, he's pacing. He's conflicted."

"Do they know we're here?"

"No, he and Autumn are focused on each other, arguing."

The odd thing was that Quin sensed and recognized Dillan's presence here too.

"Dillan, were you viewing earlier tonight?"

"Like I said, Kruse had a late-night session with me and then Rachel."

"What did you see?"

"You know we can't talk about our sessions, but what the hell, I think I was off target, walking around a cave somewhere in the desert."

"Did Kruse give Rachel the same target for her session?"

"Not sure."

The presence that Quin had felt earlier in the evening at the tunnel entrance had to have been Rachel. Kruse was hedging his bets, using both Dillan and Rachel to follow Quin's movements.

"Is she in a session with Kruse right now?"

"No, she left her session an hour ago, all crazy upset."

"What else do you see inside the warehouse?"

"Ah, I lost it. Kruse and I don't have conversations like this during a session. Sorry, man."

"No, that's my bad," Quin said. "I'll check it out."

"Quin, wait," Dillan said. "The man with Autumn has a gun."

Quin looked over at Lopez, who couldn't believe the conversation she was hearing.

"Thanks, Dillan, and remember, you shouldn't talk about your RV sessions. Let's keep tonight's viewing between you and me. Agreed?"

"Cool, good luck!"

He turned to Lopez. "It's happening now. I'll go in, and you stay outside here at the truck."

"You sure you want to go in alone?"

"One hundred percent."

Lopez reached across to the glove box and pulled out a Glock 17 and unholstered her Glock 23, showing them to Quin. "It's up to you."

"You're possessive of that Glock 23," he said.

"The 17 actually holds more ammo," she said. "If you go in there alone, take it. I'll back you up with the 23."

He took her advice, stepped out of the truck, and ran to the warehouse with the 17 at his side. The door was locked. No surprise. He listened and heard voices inside. Dillan was right, Autumn and a man were in the midst of a heated conversation. He could try kicking in the door, but that would ruin the element of surprise. He knocked instead, and then waited as he heard the voices whispering and somebody coming to the door. At that point, it was anyone's guess as to who was on the other side. He knocked again, louder this time. The ravens hopped to the edge of the roof above the door, agitated, making a ruckus that only he could hear.

"¿Quién es?" *Who is it?* a man said through the door.

Quin waited in silence, holding his breath. He knew Lopez was watching from the truck.

The door opened and the man leaned out with his pistol extended in front of him. *Idiot move*, thought Quin. In a burst of black and white flashes of light and shrieks from the ravens above, Quin kicked the gun upward with the toe of his boot. It spun out of the man's hands and landed on the ground. It was an FN-57, or what's known in the States as a "cop killer"; carried by all the drug thugs. More flashes: black on white and white on black. The man dove for it, another idiot move that Quin anticipated, kicking him in the ribs before he pressed the Glock to the back of his head.

He heard Lopez racing toward them, shouting, "Keep your ass on the ground!"

Quin pulled the man's arms behind his back and cinched his wrists with a zip-tie.

"Buena noches," Quin said to him.

"What's your name? ¿Su nombre?" Lopez said between breaths.

Quin stepped off of him, recognizing the man. "He's Jefe," he said to Lopez, watching the man struggling on his stomach, cursing in Spanish.

"Quin!" Autumn shouted, running with Marta to Jefe's side.

Quin lowered his gun and motioned to Lopez to do the same. They were a family, therefore, part of Quin's family: a sister, an estranged brother-in-law, and a niece. And here he was, the impatient American, pushing them around and terrorizing them.

"I heard arguing," he explained to Autumn, "and he had a gun."

"We were discussing my leaving. Jefe, esto es Quin," she said, introducing them.

Well, this is awkward, thought Quin. He reached down to his boot, removed his knife, and cut the zip-tie. His brother-in-law sat up in the dirt. Quin reached out a hand to help him up but Jefe refused assistance. He stood up on his own, wiping sand and dirt from his face.

"She's the one you're looking for?" Jefe said in pretty good English. "You're her brother?"

"Yes."

"I've heard about you," he said.

Unfortunately, Quin couldn't say the same about Jefe. He knew absolutely nothing about him or Marta, and very little about his own sister.

"I'm here for you and Marta," he said to Autumn, nevertheless. "It's time to go."

"Now?" Autumn said in disbelief.

"I'm an American on Sinaloa land, so I suggest we move quickly," he said. "I've got transportation waiting."

"Come with us, Jefe," she said, holding Marta's hand and reaching for his.

Jefe was a gaunt man who looked younger than Autumn, in Quin's opinion. He wondered how they'd met, and guessed he'd learn that at some point.

"You could start a new life," she pleaded with him.

This was what the argument was about, whether Jefe would join them on their journey to the States. If they were splitting up, this could be a painful good-bye that might draw a lot of unwanted attention.

"Come with us to the border, Jefe. You can decide there," Quin said.

His brother-in-law went along with the idea and they walked to the Chevy Suburban, where Quin rode in the back seat with his gun and Jefe's, in case there was trouble. Marta, clutching a threadbare stuffed teddy bear, was sandwiched between her parents in the bench seat in front of Quin. He watched as Autumn and Jefe looked back at the warehouse for what could be the last time. They were leaving everything behind, fleeing in the middle of the night with nothing but the clothes on their backs. For Jefe, this must be a tougher decision; he was a local who had family here. For Autumn, it was a chance to return to a home she once knew and loved.

Lopez steered off the highway onto the uneven hard-packed clay and rock. In the moonlight the saguaros, the tallest cacti, stood like ancient desert gods, their arms stretched to the heavens. Hawk would certainly think it was a sign.

When they reached the outcrop of rock, Lopez stopped and parked the truck. "This is your stop."

"Where?" Jefe asked, looking out the window.

"Up ahead," Quin said, pointing to the hole in the rock where Jimmy and Hawk were seated in their golf carts, waiting. They were ghostly moon shadows in front of an outcrop of boulders.

"Underground?" Jefe said to Autumn.

Autumn nodded.

Jefe turned to Quin, asking, "Why underground?"

It was clear that Jefe had thought they would use the official border crossing in Nogales. There must be a reason that Autumn hadn't told him about the tunnel until now. Maybe he was afraid of it, like Hawk.

"You got a passport?" Quin asked.

"No."

"Autumn is a natural-born US citizen and she could have a child out of the country, such as Marta, who would ordinarily qualify as a citizen," Quin said. "But a US citizen parent must have been physically present in the US for five years before the child's birth, and at least two of those years must have been after age fourteen."

"Marta isn't a US citizen?" Autumn said.

"Not yet," Quin said.

"Then I'm not leaving."

"We can do this the hard way and cross through the tunnel, or we can do it the harder way, have you sit in immigration services for days, if not weeks, while it all gets sorted out," he said.

"Come with us," she said to Jefe.

"Incicio está aquí." *Home is here*, he said proudly. He opened the truck door and as he stepped out, he grabbed Marta.

"Jefe, no!" Autumn shouted.

Quin jumped out of the back seat and followed Jefe. "Let her go."

As Jefe quickened his pace Marta stumbled and looked back, calling, "Mama!"

Autumn gave chase, running past Quin in a maternal rage toward the father of her child. She began slapping him on the head, kicking his legs. This was spiraling into a domestic dispute and he knew it was always better to stay out of it, to let the couple blow off their steam before breaking it up.

But then Marta broke free, and to Quin's surprise, she sprinted toward *him*. He knelt with his arms open and embraced her as she collapsed into his arms. He covered the girl's eyes as he watched Autumn and Jefe pushing one another until Jefe shoved her to the ground and left her. Autumn pulled herself up, brushed the dirt and sand from her jeans and walked back, wiping tears from her eyes.

"Estoy aquí." *I'm here*, she said to Marta.

"You okay?" Quin asked, handing her daughter back.

"Yeah, that about sums up our marriage," she said. "Let's go."

Quin escorted them up to the golf carts, where he introduced them to Jimmy and Hawk, who both smiled and put them at ease.

"Autumn, you and Marta will ride with me," Quin said. "Hawk, you'll ride with Jimmy and follow behind us. Agent Lopez will drive the truck through customs and meet us back at the house."

Lopez stepped out of the cave and Quin helped her walk the metal door forward along its track. He waited for her to lock it and when he heard Lopez start up her truck, he returned to the golf cart and started the engine.

The headlights illuminated the walls of the tunnel, accenting shadows in the rock crevices. Quin drove forward slowly as they descended the steep ramp, the cart sliding even as he applied the brakes. Jimmy's cart bumped Quin's again, launching them down the ramp into an uncontrollable slide.

"Momma!" Marta said, tucking in closer and clutching her mother's arm. Autumn comforted her, stroking Marta's hair.

Quin accelerated to gain better control of the slide as the rock walls seemed to close in on them. He understood why his niece was afraid; it smelled musty in here and was cooler than up top. When he hit the flats, he continued faster, with Jimmy and Hawk trailing.

"How far do we have to go?" Autumn asked.

"Exact distance? Not sure. It took us forty minutes to get here."

"We'll be down here for forty minutes?"

"If all goes well. It's the only way to get across the desert without the border patrol spotting us," he said, steering over a rut. The cart scraped the wall on Autumn's side.

"I hate this place," she said. "You never forget the smell."

"You've been here before, haven't you?"

She was silent, clutching her daughter.

"Autumn, the night you disappeared, did they bring you through the tunnels?"

She nodded and wiped another tear. He drove with his eyes locked on the bouncing high beams, waiting for her to explain how and why she'd been kidnapped.

"What happened?" he asked.

"I don't want to talk about it."

"The bureau will want to know. They've invested resources to find you. Hell, *I* need to know before you tell *them*. For years I've lived under a cloud of suspicion. Some people think I killed my parents and my sister."

"Not in front of Marta," she said. "Get us to the other side and I'll tell you everything."

He drove in silence, still concentrating on his headlights. When they reached a fork in the tunnel he turned left, heading into the larger tunnel. The air felt damp and the walls were streaked with dripping water. He slowed to a stop, waiting for Jimmy and Hawk to catch up.

"What's wrong?" she asked.

"Nothing."

"What is this?"

"A cave, formed thousands of years ago."

His phone chirped that he had a voice mail, the sound echoing off the walls. The sound caused a flutter of activity above.

"Bats? Look at all of them!" she said. "Let's get out of here!"

"We all have to stay together. Jimmy and Hawk have fallen behind."

He reached for his phone. He played Lopez's message aloud as Jimmy and Hawk coasted to a stop next to their cart: "*Quin, it's me. I'm on my way toward the border. Thought you should know, a guy on a motorcycle passed me, looked a lot like Jefe, and he turned off the highway heading into the hills. I could be wrong but I thought I would alert you in case he's waiting at the exit.*"

Everyone sat for a moment thinking about what this meant. "Does Jefe have a motorcycle?" he asked Autumn.

She nodded. "He races dirt bikes. That has to be him."

"There's more than one exit," Hawk said. "How could he find us?"

In the movement above his head, Quin noticed larger black wings flapping in the air. His ravens had arrived, flying back and forth from one rock ledge to the other. And then he heard it, the distant hum of an engine.

"He's not waiting at an exit, he's following us," Quin said.

They listened, but nobody else heard it.

"How could he get in?" Jimmy said. "Agent Lopez locked the door."

"There have to be dozens of crevices and openings that he could fit a dirt bike through," Quin said.

"He's right, Jefe's coming!" Autumn said.

The ravens flew in circles in the high dome ceiling of the cave and Quin watched them descend into the tunnel with the running stream.

"What's with him?" Jimmy said.

"Shhh, he's having a vision," Hawk said. "Quin, what do you see?"

"A different way."

"No, we're taking the same route that got us here," Jimmy said. "Follow the map."

A shriek of Jefe's engine echoed in the tunnels and this time they all heard it.

Quin turned to Jimmy and Hawk and said, "We need to follow the ravens." He started the cart and led them downward, deeper into the earth, with Jimmy and Hawk following. He drove across the stream, water splashing up into the cart, where Autumn shielded Marta from the spray. He parked on the edge of the water and turned off the motor and headlights. Jimmy did the same. When Quin looked back up toward the main cave passage, all he saw was darkness, except for the soaring wings of a raven that appeared as a pale shadow of gray. It flew down into a smaller cave and the other raven followed.

"Grab your flashlights," he said, following the ravens into the narrows, where he could barely stand upright.

Autumn cradled Marta in her arms, quietly singing her "Shii Naashaa," a Navajo lullaby that their mother used to sing to them.

Then they walked into the earthen chamber with nothing but the yellow glow of two flashlights. Quin found a flat, dry surface and motioned for them to sit. He sat with them and told Jimmy, "Turn off your light."

There was dark, and then there was completely blind, which was how Quin felt, his eyes wide open, craving even a speck of light. Just as a desert embraces heat and light, an inner cave imprisons cold and darkness.

"Caw! Caw!" a raven cried. *Quiet! Quiet!*

The groan of Jefe's motorcycle engine echoed in the cave above them. He had slowed, possibly stopped.

"Shhh," Quin whispered to the group.

They were silent except for the faintest whispers of Autumn reassuring her daughter that Uncle Quin would lead them to safety.

"Marta, estoy solo sin ti," Jefe called out. *I'm lonely without you.*

How cruel that Jefe would lean on his daughter to give up their hiding place. But she was tough, though, barely making a sound except for a sniffle.

"¿Marta? ¿Marta?" he cried out louder, his voice echoing.

He must've noticed the golf carts and tracks leading down to the stream. Now Quin could hear Jefe's footsteps sloshing along the water's edge, the beam of his flashlight bouncing off the walls. Quin had no choice but to protect his group. He could use the Glock, but didn't want to shoot where the ricocheting bullets could harm somebody. He slid the knife out of his boot and grabbed his flashlight.

"Everyone wait here," he said.

"I'm going," Hawk said. "I'll distract him."

Hawk ran ahead into the darkness toward Jefe's light, shouting in shrieks and howls that sounded like a pack of coyotes. Jefe spun around toward the moving sounds. The echoes must've confused him and he began shooting wildly in different directions. Quin counted at least a dozen shots ricocheting off the rock walls. The muzzle flashes were a reminder that Jefe had his FN-57, a gun that could have a twenty-bullet magazine but was more likely to have a magazine with thirty bullets. Even a blind shooter with a full magazine clip could eventually hit a moving target like Hawk.

Quin ran out of the narrows into the open chamber and drove his knife into Jefe's right shoulder to disable his shooting arm. The man screamed, but the gun didn't drop from his hands; instead, he fired three more shots. Quin pulled him into a chokehold, pressing the knife up under Jefe's chin where he could feel it. "Drop it, drop the gun!" he yelled, dragging him back away from wherever Hawk was hiding.

With his arm extended, Jefe turned his wrist and fired another three rounds toward Quin's head. Quin sliced at Jefe's gun arm, tearing into flesh, and the gun finally dropped to the ground. He tightened his chokehold, forcing Jefe to gasp for air.

"Grab the gun!" Quin said to Hawk.

In the darkness, he saw a flashlight beam on the ground. A hand picked up the gun, but it wasn't Hawk's leathery hand, it was Jimmy's.

"There's zip-ties in the golf cart," Quin said, "and bandages. Grab those too."

Jimmy ran up the path to the carts and Quin searched for Hawk.

"Hawk?" Quin called out. "Hawk?"

Jimmy returned with the ties and held the Glock pointed at Jefe. Quin tied the man's wrists behind his back and wrapped a bandage around his bleeding forearm.

"Where's Hawk?" Jimmy said.

"Here."

Jimmy raised his other arm with the flashlight toward the sound of the voice. Hawk was on the ground, squinting in the light.

"You hurt?" Jimmy said.

"Yep."

"You shot my granddad?" Jimmy said to Jefe.

Jefe shouted and went on a rant about something that only Autumn understood as they all walked back up to the carts. Quin seated Jefe and tied his wrist to the back of the seat post.

He and Jimmy tended to Hawk, who had taken a bullet through his lower right back. There wasn't much blood, but he was in terrible pain, his breathing labored.

"What were you doing out here?" Quin asked.

"Distracting him," Hawk said. "It worked, you got 'im. We make a good team, the three of us."

Everyone piled into the carts; Jimmy followed with Jefe and Hawk rode with Quin, Autumn, and Marta in her lap as they drove up to the main tunnel. They drove past Jefe's dirt bike and Quin considered strapping it to the back of Jimmy's cart in case they needed it. But with Jefe on board, they were hauling too much weight already.

"Let me go, man!" Jefe said.

"No, you've earned yourself a ticket to the USA," Quin said.

"They know I'm down here," Jefe said. "My bros will come looking."

That sounded like classic bullshit bargaining from a skip, but Quin decided not to take any chances. He got out of the cart, lifted the dirt bike, and walked it to the edge of the drop-off over the stream. He pushed it over and it splashed with a thundering clang as it hit the rocks below.

"What? Why?" Jefe said.

"If your friends come searching for you, they'll think you escaped to the other side with us."

He got back into the cart and punched it, and had been speeding through the tunnel for a good twenty minutes when he realized it was hard to see up ahead. At first he thought there was more dust, and then it occurred to him that his headlights were dimmer. Jimmy's lights behind him were dimmer, too. Despite their having installed fresh batteries yesterday, the subterranean conditions had drained them. The high speed combined with the loose sand and the extra weight took their toll.

"How much further do you think we have to go?" Quin asked Autumn, who was holding his phone. Hawk had all he could do to manage his pain on the bumpy ride.

"We're more than halfway there," she guessed, reading the map on his phone. "What's wrong?"

"Nothing."

Jimmy had faded back and Quin slowed so he wouldn't lose him. When Jimmy caught up, he was shouting in frustration, "Almost out of juice!"

"What's that mean?" Autumn asked.

"We're losing power," Quin said.

"You're all gonna die down here," Jefe said.

"Shut up, Jefe!" Autumn said.

Quin drove on at half-speed and as the light dimmed, he scanned the floor ahead for signs and debris that he'd recognize—soda cans, beer bottles, anything to reassure himself that they hadn't missed a turn. So far, it all seemed familiar—or was he imagining it?

Jimmy had fallen behind again. He flashed his headlights on and off. Quin slowed and realized he wasn't playing with his lights to get his attention; Jimmy's batteries were dead. He and Jefe were back there in the blackness.

Quin stopped and set the cart in reverse. It beeped and beeped as he drove backward toward Jimmy's cart, scraping the walls. He handed Autumn the flashlight and she pointed it back so he could see where he was driving. There were Jimmy and Jefe, their cart completely dead.

Jefe laughed like a crazy man Quin had once met in the psych ward who had a cackling laugh that often ended in coughing fits.

"Now what?" Jimmy said.

"You drive the front cart, we'll leave this one behind," he said. "Get moving, while you still have power in my cart."

"See ya, bro," Jimmy said, elbowing Jefe.

"You're coming with us, Quin," Autumn insisted.

"No, there's too much weight in that cart and Hawk needs medical attention. I'll walk or run and catch up."

"What about Jefe?" Autumn asked.

"He'll come with me." He took two flashlights and handed Jefe's gun to Autumn. "Go on, hurry."

Jimmy drove the cart barely twenty miles an hour. The halo of light faded into a candle glow as the rumbling of the motor evaporated in the distance.

"Cut me free, man."

The only weapon Quin had left was his knife, which he used to cut the zip-ties that secured Jefe to the cart seat. He didn't cut the tie that held Jefe's wrists bound, however.

Quin turned him around, facing toward Mexico. "Start walking."

"Let me go."

He shoved Jefe, forcing him into a trot with his hands still bound behind is back.

"You gonna cut me again, kill me?"

"Maybe. More walkin', less talkin'."

"Can't see."

Quin shined the light over Jefe's shoulder; the other light was tucked into his belt in the small of his back. He wasn't sure what to do with Jefe other than put as much distance between him and his escaping family as possible. The guy needed to cool off and lick his wounds, and a walk would give Quin a chance to drag information from his brother-in-law. There was so much he needed to know, and family members are always the best source of family dirt.

"How long have you known my sister?"

"Quatro o cinco anos."

"Speak English. What's your story?"

"Huh?" Jefe asked, looking over his shoulder.

Quin shoved him again for effect. "How'd you meet her?"

"Through the company. Workin' my way up through Sinaloa," he said. "She was with them."

"She worked for them?"

"Worked, lived, it's all the same. When you're in, you're in. Her family needed money. They had her run drugs, like me. That's how we met."

"Who's this family on the Mexico side? Her real family was in Arizona before somebody attacked us."

"A man named Santana," Jefe said. "A fat gringo, with pink skin. Kids in the street call him Santa."

"He's American?"

"He's fat with pink skin, obviously he's American." He laughed, stumbling forward.

"What does Santa do?"

"Does what Santa always does, delivers gifts."

"What? Drugs? He's a drug runner?"

Jefe shook his head, chuckling, enjoying the guessing game. "What's more precious than drugs?" He began singing "Feliz Navidad" as Quin thought about the riddle.

What's more precious along the border than drugs? Quin guessed again. "Gold? Diamonds? Weapons?"

"Incorrect, incorrect, incorrecto! See? Ah, when you have so much of it, it has no value. My hands are tied, your American hands are not—"

It hit Quin. "Freedom!"

"Si, Señor!"

"This man you call Santa brings people across the border."

"For a price, mucho dinero," he said in a mock Spanish accent.

"He sells them freedom."

"The *idea* of freedom," Jefe said. "Men slave in the fields and women slave on their backs, or knees...you know."

"I'm familiar with human trafficking. But how did Autumn get caught up in it?"

Jefe stopped and turned to Quin, squinting. "Caught up in it? You and she were born into it."

"Explain," he said.

"She hasn't told you?"

"Told me what, Jefe?"

Jefe spun around and walked away, mumbling to himself, and Quin followed. He was practically running back to Mexico in the dark.

"What is it that she has to tell me?"

"It's a family thing."

"You're family. Tell me," he said, grabbing Jefe from behind by this injured arm.

"Ahhh! Dios mio! Watch it, wouldja?"

"Sorry, I didn't mean to hurt you."

"Really? You took my wife, my child, stabbed me, tied me, and now you're sorry?"

"What do mean Autumn and I were born into it?"

"Your father worked with Santa, helped him ship people across."

Quin took a step back. He spat and inhaled a breath of musty air. Jefe, who lived in Mexico, was confirming Nizhoni's theory about his father's business.

"How come Autumn was kidnapped, living with this scum of a profiteer?"

"I dunno," Jefe said. "My phone is vibrating in my pocket. I better answer it."

Quin realized they were only twenty yards from the interior cave where cellphone reception was available. He slid Jefe's phone out of his pocket and held it to Jefe's ear.

"Don't say anything you'll regret," Quin warned him, "or I'll slit your throat."

Jefe mumbled something in Spanish into the phone. There was no way he could know for sure whether Jefe had just tipped off his friends that Autumn and Marta were escaping. Quin had to get moving.

"Thanks for the info about Autumn," he said.

"You owe me, brother," Jefe said. "When I shot at you earlier? I could've killed you. I spared you because you're Autumn's brother."

That could have been bravado, but Quin knew it might also be the truth. The fight in the cave was Jefe's way of coming to terms with his new reality. His wife and daughter were leaving him, crossing under the fence that separates the haves from the have-nots, and there was nothing he could do but rage against it before he let go.

Quin cut the zip-ties and handed Jefe one of the two flashlights, and then they went in separate directions, Jefe down to the stream to retrieve his busted dirt bike, and Quin back into the tunnel leading to the States.

Jefe called back over his shoulder, "Life in the States isn't so great. They'll come back."

Quin walked off, thinking about what Jefe had told him, and the more he thought about it, the faster he walked. Soon he was jogging, the flashlight beam bouncing in front of him on the ground and walls depending on the contours of ground under his boots. In the distance he saw a reflection of light, two small eyes, and then a rat the size of a raccoon turned and scampered ahead along the wall and buried itself under a pile of trash.

He slowed, told himself it wasn't the rat. He just needed to catch his breath, to pace himself. It was more eerie down here alone with a single beam of light than moving thirty miles an hour in a cart. That would be his first goal, to get to the cart that had been left behind and see if any of the batteries were working. Quin wondered if Jefe had tampered with them before the fight broke out. He should have asked him. *Shoulda, woulda, coulda,* he thought. He reached for his phone to call Jefe and ask him, but there was no cell signal. Damn, he was too far underground or in a no-man's-land of no cell phone service. A cobweb blanketed his face and he wiped it off with his sleeve. That gave him the shivers and made him feel like something was behind him, following him, stalking him. He started running again, counting his strides, distracting himself from the patches of graffiti on the walls: names of people who had made it—or died trying.

How could his father risk everything to bring people across? Did his mother know? She must have known. Is that what their late-night fights were about?

He ran faster to burn off his anger and fear, to push through the darkness, to leave the black, murky border behind. He sprinted faster, his boots pounding sand, and as he lengthened his stride, he seemed to float above the ground. If he could maintain this pace, he'd be on the surface in no time at all. He leapt over a crushed water bottle, counted three more strides, and jumped over a large rock. This was it, he had a rhythm, he was in a zone, and then something caught the toe of his boot and he was aloft, the silver handle of the flashlight tumbling ahead of him.

Pitch…black…hard ground.

Lying on his stomach, he rolled over and saw nothing. Blinking, he still saw nothing. He felt his arms and legs. His left kneecap hurt from the landing, but nothing was broken.

Now what? Where's *the flashlight? Think.*

It had to be ahead somewhere. He reached out, sweeping his arms around him. Nothing. He had an idea and pulled his phone out.

A glow!

He could see four or five feet around him with the glow from his phone as he searched for the flashlight. He thought it ironic that the very phone he couldn't use to call for help could show him where to find a brighter light. He stood up to search the ground and spotted a shiny reflection. He ran toward it.

Bingo!

He picked it up and turned it back on, but it still didn't produce any light. He shook it, hearing the batteries inside. He looked at the end and the lens and bulb were shattered.

Damn! Isn't the glass supposed to be shatter-proof? There's a lifetime warranty for this thing! he thought angrily. He turned and threw it into the tunnel, listening to it bounce and skid across the floor. *No wonder there's so much trash. Nothing works down here. The place is cursed.*

All he had left was his phone and its battery was fading, too. It should get him to the other side if he ran without stopping. He started again, holding the phone in his left hand as he trotted, and tried to adjust to the dim light. The trot became a run, a man on the run, underground in the cold depths of the desert. Each stride carried him closer to his single goal, the abandoned golf cart. His feet slipped in his boots, a blister rising on the back of his right heel. What was his heart rate at this moment? Kruse would want to know; he'd record it in his database. He had to capture everything a Remote Viewer did while on assignment. Quin thought about what Jefe had said about his father and he pushed harder, knowing that Autumn, further up the tunnel, had to know the answer.

He was relieved when he saw the abandoned cart in the distance, it was a confirmation that he was making progress in the dark. He lifted the seat and shone the phone's light onto the batteries. The connections looked good; Jefe hadn't tampered with them at all. He lowered the seat, sat in the cart, and turned the key. No sound issued from it. He sat there catching his breath for a moment, then noticed Marta's stuffed teddy bear on the floor of the cart. He scooped it up, stepped out of the cart, and started running again.

That was when he heard voices behind him crying out for help. He knew they weren't real, or he would have run into them already. Some were begging, others were laughing and mocking Quin as he ran.

"You're never gonna make it," a man shouted from behind. "Give up!"

Quin looked back, shining his phone at the empty corridor.

"What are you looking for?" a woman said. "A way out? You lost?"

He tried plugging his ears to block the voices as he ran, but he couldn't see without the glow of his phone. And they only shouted louder anyway.

"Come back, take us with you!" a man begged.

"Shut up! Shut…up!" Quin shouted back as he stumbled forward on the sand. They laughed, enjoying every moment of his fear and confusion. Was Hawk right? Was this a gravesite, an underworld of lost souls? Or was Quin imagining all of this—one big hallucination, dragging him down into the corridors of his own mind?

He got up from his knees and walked, ignoring their shouts, counting his strides: one, two, three...seven... ten. Tired and thirsty, he made steady progress even as the voices followed from behind. And then, as if a breeze had blown out a candle, the dim glow of his phone vanished—another battery gone dead.

"Aaaah! Give me a fucking break!"

They all jeered and laughed at him. He spun around, cupping his ears, and then he realized what a bad move that was. Which direction was he facing now? Mexico or the states?

"You idiot, you're lost!" an old man laughed.

The voice was still from behind, so it was possible that Quin was once again facing in the right direction; but how could he know for sure? He had nothing to guide him, nothing to follow, except maybe...the ravens.

"Caw!" he shouted, and listened as the echo of his voice faded.

In the distance ahead, he heard a faint reply, "Caw! Caw!"

His raven guides were there. He walked toward them.

"Wrong way!" the old man shouted.

Quin ignored the voice. He tucked Marta's teddy bear into his belt and continued walking blindly through the tunnel, calling to the ravens as they called back to him.

"Don't leave us!" a woman cried out in desperation.

These were the voices of chindi, the spirits of those who never made it to the other side. He felt sorry for them.

"Where *you* going?" the woman pleaded.

"Home," Quin said, without breaking stride. "Come with me."

And with that, he felt a wind rush from behind—the spirits were soaring, carrying him forward! He ran with them, his arms outstretched like wings, and he flew through the tunnel without touching the ground or brushing the walls. He was in flight; they were all in flight. The closer he got to the tunnel exit, the more powerful the rushing tailwind became and the louder and more beautiful the ravens' calls. They were climbing higher and higher in an updraft over the other empty golf cart at the bottom of the ramp. It must have died there, unable to make the final climb. He soared above the ramp toward the tunnel entrance, where he saw a mosaic of stars in the night sky.

He collapsed onto the rocks as the chindi swooshed past him toward the stream and a sparkling, silvery moonlight on the waters. The spirits, a dozen or more, followed the ravens across the running stream and vanished into a mist.

A pair of boots stepped closer to his face and the stranger crouched lower, toward him, dangling a cigarette.

"It's all right, you made it," Lopez said. "I heard you screaming down there. Sounded hellish. You had me worried."

He sat up. "What about Hawk?"

"Jimmy carried him up out of the tunnel back to the safe house. Hawk lost a lot of blood but he was conscious. Paramedics are transporting them both to the hospital."

She reached out her hand. He accepted it and rose up, brushing dirt off his jeans. Fresh air never tasted so good, so sweet. He felt the bear stuffed into his belt. He removed it and said, "Where's Autumn and Marta?"

"Back at the safe house," she said, walking the metal door back across the cave entrance.

"What happened in there?" she asked, locking the door.

"Jefe and I walked back to the cave, where I let him go."

"No, I mean on the way out, what happened? I heard you talking to somebody. You came running out of there like a bat out of hell."

He thought for a moment and brushed it off. "Lost my way and panicked."

"I left the door open, thinking you might follow the air draft."

"Thanks, that seemed to do the trick."

"Hey, you got my back, and I got yours," she said.

Agent Kruse was usually a three-cup-in-the-morning coffee drinker. But now, he was already on his fourth and it was only 6:00 a.m. Rachel and Dillan sat across from him at a large conference table, while Dr. Hayden sat next to him. He was both elated and frustrated. Quin had left him a cryptic message four hours ago: *Target Retrieved.*

Kruse had a million questions running through his mind: Did Quin actually have Autumn? Was he in Mexico or had he brought her across the border? Why didn't he wait for Kruse to give the go-ahead? The list went on and on, and with each sip of coffee, he thought of another question.

"Quin called you at what time?" he asked Dillan.

He looked at his phone. "Two in the morning."

"How did he sound?" Dr. Hayden asked.

"Like Quin," Dillan said.

"Frightened or irrational?"

"No, he was totally cool."

"You said earlier that Quin called you just to check in and say hi?" Kruse asked.

"Yeah."

"At two in the morning?" Kruse said. "What are you withholding from me, Dillan?"

He squirmed in his seat. "Nothing."

"Did Quin ask you to view a location for him?" Kruse asked.

Dillan drummed his fingers on the table, averting his eyes. He was going inward, something Kruse had seen before. He could retreat into a shell and not talk for hours.

"Dillan, if it's easier, go ahead and use sign language," Dr. Hayden said. It was a technique she taught hospital patients to get them to express themselves when words failed.

Dillan raised his left hand and gave Kruse the finger.

"Let's give Dillan a break," Dr. Hayden said to Kruse.

He turned his attention to Rachel. "You and Dillan talk…what's he holding back?"

He waited for the girl to gather her thoughts. She was a nervous person, too, but far less stubborn than Dillan. And she was generally compliant and cooperative. If he coaxed her into talking, she'd spill it.

"Tell the truth, Rachel."

"How come this is falling apart?" she asked Kruse.

"Huh?"

"When we started this, we were a team. You taught us RV and showed us how to help our country," she said. "Now you're turning on us, always yelling."

Kruse caught himself before he launched into another condescending lecture. "You're right—"

"We work for hours in rooms that are barely larger than closets, searching for unknown targets. You don't share any information with us, whether we're succeeding of failing."

"I know, it's the protocol."

"This is the only assignment where you shared a few pieces of intel with us, and Quin out there finally confirmed that we're right!"

Dillan cleared his throat. "Quin asked me to view inside the warehouse before he went in."

"You witnessed him saving Autumn?" Kruse asked.

"No, I gave him the intel he requested and went back to bed," Dillan said. "I won't spy on my friends. Not anymore."

"Is there anything else you can share with me about last night?"

"Obviously he found her, we all found her. Why not stop there, end on a high note?" Dillan answered with a smirk.

Good idea. They had succeeded, after all. What more could he expect of them? It was now up to Quin to bring the evidence home.

"Thank you for your candor and your patience with me," Kruse said. "Take the rest of the day off."

Dillan pushed his chair away from the table. "Come on," he said to Rachel.

She rose and followed him to the door. He opened it like a gentleman and she passed through the doorway, giggling. When Dillan closed the door, he acted as if he were locking it from the outside and shouted to Kruse and Dr. Hayden, "Get back to work!"

Their sophomoric rebellion wasn't entirely unexpected. His colleague had predicted it would happen. "Satisfied, Dr. Hayden?"

"You know the phrase, 'The mind, once stretched by a new idea, never goes back to its original dimensions,' " she said, crossing her arms.

"Who said that? Jung? Freud?"

"Neither, Ralph Waldo Emerson. Once your recruits learn an important skill like RV, they'll naturally develop new confidence. NIH will applaud this positive change in their behavior."

"We're not here to build their self-esteem, we're training psychic warriors. To accomplish that, we must deliver proof that what we do actually works."

"You've done at least twenty assignments for the NSA and CIA over the past year," she pointed out. "They wouldn't come to you if it wasn't working."

"Locating a Russian submarine is one thing, but any satellite can do that. Finding evil-doers, tracking and stopping them moments before they strike, that's an entirely different kind of weapon. This assignment, finding Autumn, is critical, because we have the evidence in hand. Instead of forwarding it to somebody up the chain of command, we hold onto it, we present it to the bureau and Homeland Security."

"Then what?"

"We get better funding, and RV finally gets the credit it deserves."

CHAPTER 8

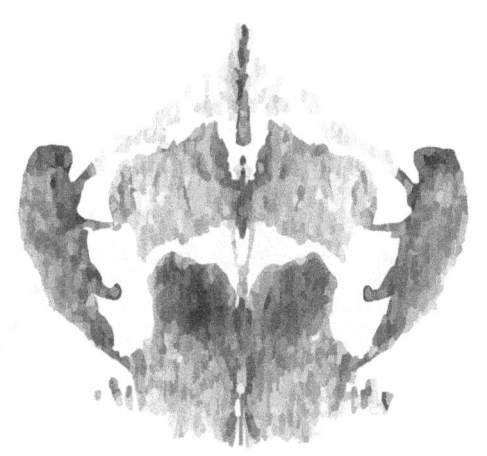

Locating Dillan wasn't as difficult as Candace had expected. He wasn't in a locked ward that would have made it nearly impossible to reach him. He was living at home with his parents in a quiet, upscale neighborhood, with a backyard swimming pool surrounded by a garden wall of brick and ivy.

Candace was seated with him at the pool's edge, both of them dangling their bare feet in the cool water. She wondered what he was thinking, but she offered him an easier question.

"How did you meet Quin?"

"At the hospital," Dillan said. "He'd check in for a week, then he'd check out."

"When was this?"

"Three years ago they brought him in in restraints. I feared him back then. Not anymore. We took art classes together. He draws wildlife art; I like landscapes," he said with a smile that reflected off the water's surface.

"Do you draw from pictures or out in nature?"

"From my imagination."

"Quin says you both draw objects you see in faraway places."

"CRV."

"What's that?"

"Coordinate Remote Viewing. Agent Kruse gives us a target and we see it, draw it. Rachel is better at that kind of art," he said, splashing the water with his toes.

"What kind of objects did you draw?"

"Can't talk about it. Not allowed to."

"Why not?"

"We're not supposed to talk about what we see."

"You have a government security clearance? You can't share what you know?"

He nodded, raising his toes out of the water. Candace felt as if she were talking to a socially awkward teenager.

"You enjoy RV?"

"At first, but then it made me sick. You thirsty? Want something to drink?"

"No thanks," Candace said. "RV made you sick?"

"Migraines, insomnia, panic attacks."

"Sorry to hear that. It's why Quin asked me to check on you," Candace said. "He wants to know how you're doing."

Dillan smiled again. "Why isn't Quin here?"

"He's busy on an assignment with Agent Kruse."

"That's why he's not supposed to talk to me directly, AOL."

"What's that?"

"Analytical Overlay. If two viewers are tasked with the same target, they might influence each other if they share information. Tell him I'm better this week. No panic attacks. The medication they give me helps me unplug."

"Unplug from what?"

"The more time you spend there, the harder it is to come back here, home," he said.

"The more time you spend where? At the hospital?"

"In here," he said, tapping a finger on this temple. "In your mind." He stood and walked back to the sliding-glass door, leaving a trail of wet footprints on the slate pool deck. "Thirsty?"

Candace stayed with him for another thirty minutes, their conversation bouncing from music to Dillan's favorite topics, skateboarding and gaming. He talked, rarely making eye contact with Candace, which wasn't as noticeable at poolside as it was sitting across from him at the kitchen table.

"How did you find this paranormal group?" she asked, redirecting him.

"Agent Kruse invited me into the program."

"How did he know that you'd be a good candidate for this work?"

"Oh, Dr. Hayden, my therapist, thought I could start working again. She gave me some tests and I showed potential, so I gave her permission to contact Agent Kruse."

"You enjoy RV?"

"It was fun for a while," he said with a look of longing. "If you show signs of stress, they give you time off and they screen you when you return."

"Screen you for what?"

"Stress. If you're not well, they put you in the locked ward. Susan's there now, on suicide watch."

"She's a Remote Viewer?"

"Quin knows her."

"What happens if you're in the locked ward?"

"They wait until you're better, but you can't come back," he said. "They dismiss you from the program."

"Do you know of others who've left the program?"

"A few, but we don't keep in touch."

"How many others would you guess have been dismissed?"

He shrugged as if he had no idea.

"Could you introduce me to Agent Kruse?"

"Seriously? No."

"Why not?"

"I've already told you, we can't talk about it."

"Then why are you talking to me now?"

"Because Quin sent you here." He looked up at the ceiling and then down at the wood floor as if searching for more reasons. "And I trust *him.*"

"Why do you trust Quin so much?"

"He's not afraid of Kruse."

Jimmy was still at the hospital with Hawk, who was in stable condition. Agent Lopez was in town as well, talking to Nogales police and the DEA about what had happened the night before while she waited for detectives from the Phoenix Office to arrive.

Quin poured a cup of coffee and set it on the table next to the couch, where Autumn slept with Marta in her arms. Quin noticed Marta was holding the stuffed bear. He sipped his own coffee, watching the steam rising from Autumn's. He didn't even know if she liked coffee or tea or an ice-cold Coke in the morning. All those idiosyncratic rituals that siblings share or even fight about didn't exist between them. They had lived apart for so long that whatever similarities they shared had to be innate, genetic traits.

Her nose twitched, her eyelids opened and she smiled at him as she stretched her arms overhead. He hadn't seen her do that morning move in twelve years, not since they shared a bedroom in this old house.

"You like coffee?" he asked, pointing at it.

"Thanks." She sat up, wrapped Marta in the blanket, and reached for the cup. "What time is it?"

He sat in the leather chair next to the couch. "Almost ten."

"Where is everyone?"

"In town."

"How's Hawk?"

"He's okay, everyone's okay. Jefe texted you a couple of hours ago. I saw it on your phone. He misses you."

"Now he misses me?" she said, holding the cup with both hands as she sipped. "He always wants what he can't have."

"He had a hard time letting you go."

"He said that? What else did he say?"

"That Dad had been moving people across the border."

She sighed without confirming or denying what Jefe had said.

"You want to tell me anything?" he asked.

She looked at Marta, still in her deep sleep. "Maybe you and I should talk outside."

He got up first, and Autumn tucked Marta in tighter and followed Quin out the front door. They walked across the front yard to the old swing set they'd once played on together. She sat in one swing, balancing with her free hand while the other held the coffee mug. Quin sat in the swing next to her and they stared out at the horizon of red rock and clay, and the wavy pattern of heat rising on the horizon.

"What exactly did Jefe tell you?" she asked.

"That Dad teamed up with somebody in Mexico to bring people across."

She lifted her feet and swung forward and then back again. "Is that so hard to believe?"

"No, he was a trucker."

"Remember how he'd sometimes park the trailer to shade the house from the afternoon sun?"

"Yeah," he said, smiling at the memory.

"Most truck drivers live in town," she said. "Not out here where it's hotter than hell."

"But why would he do it?"

"Because he could. He had the means to do so," she said.

"He was heading north anyway," he suggested. "Why not bring some illegals along?"

"Don't say it like that."

"That's what you're telling me, that Dad had a truck and an isolated house in the desert. He could make tax-free money on the side hauling human beings."

"I never said he did it for money."

"Then why the hell would he do it?"

"Families were dying out there," she said, sweeping her hand across the horizon in front of them. "You remember? The clothing we'd find on our walks, dolls that I'd bring home to show Mom?"

He did remember: the junk treasures they'd collected—empty beer cans, hooded sweatshirts, piles of socks.

"Why do you think Mom didn't want us wandering far from the house? How she'd tell us stories of beasts out there?"

"Chupacabra."

"Yes! Oh my God, chupacabra will bite you, suck your blood," Autumn said, imitating their mother's stern voice.

"Mom was aware of what Dad was doing?"

"She's the one who begged him to do it. Anybody who was desperate enough to stop here, she gave them food and water. Then, instead of sending them back into the desert, she asked Dad to drive them north. You do that a couple of times and word gets out that this is a safe place. They only have to make it this far, to the other side of Nogales."

"He'd drive them north to work in the fields?"

"Up through California and even into Canada, depending on the season. And he'd bring them home, too."

"Mom and Dad didn't do it for the money?"

"They wouldn't take it. People offered gifts, wine, handmade blankets, jewelry, whatever they could easily carry. Mom donated all of it. She couldn't sit by and watch as families carried their children into the desert."

"How do you know all this?"

"When I was taken to Mexico, I learned of Mom and Dad's reputation, how the people respected them for protecting poor, struggling families."

"If they had such a good reputation, who attacked us?"

"Coyotes. When you offer a service for free, you make life difficult for people who could easily profit from it."

Coyote was a term for those who smuggle people into the States for hefty fees, with no guarantees that their clients will actually make it to their final destination. Smuggling isn't the same as human trafficking, but it's close. Coyotes sometimes diverted their clients into the hands of *wolves*, men who run human trafficking rings. Quin realized his parents weren't only saving families from the desert heat, but from a life of misery and slavery.

"Do you know the men who did this to us?"

"No," she said. "They were hired hands. Gangbangers."

"Why did they take you and leave me for dead?"

She leaned back in her swing, looking up at the sky. "Girls are worth more than boys."

He felt sickened at the thought of it. "I'm so sorry, Autumn."

"It's ironic, how Mom and Dad saved so many other families at the price of their own. I've thought about that so many times."

"Jefe mentioned the name Santana, that you lived with him. What does he know about this?"

"He's an ex-pat, a coyote who protected me from the traffickers. I wouldn't be alive if it weren't for him."

"Would he know who's ultimately responsible for our parents' deaths?"

"Gangs come and go like tumbleweed around here," she said. "It's too late. Nobody in the States cared enough to search when they had the chance."

That was true. Quin had often felt that nobody really cared about the case. The DA and police assumed the family had been smuggling drugs and got attacked by a rival gang entering the territory. Of course, others thought Quin had killed his own family, but no charges were ever brought against him, only vicious rumors that left him alone, drifting through the foster care system like a tumbleweed himself.

"Admit it, Quin. The police, DEA, and FBI turned their backs on us."

"Not anymore," he said. "A team within the bureau sent me here."

"You're one of *them*."

"No, it's not like that."

"In the tunnel Hawk told me you're an informant for the FBI."

"I'm a bounty hunter, a *contractor* hired by the bureau."

"Is this a rescue mission, Quin, or am I under arrest?"

"Rescue. I'm not here to drag you in."

"This house that was once our home now belongs to the bureau," she said. "And they hired you to find me after I was missing for twelve years. It all seems so... orchestrated."

Her mood had shifted from proud memories of their family to suspicion of Quin's motives. He couldn't blame her; she'd felt abandoned and forgotten all these years and the circumstances surrounding her rescue, if he could even call it that, were shady indeed.

"How did they track me down after all this time? They use a satellite or one of those drones?"

Skips often asked this question: "How did you find me?" as if the bounty hunter had an obligation to share what the skip did wrong before dragging his or her ass back to jail. Quin never talked about how he did it because he knew it would never make sense to a skip—that he'd see them, feel them out there hiding, and anticipate their next move.

"Remember how we'd play hide and seek out there beyond the rocks?" he asked. "It's something like that."

"You close your eyes, count to twenty, and then come find me?" she joked.

"Correct."

"I knew you were searching for me, Quin. Lately I had this feeling."

"Describe the feeling."

"That your presence was nearby. I hadn't felt that until recently."

"When I came to your back door, did you recognize me?" he asked.

"No, but I knew it was you."

"If you sensed my return and were afraid that I might arrest you instead of rescue you, why not run?"

"I knew I couldn't, it was over. The whole nightmare would end if I'd surrender. And I trusted you because you're my brother."

It was possible, he thought, that she, too, had the gift, but she hadn't used it or learned how to control her instincts. His time in the field bounty hunting had helped him hone his skills, and with Kruse's help, he took it to another level.

Quin's phone vibrated in his pocket. It was Kruse calling again. "I'd better take this call."

Autumn stepped off the swing. "I'll check on Marta."

He watched her walk back to the house, her light frame reminding him of their mother. Kruse answered on the first ring.

"What happened?"

"We got her."

"You're sure this time? Because the other day you acted as if it might not be her."

"I spoke with her this morning."

"Who are you with? Agent Lopez said a man was shot," Kruse said.

"Hawk and Jimmy are friends of mine."

"You're on official business, Quin."

"Working vacation, remember? I couldn't have done it without them."

"You have no idea how everyone in the Phoenix office is buzzing about this."

"Dillan and Rachel were amazing."

"Of course, it was a team effort," Kruse said. "How's Autumn?"

"Better than I expected," Quin said. "Marta is in good shape, too."

"How did you cross the border?"

"I'll explain later. We're all here catching our breath from a long night of traveling."

"Bring her home," Kruse said.

"This *is* home...or it was."

"Get Autumn up here as soon as possible. I need to interview her."

"How about I bring her to the Phoenix office where they can take her statement?"

"No, bring Autumn here, where I can speak with her, get her statement on video. We don't want the Phoenix office taking credit for this."

"They can't fly commercial air, they don't have passports or ID."

"I'll arrange a private jet. You can fly out of Tucson in a few hours."

Kruse sounded anxious, a little too eager to lay claim to Autumn's rescue. Quin had questions of his own before he'd hand his sister over; besides, he couldn't fly out. "Even if they discharge my friend Hawk from the hospital, he won't fly. I'll drive him home. We'll be there in a few days."

Kruse exhaled into the phone. "Get on the road as soon as possible."

Quin hung up and realized that as he'd been standing outside on the phone, Autumn had been watching him from the house, the blinds pulled back a couple of inches. She had to be nervous. She'd already expressed her distrust of the bureau, and now she'd have to explain to them how they screwed up, left her for dead, only to have her resurrected by her own brother? He walked back to the house and opened the door, where he found Autumn sitting on the couch with Marta.

"We're leaving."

"Where to?"

"Home. Minnesota."

"That's not *my* home," she said defiantly.

"I've seen where you lived, now you can see where I've been living," he said, trying to calm her down.

"Are they going to ask me more questions? I've already told you what little I know."

He reached out and held her trembling hands. "They'll record your statement, and then you're free."

How much longer could Agent Kruse mask his irritation toward Agents Backstrom and Clark, seated across from his desk, their suit coats unbuttoned, playing good cop, bad cop? He knew what this visit was about; his remote viewing demonstration had been a success, but somebody in DC didn't appreciate his most recent results. Agents from the J. Edgar Hoover building on Pennsylvania Avenue don't show up unannounced unless there's a problem.

"Where are they?" Backstrom said, bad-copping him.

"Quin's driving Autumn back as we speak," Kruse said.

"Why not stop in Phoenix so we can verify that she *is* Autumn?" Clark suggested.

"Phoenix isn't hijacking *this* case."

"Let's not get territorial here," Clark said.

"You knew I was searching for Quin's sister. Why didn't you stop me weeks ago? Because you thought I'd fail, that I'd hit a dead-end. Well, surprise, gentlemen, there really is a pot of gold at the end of this rainbow."

"Your job is to accept assignments handed to you, uncover intel, and forward it back to the appropriate agency," Backstrom said.

"You know how few assignments I've received over the past year? Five from the NSA, a dozen from the CIA, and only three from Homeland Security. That leaves me with a lot of free time to recruit and train, but eventually I have to give the remote viewers something real to hunt, to chase."

"You can't go rogue, creating your own assignments," Clark said.

"Why, because I might uncover something that should be reported to Internal Affairs?" Kruse threatened.

"I don't know what you're implying, but at this point we have no evidence that you've found anyone. Where is she?" Backstrom said.

"I don't know," he said, which was technically true. He knew Autumn was with Quin but where at this moment, he wasn't sure.

"Is she hiding on one of the reservations?" Backstrom asked. "The bureau has jurisdiction over all Indian reservations."

Kruse couldn't take the posturing from these testosterone-fueled agents. They had no idea of Kruse's longevity with the bureau. They hadn't done their homework and were about to get schooled.

"Don't lecture me about our relationship with indigenous cultures, Mr. Backstrom. For twenty years I worked in the Indian Country Crimes Unit (ICCU), assisting tribal police, but more often than not apologizing to tribal members for our ignorance and arrogance when working with tribes. We only have jurisdiction over 200 of the 565 recognized tribes in the United States. If we want to win the war on terror, I suggest we become better neighbors, especially with those within our borders."

Agent Clark leaned forward. "Cool it, we're here to assist you."

"The Phoenix office knew of Autumn's disappearance. Why didn't they solve the case years ago?"

The question hung in the air like a feather floating between them, both men pondering it, but neither of them reaching for it until Backstrom gave a stock answer: "Limited resources," he said, shaking his balding head, "and Quin's family *chose* to live in the borderlands."

Kruse was well aware that all branches of law enforcement had their backlogs. Some criminals were caught, others got away, some were prosecuted, others plea-bargained, with little to no time served. But cold cases like this one were cold for a reason—poor families living along the border are a low priority, presumed guilty of something, or why else would they live there? The poor didn't matter, which to Kruse was the biggest crime of all.

In a way, Autumn was more valuable to Kruse and his team than to the FBI. She was living proof that what they did worked, that they were contributing to the greater good. He decided to run a new idea past them, an idea he knew they'd like. "What if it's not her after all? What if Quin is wrong?"

"No harm. Mistakes happen in the field all the time," Clark said.

"She might've lied to get a free ticket across the border," Backstrom suggested. "Some people will tell you whatever you want to hear."

"And if this woman wants to stay and live a quiet private life, that's fine," Clark said.

Kruse riffed on their bullshit narrative. "It's possible that I front-loaded the task, planting the idea in Quin's mind that this woman is his sister."

"Quin's a psych patient, sees what he wants to see," Backstrom said.

"Remote Viewing can't be 100 percent accurate," Clark said. "You'd document in your report that the target you found is not the target you were searching for."

"Of course."

"And upon receiving your report, we'll see to it that your department gets other assignments," Backstrom said, "more pressing cases for Homeland Security. Until then, funding for your department is frozen."

"You can't do that!" Kruse said.

"Can't cut off funding to a department that doesn't officially exist? Of course we can," Clark said with practiced empathy.

Backstrom leaned forward and lowered his voice. "This nation faces a rising tide of threats, from hostile foreign intelligence looking over our shoulders to homegrown extremists. Not to mention the violent gangs running the streets and corporate fraud built on pyramid schemes that leave our government footing the bill. Despite that, the $120 million Criminal Justice Information Services (CJIS) is about to get cut in order to fund the Intelligence Community Information Technology Enterprise (ICITE) for the FBI. So if you see yourself working with us in the future, helping us track threats or the next lone wolf attack, then you'd best get your house in order."

Nogales is a rugged border town where the Emergency Department of Holy Cross Hospital was conveniently located on Target Range Road. Quin parked and walked with Autumn and Marta across the hot blacktop parking lot to the main entrance. The doors opened automatically and a blast of cold air enveloped them. Marta smiled and looked up at her mother, as if she'd never felt air-conditioning before. Quin approached the front desk and an elderly woman with sun-dried, leathery skin pointed down the hall to Hawk's room.

Quin led the way and rounded a corner, finding Agent Lopez seated outside Hawk's room, checking messages on her phone. When Quin, Autumn, and Marta approached, Lopez stood to attention.

"How is he?" Quin asked.

"Good, the bullet grazed him. He's got a couple broken ribs and a dozen stitches," she said. "He's tough for a guy his age."

"If I can get him discharged, you okay with me taking him out of here?" he asked.

"Detectives want to talk to him—and you as well, Autumn," she said.

Autumn pulled Marta in tightly to her side. "I'll give my statement in Minnesota."

She had no interest in talking with the FBI, especially the Phoenix office, she'd told Quin. She didn't trust them. Quin would have a hard enough time getting her to Minnesota, but he knew he couldn't leave her here.

"Agent Kruse wants to do all this in Minneapolis," Quin said. "We reopened the case up there, we might as well close it. Sorry to play inter-office politics."

Lopez shook her head. "I can't let you do that, Quin."

"C'mon, Lopez, look the other way."

"And play the fool by letting you waltz off with them?"

"You said you had my back."

She folded her arms, whispering, "You're an ass, you know that?"

"Tell them there was a miscommunication between the two departments. Blame it on Agent Kruse," he said.

"I could lose my job over this."

"They won't fire you, Kruse will see to that. Maybe they'll suspend you with pay. You wanted a break anyway, right? More time with your kids?"

She looked at Autumn and Marta, mother and daughter standing together. It must have tugged at her heartstrings. "I'll tell the nurses I'm transferring you. Meet me outside once Hawk has checked out."

Hawk signed his release forms and an orderly wheeled him to the front door, where Quin and Jimmy walked him to the truck. Carefully, they helped him into the passenger seat, riding shotgun as Hawk reminded them. Jimmy, Autumn, Marta, and the teddy bear squeezed into the bench seat in back. Quin put the truck in gear and drove off slowly over a speed bump.

"It's a good twenty-four-hour drive from here," Quin said. "Jimmy, Autumn, and I will do all the driving. You rest, Hawk."

"We gotta make a stop on the way, though," he said.

"Where?" Quin asked.

"Window Rock, to reunite you and Autumn with your family, to see Nizhoni."

"That will add another four hours."

"It's worth it," Hawk said.

Quin looked in the rearview mirror at Autumn. "You okay with seeing her?"

"I would love to see Nizhoni again."

Quin continued through the hospital parking lot. Hawk lowered his window as they approached Agent Lopez on the edge of the hospital grounds, smoking. Quin slowed.

"Thanks, Lopez," Hawk said, "for saving this old life."

She smiled and turned her back on them, letting them go. After puffing beautiful silky smoke rings upward into a deep blue sky, she said, "This is my last cigarette, I swear."

CHAPTER 9

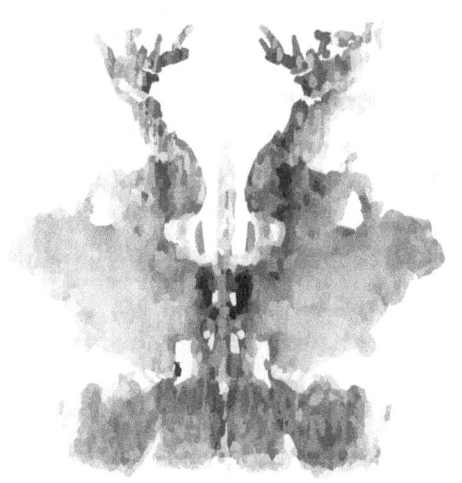

The desert landscape near Nizhoni's home hadn't changed much over the years. Quin and Autumn must have been eight or nine years old when they had last sat on Nizhoni's deck overlooking a hoodoo, a tall spire of red rock. She told Marta it was a fairy chimney before she carried her on her hip inside and laid her on the couch for a nap. She returned with a pitcher of ice water and poured them each a glass and as they sat down.

"Drink more, Hawk," she said.

He guzzled the water, then wiped his mouth with the back of his hand. "You're gonna drown me."

"It's a miracle that you're both here," Nizhoni said, wiping a tear, smiling at Quin and Autumn. "When Hawk told me what you were up to, Quin, I never imagined you'd find each other so quickly."

"He was very brave," Autumn said, patting him on the knee.

"I couldn't have done it without Hawk and Jimmy's help. And the bureau's."

"Nizhoni, tell them what you told us," Hawk said.

Quin listened to her describe the struggles their parents had endured in their marriage, and how Quin and Autumn's grandparents had never accepted their father as a member of the clan. It hurt listening to her relive the day their mother left the reservation for good. Autumn crossed one leg over the other, her knee bouncing nervously.

"I'm so sorry," Nizhoni said to her. "I should've done more to look for you."

Autumn shook her head. "It's not your fault."

"The bureau dropped it," Hawk said, "or covered it up."

"Why?" Quin asked.

Nizhoni sighed. "Remember the DEA's War on Drugs? Then suddenly immigration became the new war. They built walls on the border, splitting towns, separating families. People were desperate."

"That's when our parents began bringing people across?" Autumn asked.

"Yes, a dangerous thing to do," Nizhoni said. "But that's how your mother was, always caring. Never turned her back on anyone in need."

"And the coyotes killed them to take over the territory," Autumn said.

"But why would the bureau not pursue the case?" Quin asked.

"It's corrupt down there," Nizhoni said. "Lot of people looking the other way when it benefits them."

"See?" Hawk said to Quin. "You can't trust the government."

Jimmy spoke up. "But the bureau helped him find Autumn."

To Quin's surprise, Jimmy was actually defending Quin's decision to work for the bureau. After all the bickering and arguing, they actually agreed on something; the bureau found Autumn. But he had a sinking feeling.

What if it wasn't true?

All this time Quin had his doubts about RV but he hadn't considered the possibility that Autumn's rescue could be a hoax. What if Agent Kruse coordinated everything to make it look as if the paranormal team had found Autumn? He had access to FBI and DEA files. He could've known exactly where Autumn was living all these years.

Kruse certainly had a motive. He was desperate to prove to Quin and others in the bureau that RV was an effective crime and terror-fighting tool. What if the cameras and the audio equipment weren't for the paranormal team's benefit, but so Kruse could edit the footage later? He could recreate the event with his own Hollywood ending. And Agent Lopez let him pull Hawk out of the hospital without any resistance. Was she part of an elaborately orchestrated plan? Was Autumn part of it, too?

He decided to test her. "Ready to head back to Minnesota?"

She looked past him to her daughter on the couch and then to Nizhoni. "I'm not ready to talk to anybody."

"You should meet with Agent Kruse," he said. "He'll need proof."

"Say I escaped, ran away."

"He wouldn't believe it, Autumn. I'm a bounty hunter. Never had a skip escape after I caught him."

"Tell Kruse you underestimated your sister and that I got away."

Her responses seemed genuine. She seemed more comfortable here with Nizhoni than traveling back to meet the Agent Kruse. That was good enough for Quin, at least for now.

"Hawk, Jimmy, and I will go back to Minnesota without you," he said, "as long as you promise me you won't leave Window Rock."

The word *stress* is what Candace gleaned from her conversation with Dillan. And the more she researched it, the more Post-Traumatic Stress Disorder (PTSD) seemed to fit the description. She'd spent quiet hours in her apartment on the couch researching PTSD, and learned that the condition manifests itself within four major groupings:

Intrusive Memories: reliving traumatic events as if they are happening again, having flashbacks, or reacting to events that trigger memories.

Avoidance: Obsessively blocking memories or avoiding people or places connected to the events.

Negative Moods: Low self-esteem, feeling emotionally numb.

Shifts in Emotional Responses: Outbursts, aggressive behavior, shame, insomnia, self-destructive behavior, and drug abuse.

Dillan had displayed several of these symptoms during their conversation. Quin, too, had symptoms. He'd avoided Candace for months, seemed emotionally detached, and sipped ayahuasca as if it were nothing more than an herbal tea.

She followed the trail of health articles, links, and videos, all leading her down a strange dark path of psychiatric disorders. It was there that she found references to the Minnesota Security Hospital, a facility an hour south of Minneapolis, nestled in the Minnesota River Valley. It was home to more than 400 adults, some of them psychiatric patients with histories of murder, arson, and other violent crimes. The violence didn't always end when a patient was admitted to the facility. Patient assaults on hospital employees and other patients were a fact of life in such a facility.

That was where Dillan said he'd lived and worked for the last five years before returning home. It was also where Quin had spent time, according to online news reports of his "aggressive use of force" while bounty hunting. He'd never served time behind bars other than the fence crowned with razor wire surrounding the hospital grounds.

Why would Agent Kruse run his remote viewing team from such a facility? Were psychiatric patients the best talent pool or were they the best lab rats?

A text message came from Jimmy's phone: *Quin wants to talk.*

Candace replied: *Call me now.*

Her phone rang and she answered to hear Quin, Jimmy, and Hawk bantering among themselves. "What's going on?" she asked.

"We found Autumn," Quin said.

"Congratulations!"

"What have you found out about RV?" he asked.

"I met with Dillan," she said, pacing her apartment, looking out the sliding-glass door beyond the balcony at the traffic three floors below.

"And?"

"He seems messed up."

"Everyone from that facility is."

"Of course, but Dillan mentioned a side effect of Remote Viewing. He has trouble unplugging. Does that mean anything to you?"

Candace heard silence except for the hum of the road and Hawk's tribal music on the stereo.

"Quin?"

"Yeah, I understand."

"And he mentioned stress that comes from RV, that there are harmful side effects. Dillan's symptoms seem to fit PTSD." Again, she waited. "Quin, is it hard to unhook from it?"

"For some remote viewers it is."

"And what happens?"

"They get sent back to the psych ward, or released from the program," he said, with frustration in his voice.

"Dillan said somebody named Susan is now in the locked ward."

"They put Susan away?" Quin said.

"You're right, there's something about Remote Viewing that's having a negative side effect on the viewers," she said.

"Thanks for confirming it. Send me what you have," he said. "I thought about what you said the last time we talked, about being cautious with the FBI. Jimmy, Hawk, and I have been talking and using our phones to search the Internet while we drive. Look up these search terms: *FBI, war on terror, psych patients.*"

She sat back down on the couch with her laptop and found several news articles about the FBI's counter-terrorism efforts.

"Look for the name Sami Osmakac," Quin said, spelling it for her.

She found an article about the man. "Who is he?"

Quin gave her the highlights of the article. "Sami Osmakac was recruited by FBI informants in a sting operation that made him look like a terrorist who was about to shoot up a Tampa bar and casino before blowing himself up. Yet he had no connections to international terrorists and no money to purchase weapons. The money and guns were funneled to him by the FBI, who filmed the weapons exchange in a hotel room. Before the bust, they helped the nervous and confused Osmakac record his martyrdom video."

"Okay, now we've got something here," she said, scrolling the page, reading along.

"Apparently informant-led sting operations are a main staple of the FBI's counter-terrorism program," Quin said. "Since 9/11 more than 500 defendants have been prosecuted in federal terrorism cases, and 243 involved FBI informants. The FBI claims these cases stopped attacks, but Human Rights Watch reported that the FBI often sets up economically disadvantaged citizens, or worse, the mentally ill. Sami Osmakac was one example; a court-appointed psychologist diagnosed him with schizoaffective disorder. Despite his mental illness and the FBI's use of entrapment tactics, Osmakac was sentenced to 40 years in prison."

"You've hit the mother vein," she said.

"Autumn's rescue..." Quin said. "It all happened so easily."

"You're suggesting that Kruse staged the event like this Osmakac case?" she asked.

"It's possible. He had me wearing a camera to record it, right?"

"But you and Agent Lopez removed the cameras."

"And Kruse was angry about it. Kruse wanted to edit a story showing the FBI waltzing past the Sinaloa drug cartel to rescue an American."

She thought about it for a moment. "You might be right."

"Kruse said Sinaloa allowed us on their land, that he'd made a deal with them."

"What kind of deal?" she asked, waiting for his response, but all she could hear were the muffled voices of Quin, Hawk, and Jimmy.

"What kind of deal?" she asked again.

"I don't know. We've been to hell and back, Candace. It's time for Agent Kruse to provide some real answers. I need answers or I'll…"

"You'll what?" she dared ask. "Quin!"

CHAPTER 10

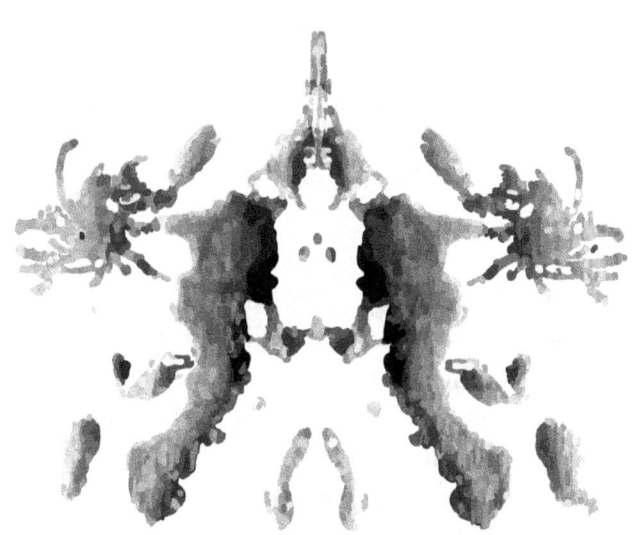

Dr. Hayden checked her phone again, hoping Quin would call back and explain his threatening voice mails. He "needed answers" from her and Kruse.

She set stacks of reports on the conference room table. It was almost midnight and Agent Kruse had just arrived without his suit jacket, his white shirt unbuttoned at the collar, wet with drops of rain.

"You obviously didn't call security."

"No," she said. "It would only set him off."

"He could be in a negative spiral," Kruse said. "He could lose his cool and God knows what he'd do."

"If he wants to harm us, there's no stopping him," she said, "unless we give him answers."

"What's all this?" he said, picking up a document off the table.

"Before he gets here, I need to bring you up to speed on his condition."

She sat, and he joined her at the table.

"When Quin was first admitted to this facility, he had a complete physical. Because of his violent past and his hallucinations, he was tested for temporal lobe epilepsy. The seizures cause sensory changes, such as olfactory or visual hallucinations. People with this condition sometimes display unusual behaviors, such as hyper-religiosity. Quin's intense focus on indigenous traditions and beliefs, his use of ayahuasca to go deeper into a hallucinogenic state, are examples. And his blackouts are a form of collapse. But after running the tests, the neurologist ruled out epilepsy and suggested we test for Bonnet Syndrome."

"Never heard of it," Kruse said.

Dr. Hayden handed him a report from the *Journal of Neuro-Ophthalmology*. "People with cataracts or macular degeneration can develop a syndrome where they see images that aren't there. Birds are a common hallucination for this condition and I figured that must be it, but again the medical team was incorrect. Quin has healthy vision; his optic pathways are normal."

"What's your point, Dr. Hayden?"

"Before Quin became a patient of mine, his previous doctor documented in his medical chart that he had a mild form of schizophrenia, a complicated condition. There's no single cause for schizophrenia, but research has shown that the disorder is more common among socially disadvantaged groups, those who live in poverty, over-crowding, or even isolation. And a person is vulnerable to the disorder in the earlier stages of life."

"You've just described Quin," he said.

"Right! Quin was orphaned after his parents' deaths and moved into the foster care system at a vulnerable point in his life, which can be isolating and lonely. But there's no test for schizophrenia. It's up to a doctor to evaluate a patient to make a diagnosis. And based on my re-evaluation, I don't think he has it."

"But the medication stopped the hallucinations. He said he felt numb."

"It's possible Quin lied, told us what we wanted to hear," she said.

"And that he never stopped seeing the unseen?" Kruse added.

"It gets even more interesting. The brief period when Quin wore the glasses in Mexico, we watched and recorded him approaching Autumn's location. We also recorded his vitals, including heart rate and sweat rate, measuring his autonomic fight or flight nervous system.

If you go back and watch what happens on the video, what he sees, and compare it to what happens, it seems as if his brain anticipates what will happen next."

"I've been saying that all along," Kruse said.

"It's as if his subconscious mind feeds him information," she said. "In those moments, he has no eye movements. He's in delta sleep, the deepest sleep phase, while walking around, and then he's suddenly awakened for his conscious mind to take action. This happens in short bursts, but we've recorded it. We only use 12 percent of our conscious mind; the subconscious mind represents the other 88 percent of our mind space. And if Quin slips into his subconscious mind more often and has the ability to stay there longer, then that might explain why he's more mobile than other viewers."

"He's sleepwalking," Kruse suggested.

"Or is he really *more awake*? What's more real—the 12 percent of the time we live in our conscious mind, or the 88 percent we live in our subconscious mind? Dr. Carl Jung called the subconscious the super-conscious."

Kruse seemed confused as he looked at all the research on the table. "He either has a neurological condition or a psychiatric condition. Which is it?"

"It's very possible he has neither," she said. "He might've developed a skill, or what you've already called a sixth sense."

"He's an enigma," Kruse said.

"Yes, but he has a technique that might benefit the other viewers. There's something about that tea."

"Really?"

"I've learned of patients, even US veterans, who've flown to Peru for it, to ease or even cure symptoms of PTSD. It occurred to me that maybe the tea helps Quin unplug, or transition out of the subconscious state without the side effects that the other remote viewers experience. When you suggested we give the others the tea, you were probably onto something."

"We should certainly test that," Kruse said.

"Even if the patients agreed to it, you'd never get approval or funding to use a Schedule 1 drug in this way."

"Never say never, Dr. Hayden," Kruse said, leaning back in his chair.

She had to somehow wipe the arrogant smile off his face before Quin showed up, so she said, "Now that you know what I plan to share with Quin, what will you say to defend the bureau?"

He took a deep breath and said, "The truth."

Quin sensed that Hawk had a bad feeling about this place. The final stop on their journey, the state security hospital, wasn't exactly on Hawk's bucket list. The rain pounded hard on the truck roof, the windshield wipers mopping sheets of it as they drove through the security gate. Hawk hated fences; Jimmy did, too, and Quin knew the razor wire only made the place *look* like a prison or internment camp.

"This is home away from home?" Jimmy asked from the back seat.

"Sometimes," Quin admitted.

"Turn around, let's get out of here," Hawk said.

"We need answers," he told them.

He checked his phone for the string of text messages he'd exchanged with Agent Kruse over the past thirty minutes. He and Dr. Hayden would be waiting for him in the first-floor conference room.

"Don't surrender to them, Quin," Hawk said. "When has it ever been good to hand over your freedom?"

That was a fair question, and one that Quin had pondered on their drive back from the Dakotas. The hours of thinking had created in him a rolling boil of anger toward the bureau. And they could easily lock him up here again.

"They owe me the truth," he said, parking the truck near the entrance that glowed with a hazy light in the rain. "Wait here."

Hawk grabbed his arm. "Listen to me."

Quin looked into his tired eyes and said. "Say it, Hawk."

"Have I told you the parable of the wolf?" Hawk asked.

"You've told me," Jimmy piped up.

Now wasn't the time for a lesson, but Quin didn't have the heart to cut him off. "I don't know, Hawk. Have you?"

"An elder was teaching his grandson about the ways of life," Hawk said. "He told his grandson that a fight was going on inside him, a terrible fight between two wolves. One wolf was evil, full of anger, revenge, pride, resentment, and superiority. The other wolf was good, full of kindness, joy, forgiveness, and compassion. 'The same fight is going on inside of you,' the chief said to his grandson, 'and everyone else, too.' The grandson asked, 'Which wolf will win?'"

Jimmy had obviously heard this story many times. "The one you feed," he said, patting Quin on the shoulder. "The one you feed."

"What happens in there is up to you; how you choose to react," Hawk said.

"I get it," he said to them. "I won't lose my temper."

"I'm coming," Hawk said, opening the truck door into the rain.

"Me, too," Jimmy said.

"Hurry up then," Quin said, leading them through the rain to the hospital entrance and the security window, where they showed their IDs and signed in. They waited in the lobby, dripping wet, until Dr. Hayden came down the hallway, her hand outstretched.

"Quin, welcome back!"

He shook her warm hand and noticed her looking at his friends. "This is Hawk and Jimmy."

"Nice to meet you both," she said, but neither of them met her halfway for the handshake. "Can I get you anything to drink, coffee?"

"No," Hawk said.

Jimmy shook his head, droplets of rain splashing to the floor.

"Follow me then," she said, and Quin walked with her down the quiet hallway, Jimmy and Hawk lagging behind.

"Congratulations," she said. "I hear you had a successful mission."

"Thanks," he said. "I just need information and I'll be on my way."

He followed her into the conference room where Agent Kruse was waiting at the far end of the table, hands in his pockets, as if he were ready for another remote viewing training session.

"Agent Kruse, these are Quin's friends, Hawk and Jimmy."

Kruse gave them a cordial nod and looked past them toward the door. "Where's Autumn?"

"What? No hello, welcome back? No 'atta boy'?" Quin said.

"You're supposed to bring me Autumn."

"Bring *you* Autumn?" Quin said. A surge of energy propelled him forward, rushing Kruse, grabbing him by the collar and pinning him to the wall.

"Quin, no!" Dr. Hayden shouted, her voice a distant echo muffled by the sound of blood throbbing in Quin's ears.

He ignored her, holding Kruse tightly with one hand. "Where's Autumn? After all these years, you finally want to know where she is?!"

Kruse choked as he tried to speak, gripping Quin's arm. "Let me explain!"

"Quin, please don't hurt him," Dr. Hayden repeated. "Don't make me call security."

Jimmy closed the conference room door and Hawk stood in front of the phone hanging on the wall.

It would be so easy for Quin to tighten his grip, to strangle the bureau's throat, to snuff out the liars who covered up the truth. He could set an example right here, right now.

"Which one will you feed?" Hawk whispered to Quin.

Quin heard the wind outside and a howl deep within himself. *Which wolf should I feed: the angry, self-righteous wolf, or the forgiving and compassionate wolf?*

A wave of calm came over him. He let go of Kruse and stepped back, saying, "It doesn't make sense."

"What, Quin?" Dr. Hayden asked.

"For twelve years nobody cared."

"I cared," Kruse said, tucking in his tousled shirt.

"Really? Why?"

"I thought if we found her, you might see value in Remote Viewing," Kruse said.

"In other words, for your own selfish reasons," he said.

"I wanted an assignment where we all saw the final results, the proof to share with the team that what they do every day has value," Kruse explained. "Is it so selfish of me? You got your sister back."

"But it's not real," Quin said. "You orchestrated the event to make it look like a real rescue."

"What are you talking about?" Kruse said.

"It was too easy. After all these years we find her?" he said.

"That's the power of a good paranormal team," Kruse replied.

"You had access to FBI and DEA files. You knew where she lived, and you convinced Dillan and Rachel that they located Autumn."

"Sure I had access to some bureau files, so maybe I'm guilty of front-loading their RV sessions," Kruse admitted. "But I never knew Autumn's location. I wasn't even sure if she was alive."

"But the bureau has been known to fabricate events to suit its own purposes," Quin said.

"I'm not one of those agents, Quin. Look at me; I'm a paranormal researcher. That's not exactly the career path one takes to climb the corporate ladder here."

"If it's real, why did the bureau give up on my family?"

"Tell him everything," Dr. Hayden said to Kruse.

Kruse sighed. "If they had pursued an investigation against the people who killed your parents, they would've jeopardized undercover agents and informants in the field."

"That's it? My parents' lives weren't worth pursuing justice?"

"Your parents smuggled people across the border, Quin."

"To save them from the coyotes!"

"It's hard to tell one coyote from another," Kruse said. "That's how the bureau saw it at the time."

"That sucks, not fair," Jimmy said.

"I don't like it any more than you do," Kruse said to them. "I put my career on the line digging up this case. This entire division is hanging by a thin thread, but RV is real. You helped prove it."

"Let's go, Quin," Hawk said.

"I'm not done yet," Quin said. "What's happening to the remote viewers?" he asked Dr. Hayden.

She looked at Kruse, as if waiting for permission to speak. He nodded.

"This is the best team we've trained, but they're showing signs of post-traumatic stress," she said. "It's not life-threatening."

"Unless they take their own lives," Quin said. "Dillan's a mess. Susan is in a locked ward. Others have committed suicide."

"On a few rare occasions," she admitted.

"Statistically they're no more likely to commit suicide than anybody suffering from PTSD," Kruse added.

"There might be a way to prevent it in the future," Dr. Hayden said. "Where do you get your ayahuasca tea?"

Quin remained silent, unsure of where she was going with her questioning.

"When Quin first came to me, he was sick," Hawk answered her. "I had something that I knew could help him."

"Ayahuasca is a Schedule 1 drug," Kruse said.

Hawk folded his arms. "It's a root from the ground."

"And a felony if you're caught with it in the United States," Kruse said.

"There are exceptions if it's used for ceremonial purposes, but only for members of the Santo Daime Church or União do Vegetal," Dr. Hayden said.

"It's a natural medicine, like peyote," Hawk said. "Why must your government take everything away and then sell it back to its people?"

"You always said to end our sessions on a high," Quin added, poking at Kruse.

A quick smile burst onto Kruse's face before he caught himself. "I didn't mean it literally."

"We're not here to make a drug bust," Dr. Hayden said. "In fact, we're interested in your tea recipe because it might indeed be medicine that could benefit the remote viewers. It's possible that ayahuasca is what helps Quin transition between his conscious and subconscious states with fewer side effects. We need to test this, of course, but it looks promising. There is anecdotal evidence that veterans suffering from PTSD have had success with ayahuasca as well. You not only found Autumn, Quin, you found the elixir that could help the remote viewers, or anybody suffering from PTSD."

"Tell him what we learned by monitoring him in the field," Kruse said.

"It's confidential health information," Dr. Hayden said, motioning toward Jimmy and Hawk. "We can discuss it privately later, Quin."

"Tell me now."

"Shall we sit?" she asked.

She shared with Quin and the others the test results she'd gathered, all the hypotheses they'd tested and how in the end, she couldn't find an exact diagnosis for him. It was a relief, a heavy burden lifting from his shoulders, and the more she talked, the more alive and normal Quin felt. From her laptop, she showed them the video from Mexico, how his brain activity would shift in and out of subconscious states.

She spoke animatedly, smiling at times, even reaching across the table to pat his hands, and for the first time in more than a dozen years, he felt less crazy, even *gifted*.

"I don't know if you've always had it or how long it will last, but it's truly an honor to work with you," she said.

"So there's no reason for me to stay?"

Dr. Hayden blinked in surprise. "I assumed you'd stay after hearing this."

"If I want to leave, can I?"

"You can exit the paranormal program, but you'd still be an outpatient here for a while," she said.

"Quin, this program needs your talents," Kruse said.

"Why would he help a government that's always taking more from its people?" Hawk said, folding his arms.

"I understand, I know how you feel," Kruse said. "This is a tiny division in a crime- and terror-fighting bureaucracy. And within this organization, just like in any country, corporation, or tribe, there are good intentions and bad intentions. Sometimes it's only with hindsight that we realize we've veered from the correct path. I believe the paranormal division can do a lot of good. We found Autumn."

"You can't have her," Quin said.

"The bureau made mistakes, even covered them up," Kruse said. "They'd be content if Autumn never materialized. But if the team could just meet her, that's all it would take to give us the satisfaction that we succeeded. I don't want anyone to think I fabricated this rescue."

Quin was beginning to trust Kruse again. His answers seemed legitimate, but he thought of something else to ask him. "What was the deal you made with Sinaloa?"

"When Dillan and Rachel located Autumn near a known Sinaloa meth lab, I was concerned you'd run into bigger trouble than we were prepared to handle."

"What kind of deal?" Quin asked again.

"They wouldn't interfere with our rescue attempt if we don't interfere with one of theirs."

"Who are they rescuing?"

"I can't divulge that—"

"Because it might jeopardize informants in the field?" Quin said sarcastically.

"Correct, and you have to stop talking to reporters," Kruse said. "Everything we do here is top secret."

"How do you know about Candace?" he asked.

"Agent Lopez called me," Kruse said. "Candace cannot publicize any of this."

"She's a journalist. She'll claim she has the freedom to express herself," he said.

"Sometimes we give up small freedoms for bigger ones," Kruse said. "Today's world is under high-tech surveillance. Every phone call, text message, web search, and credit card transaction is recorded. The data is monitored, or even stolen by foreign governments. Our goal is to find a new way—or maybe it's an old way—of watching and listening, to stop thieves and terrorists."

"I still don't like giving up freedom," Hawk said.

"Most of my career was with the bureau's Indian Country Crimes Unit. I've been to many of the reservations," Kruse said. "May I ask, Hawk, are you Dakota or Lakota?"

"Dakota. My wife Lily was Lakota."

"And you know of the Oglala warrior who stood up against US Cavalry forces to protect his people?"

Hawk nodded. "Crazy Horse."

"And Crazy Horse eventually surrendered to save his people," Kruse said. "He gave up his freedom, hoping to preserve his tribe."

"We've been fighting terrorism since 1492," Hawk said proudly.

"You certainly have," Kruse said, "and I know I shouldn't ask any more of you. But we are all one people who have to figure out how to get along, and right now xenophobia is in the air."

Hawk nodded in agreement. "And now you know what it's like to be attacked based on another man's beliefs," Hawk said to Kruse.

At that moment, Quin noticed the conversation had turned into something far more symbolic. Kruse was attempting to bridge the gap between indigenous tribes and the FBI.

"Zealots and lawless men are recruiting vulnerable people to act out heinous crimes against humanity; but the FBI recruits, too," Kruse said. "We need gifted people like Quin."

"It's not my decision, it's his," Hawk said to Kruse and then turned to Quin. "But either way, you have my blessing, Quin Raven."

This was the first time Quin had ever seen Kruse nervous, as if everything was riding on this one decision. Kruse cleared his throat and said, "We're training a new kind of warrior to see and stop the enemy before it strikes here. And since the United States shares borders with indigenous tribes, I hope we can continue working together to protect our shared homeland. Quin, can I count on you?"

Quin enjoyed a month of vacation from the bureau and bounty hunting, fishing and camping with Hawk and Jimmy while he cleared his head. He was enjoying his new roles as brother and uncle. Autumn wasn't sure if she'd settle in with the Navajo Nation or somewhere near Quin, so he invited them to Minnesota to experience his hometown. Hawk had provided a room for them at his place and today, Jimmy had volunteered to babysit Marta while Quin and Autumn explored the city. Their first stop: Freedom Bail Bonds.

Quin waved to Sal Foster as he and Autumn stepped into the musty office, the door clanging shut behind them. Sal peered at him through the bulletproof glass separating him from two women seated with clipboards, filling out bail bond forms.

"Look what the cat dragged in," Sal said.

"What? No thanks for coming back?" Quin said.

"And you brought a beautiful woman with you. She's not a skip, is she?" he said, shuffling through his paperwork.

"Be respectful, Autumn is my sister."

"You never told me you got a sister."

"You never asked."

"Autumn, beautiful name."

"Thanks," she said. "Nice to meet you."

"It's a good day, right, Sal?" Quin asked.

"Good?" Sal said, sticking an unlit cigarette into his mouth. "I got two here posting bail but I got three more that skipped. It's a leaky bucket."

"Sounds like you could use help," Quin said, leaning up closer to the glass.

"You and her teaming up?"

"No, I'm only riding along today," Autumn said.

"Because the Finn brothers teamed up. They post all them bounty-hunting videos on YouTube. They got an agent in Hollywood that's getting them a reality TV show. You two could do that. It could be free advertising for my business," Sal said.

Quin looked at his sister, who was holding back her laughter. "She's just tagging along to see how I work."

"It's about time you got back. What took so long?"

"You knew I was on assignment with the bureau."

"Assignment? Thought you were on vacation."

"It was a little of both."

"How'd that work out for ya?"

"Better than expected."

"Where was this work-slash-vacation?"

"Nogales."

Sal rubbed his eyes and sucked on his unlit cigarette. "A border town? You bring anything back other than a cheap tattoo and a bad venereal disease?"

"Is there such a thing as a *good* venereal disease?" Autumn asked.

The women filling out bond forms laughed at her comment.

Sal liked it too. "Good one! But Quin didn't answer my question."

"I found what I was searching for, if that's what you mean," he said, glancing back at his sister.

"And the bureau paid for this vacation?"

"Of course."

"How much?"

"They pay better than you, Sal."

"The bureau pays with taxpayer money. Entrepreneurs like me create jobs and pay taxes that fund your bureau-bloated salaries," he said. "What do you care? Now that you're a hot-shot FBI man."

"Who told you that?"

"Word gets around."

"From who?"

"Hawk called me, bragging on you," Sal said.

"The bureau offered me a position but I turned it down, said I'd continue on as a contractor."

"You got time to help out old Sal?"

"On weekends now and then, sure."

Sal opened a file drawer, mumbling, probably even cursing, Quin wasn't sure. He'd only been gone six weeks from this place and yet Sal seemed to have aged another ten years. Behind Sal on the wood-panel wall, Quin spotted the latest FBI Ten Most Wanted poster.

"What are you looking at?" Sal asked.

"The Ten Most Wanted."

"Huh? Oh yeah, so what?"

Sal collected them and owned every one issued since J. Edgar Hoover thought of the idea back in 1950.

"You're always telling me how important the posters are," Quin said. "Tell Autumn how many fugitives have been caught from those posters."

"Well, 495 made the list, 465 apprehended," Sal said. "See the new face on the Top 10, Joaquin "El Chapo" Guzman? He's the drug lord who just escaped from a Mexico prison. This is the second time he's escaped."

Quin stepped closer and studied the poster with Autumn.

"El Chapo is the head of Sinaloa," she whispered to him. "Jefe works for him."

"You know how he broke out of a maximum security prison?" Sal asked.

Quin had learned of the escape while he was on vacation. "His men dug a tunnel right to his prison cell," he said to Sal.

Both Quin and Autumn had felt uneasy about El Chapo's escape because of the obvious similarities to how he rescued Autumn. The tunnel was of sophisticated design with lighting, a motorcycle on tracks, and a ventilation system to prevent suffocation while motoring underground. The drug kingpin's cell was monitored with 24-hour video surveillance. He wore an ankle bracelet right up until his escape through the floor in the shower stall.

It obviously took years of planning and corruption inside the prison. Quin and Autumn's use of tunnels couldn't have inspired the escape, but he couldn't help wondering if this was the deal that Agent Kruse had agreed to. That the FBI and DEA would look the other way, or at least give El Chapo a little room to run before they assisted in his recapture. Catch and release.

"He's a billionaire, could be anywhere in the world by now," Autumn said.

"That's why the bounty is set at $3.8 million," Quin said.

Sal finally lit that cigarette, sucked in the nicotine, and said, "Focus on *my* skips, *my* debts." He slid a manila folder under the glass.

The folder contained details on Sal's skips, their bail pieces, mug shots and any other photos he'd copied from the Internet, and addresses of family and friends. Quin grabbed it, looked up at the poster again, and left Freedom Bail Bonds with Autumn.

They stepped off the curb, walking to his truck when Autumn asked, "Would you ever hunt down a man like El Chapo?"

"Why are you interested in chasing him?"

"Well, $3.8 million is a lot of money."

"And that means every bounty hunter in the country wants to bag him," he said. "And if bounty hunters like the Finn brothers have TV cameras following them, it's gonna be a circus."

"Let that one go," she agreed.

"Ready to meet my coworkers from the bureau?" he asked.

He drove through downtown traffic, describing the people she'd soon meet: Dillan, Rachel, Agent Kruse, and Dr. Hayden. Today was the first of a new series of offsite meetings where the paranormal team could socialize with each other without the pressures of work. It was something Dr. Hayden had suggested and Kruse had agreed to, if it would keep the team together.

However, Quin thought it was odd that they were meeting at the Sculpture Garden for a picnic near the Spoonbridge and Cherry sculpture. This was one of the targets from their remote viewing practice sessions. Kruse must've chosen the location for the picnic. Work and socializing would always be more work when Kruse was footing the bill.

Quin pulled into the lot and parked in the shade. Candace was there, leaning on the back of her car, but today instead of wearing a cowboy hat and boots, she wore sandals and a baseball hat, her ponytail sticking out the back.

He stepped out of the truck and with Autumn he walked over to her. "Candace, what are you doing here?"

"Dillan told me you were all meeting for lunch," she said. "I was hoping to meet your sister."

"Oh, Candace, this is Autumn. Autumn, meet Candace," he said.

They shook hands briefly and Candace said, "They actually found you. I had to see you for myself."

"I'm here in the flesh and blood," Autumn replied.

"I apologize about Agent Kruse killing your story in the name of National Security," Quin said.

"He gave me a tear-jerking patriotic lecture about how the information could jeopardize agents in the field," she said.

"But eventually all this stuff becomes declassified," Quin assured her.

"Then I'll write the big story," she laughed.

"In the meantime you could always become an informant for the bureau," he joked.

"I hear it pays pretty well," she said with a wink, before she walked back to her car door. "Tell Hawk and Jimmy I enjoyed our road trip together," she said to Quin. "It was the best history lesson I ever had."

She sat in her car, started the engine and drove off. Quin was surprised she'd agreed to kill the story. Kruse either exerted a lot of pressure on her, paid her to not write the story, or maybe she was already an informant. He really didn't know. He was learning that in the undercover world of Homeland Security, you're not always at liberty to know.

He walked with Autumn along a limestone path through a grove of trees toward the pond where the team was setting up the picnic.

"You ready for this?" he asked Autumn.

"I think so," she said.

Agent Kruse and Dr. Hayden were standing next to a picnic table with Dillan, Rachel, and Susan. They all turned and looked as Quin approached with Autumn. How would he describe the look on their faces? It was a mix of awe and wonder.

"Everybody, this is my sister, Autumn," he said.

Kruse turned to Dr. Hayden and then back at Quin. "You brought Autumn home," he said.

Quin knew it was important for all of them to see the fruits of their labor. "We *all* brought her home."

Kruse set his drink on the table and walked toward her with his arms outstretched. "Autumn, I'm Agent Kruse. It's an honor to finally meet you."

He embraced her as if Autumn was his long-lost relative. She politely returned the hug. She was living, breathing proof that what remote viewers did behind closed doors actually worked. And Quin knew that RV was more effective when a viewer like him was in the field. He wondered how long Kruse would wait before he'd offer to test Autumn's sixth sense. And then he'd recruit her to join their team to protect the homeland from wolves. Quin knew she'd have reservations but if she joined them, they'd work together, in good company.

What Reviewers Are Saying About Larranaga's "In The Company of Wolves" series